ISAAC ASIMOV'S
ROBOT CITY™

ISAAC ASIMOV'S ROBOT CITY

BOOK 1: ODYSSEY
MICHAEL P. KUBE-McDOWELL

ibooks
new york
www.ibooks.net

DISTRIBUTED BY SIMON & SCHUSTER, INC.

A Publication of ibooks, inc.

An ibooks, inc. Book

Distributed by Simon & Schuster, Inc.
1230 Avenue of the Americas, New York, NY 10020

ibooks, inc.
24 West 25th Street
New York, NY 10010

The ibooks World Wide Web Site Address is:
http://www.ibooks.net

ISBN 0-7434-7924-6
First ibooks, inc. printing June 2004
10 9 8 7 6 5 4 3 2 1

Edited by David M. Harris

Printed in the U.S.A.

CONTENTS

For all the students
who made my seven years of teaching time
well spent, but especially for

Wendy Armstrong	Julie Merrick
Todd Bontrager	Kendall Miller
Kathy Branum	Matt Mow
Jay & Joel Carlin	Amy Myers
Valerie Eash	Khai & Vinh Pham
Chris Franko	Melanie & Laura Schrock
Judy Fuller	Sally Sibrt
Chris & Bryan Hackett	Stephanie Smith
Kean Hankins	Tom Williams
Doug Johnson	Laura Joyce Yoder
Greg LaRue	Scott Yoder

And for Joy Von Blon,
who made sure they always had
something good to read.

MY ROBOTS
ISAAC ASIMOV

I wrote my first robot story, "Robbie," in May of 1939, when I was only nineteen years old.

What made it different from robot stories that had been written earlier was that I was determined *not* to make my robots symbols. They were *not* to be symbols of humanity's overweening arrogance. They were *not* to be examples of human ambitions trespassing on the domain of the Almighty. They were *not* to be a new Tower of Babel requiring punishment.

Nor were the robots to be symbols of minority groups. They were *not* to be pathetic creatures that were unfairly persecuted so that I could make Aesopic statements about Jews, Blacks or any other mistreated members of society. Naturally, I was bitterly opposed to such mistreatment and I made that plain in numerous stories and essays—but *not* in my robot stories.

In that case, what *did* I make my robots?—I made them engineering devices. I made them tools. I made them machines to serve human ends. And I made them objects with built-in safety features. In other words, I set it up so that a robot *could not* kill his creator, and having outlawed that heavily overused plot, I was free to consider other, more rational consequences.

Since I began writing my robot stories in 1939, I did not mention computerization in their connection. The electronic computer had not yet been invented and I did not foresee it. I did foresee, however, that the brain had to be electronic in some fashion. However, "electronic" didn't seem futuristic enough.

The positron—a subatomic particle exactly like the electron but of opposite electric charge—had been discovered only four years before I wrote my first robot story. It sounded very science fictional indeed, so I gave my robots "positronic brains" and imagined their thoughts to consist of flashing streams of positrons, coming into existence, then going out of existence almost immediately. These stories that I wrote were therefore called "the positronic robot series," but there was no greater significance than what I have just described to the use of positrons rather than electrons.

At first, I did not bother actually systematizing, or putting into words, just what the safeguards were that I imagined to be built into my robots. From the very start, though, since I wasn't going to have it possible for a robot to kill its creator, I had to stress that robots could not harm human beings; that this was an ingrained part of the makeup of their positronic brains.

Thus, in the very first printed version of "Robbie" (it appeared in the September 1940 *Super Science Stories,* under the title of "Strange Playfellow"), I had a character refer to a robot as follows: "He just can't help being faithful and loving and kind. He's a machine, *made so.*"

After writing "Robbie," which John Campbell, of *Astounding Science Fiction,* rejected, I went on to other robot stories which Campbell accepted. On December 23, 1940, I came to him with an idea for a mind-reading robot (which later became "Liar!") and John was dissatisfied with my explanations of why the robot behaved as it did. He wanted the safeguard specified precisely so that we could understand the robot. Together, then, we worked out what came to be known as the "Three Laws of Robotics." The concept was mine, for it was obtained out of the stories I had already written, but the actual wording (if I remember correctly) was beaten out then and there by the two of us.

The Three Laws were logical and made sense. To begin with, there was the question of safety, which had been foremost in my mind when I began to write stories about *my* robots. What's more I was aware of the fact that even without actively attempting to do harm, one could quietly, by doing nothing, allow harm to come. What was in my mind was Arthur Hugh Clough's cynical "The Latest Decalog," in which the Ten Commandments are rewritten in deeply satirical Machiavellian fashion. The one item most frequently quoted is: "Thou shalt not kill, but needst not strive / Officiously to keep alive."

For that reason I insisted that the First Law (safety) had to be in two parts and it came out this way:

1. A robot may not injure a human being, or, through inaction, allow a human being to come to harm.

Having got that out of the way, we had to pass on to the second law (service). Naturally, in giving the robot the built-in necessity to follow orders, you couldn't forfeit the overall concern of safety. The second law had to read as follows, then:

2. A robot must obey the orders given it by human beings except where such orders would conflict with the First Law.

And finally, we had to have a third law (prudence). A robot was bound to be an expensive machine and it must not needlessly be damaged or destroyed. Naturally, this must not be used as a way of compromising either safety or service. The Third Law, therefore, had to read as follows:

3. A robot must protect its own existence, as long as such protection does not conflict with the First or Second Laws.

Of course, these laws are expressed in words, which is an imperfection. In the positronic brain, they are competing positronic potentials that are best expressed in terms of advanced mathematics (which is well beyond my ken, I assure you). However, even so, there are clear ambiguities. What constitutes "harm" to a human being? Must a robot obey orders given it by a child, by a madman, by a malevolent human being? Must a robot give up its own expensive and useful existence to prevent a trivial harm to an unimportant human being? What is trivial and what is unimportant?

These ambiguities are not shortcomings as far as a writer is concerned. If the Three Laws were perfect and unambiguous there would be no room for stories. It is in the nooks and crannies of the ambiguities that all one's plots can lodge, and which provide a foundation, if you'll excuse the pun, for *Robot City*.

I did not specifically state the Three Laws in words in "Liar!" which appeared in the May 1941 *Astounding*. I did do so, however, in my next robot story, "Runaround," which appeared in the March 1942 *Astounding*. In that issue on line seven of page one hundred, I have a character say, "Now, look, let's start with the three fundamental Rules of Robotics," and I then quote them. That, incidentally, as far as I or anyone else has been able to tell, represents the first appearance in print of the word "robotics"—which, apparently, I invented.

Since then, I have never had occasion, over a period of over forty years during which I wrote many stories and novels dealing with robots, to be forced to modify the Three Laws. However, as time passed, and as my robots advanced in complexity and versatility, I did feel that they would have to reach for something still higher. Thus, in *Robots and Empire,* a novel published by Doubleday in 1985, I talked about the possibility that a sufficiently advanced robot might feel it necessary to consider the prevention of harm to humanity generally as taking precedence over the prevention of harm to an individual. This I called the "Zeroth Law of Robotics," but I'm still working on that.

My invention of the Three Laws of Robotics is probably my most important contribution to science fiction. They are widely quoted outside the field, and no history of robotics could possibly be complete without mention of the Three Laws. In 1985, John Wiley and Sons published a huge tome, *Handbook of Industrial Robotics,* edited by Shimon Y. Nof, and, at the editor's request, I wrote an introduction concerning the Three Laws.

Now it is understood that science fiction writers generally have created a pool of ideas that form a common stock into which all writers can dip. For that reason, I have never objected to other writers who have used robots that obey the Three Laws. I have, rather, been flattered and, honestly, modern science fictional robots can scarcely appear without those Laws.

However, I have firmly resisted the actual quotation of the Three Laws by any other writer. Take the Laws for granted, is my attitude in this matter, but don't recite them. The concepts are everyone's but the words are mine.

But, then, I am growing old. I cannot expect to live for very much longer, but I hope that some of my brainchildren can. And to help those brainchildren attain something approaching long life, it is just as well if I relax my rules and allow others to make use of them and reinvigorate them. After all, much has happened in science since my first robot stories were published four decades ago, and this has to be taken into consideration, too.

Therefore, when Byron Preiss came to me with the notion of setting up a series of novels under the overall title of *Robot City*, in which "Asimovian" robots and ideas were to be freely used, I felt drawn to the notion. Byron said that I would serve as a consultant to make sure that my robots *stay* "Asimovian," that I would answer questions, make suggestions, veto infelicities, and provide the basic premise for the series as well as challenges for the authors. (And so it was done. Byron and I sat through a series of breakfasts in which he asked questions and I—and sometimes my wife, Janet, as well—answered, thus initiating some rather interesting discussions.)

Furthermore, my name was to be used in the title so as to insure the fact that readers would know that the project was developed in conjunction with me, and was carried through with my help and knowledge. It is, indeed, a pleasure to have talented young writers devote their intelligence and ingenuity to the further development of my ideas, doing so each in his or her own way.

The first novel of the series, *Robot City Book 1: Odyssey*, is by Michael P. Kube-McDowell, the author of *Emprise*, and I am very pleased to be connected with it. The prose is entirely Michael's; I did none of it. In saying this, I am not trying to disown the novel at all; rather I want to make sure that Michael gets all the credit from those who like the writing. It is my role, as I have indicated, only to supply robotic concepts, answer (as best I can) questions posed by Byron and Michael, and suggest solutions to problems raised by the Three Laws. In fact, Book Two of this series will introduce three interesting new laws concerning the way robots would deal with humans in a robotic society, a relationship which is the underpinning of *Robot City*.

In nearly half a century of writing I have built up a name that is well known and carries weight and I would like to use it to help pave the way for young writers by way of their novels and to preserve the names of older writers by the editing of anthologies. The science fiction field in general and a number of science fiction practitioners in particular have, after all, been very good to me over the years, and the best repayment I can make is to do for others what it and they have done for me.

Let me emphasize that this is the first time I have allowed others to enter my world of robots and to roam about freely there. I am pleased with what I've seen so far, including the captivating artwork of Paul Rivoche, and I look forward to seeing what is done with my ideas and the concepts I have proposed in the books that follow. The books may not be (indeed, are bound not to be) exactly as I would have written them, but all the better. We'll have other minds and other personalities at work, broadening, raising, and refocusing my ideas.

For you, the reader, the adventure is about to begin.

The youth strapped in the shock couch at the center of the small chamber appeared to be peacefully sleeping. The muscles of his narrow face were relaxed, and his eyes were closed. His head had rolled forward until his chin rested on the burnished metal neck ring of his orange safesuit. With his smooth cheeks and brush-cut sandy blond hair, he looked even younger than he was—young enough to raise the doorman's eyebrow at the least law-abiding spaceport bar.

He came to consciousness slowly, as though he had been cheated of sleep and was reluctant to give it up. But as the fog cleared, he had a sudden, terrifying sensation of leaning out over the edge of a cliff.

His eyes flashed open, and he found himself looking down. The couch into which the five-point harness held him was tipped forward. Without the harness, he would have awakened in a jumbled heap on the tiny patch of sloping floorplate, wedged against the one-ply hatch that faced him.

He raised his head, and his darting eyes quickly took in the rest of his surroundings. There was little to see. He was alone in the tiny chamber. If he unstrapped himself, there would be room for him to stand up, perhaps to turn around, but nothing more ambitious. A safesuit helmet was cached in a recess on the curving right bulkhead. On the left bulkhead was a dispensary, with its water tube and delivery chute.

None of what he saw made sense, so he simply continued to

catalog it. Above his head, hanging from the ceiling, was some sort of command board with a bank of eight square green lamps labeled "P1," "P2," "F," and the like. The board was in easy reach, except that there appeared to be no switches or controls for him to manipulate. In one corner of the panel the word MASSEY was etched in stylized black letters.

Apart from the slight rasp of his own breathing, the little room was nearly silent. From the machinery which filled the space behind his shoulders and under his feet came the whir of an impeller and a faint electric hum. But there was no sound from outside, from beyond the walls.

Thin as it was, the catalog was complete, and it was time to try to make something of it. He realized that, although he did not recognize his surroundings, he was not surprised by them. But then, since he could not remember where he had fallen asleep, he had carried no expectations about where he should be when he awoke.

The simple truth was he did not know where he was. Or why he was there. He did not know how long he had been there, or how he had gotten there.

But at the moment none of those things seemed to matter, for he realized—with rapidly growing dismay and disquiet—that he also did not know who he was.

He searched his mind for any hint of his identity—of a place he had known, of a face that was important to him, of a memory that he treasured. There was nothing. It was as though he was trying to read a blank piece of paper. He could not remember a single event which had taken place before he had opened his eyes and found himself here. It was as though his life had begun at that moment.

Except he knew that it had not. He was not a crying newborn child, but a man—or near enough to one to claim the title until challenged. He had existed. He had had an identity and a place in the world. He had had friends—parents—a home. He had to have had all of that and more.

But it was gone.

It was a different feeling than merely forgetting. *At least when you forget something, you have a sense that you once knew it—*

"Are you all right?" a pleasant voice inquired, breaking the silence and making him suddenly tense all his muscles.

"Who are you?" he demanded. "Where are you? Where am I?"

"I am Darla, your Companion. Please try to remain calm. We're in no immediate danger." The voice, coming from the command panel before him, was more clearly female now. "You are inside a Massey Corporation Model G-85 Lifepod. Massey has been the leader in space safety systems for more than . . ."

While Darla continued on with her advertisement, he twisted his head about as he reexamined the compartment. I should have known that, he thought. Of course. A survival pod. Even the name *Massey* was familiar. "Why are there no controls?"

"All G-series pods have been designed to independently evaluate the most productive strategy and respond appropriately."

Of course, he thought. You don't know who's going to climb into a pod, or what kind of condition they'll be in. "You're not a person. What are you, then? A computer program?"

"I am a positronic personality," Darla said cheerfully. "The Companion concept is the Massey Corporation's unique contribution to humane safety systems."

Yes. Someone to talk to. Someone to help him pass hours of waiting without thinking about what it would mean if he weren't found. The full picture dawned on him. All survival pods were highly automated. This one was more. It was a robot —presumably programmed as a therapist and charged with keeping him sane and stable.

A robot—

A human had a childhood. A robot did not. A human learned. A robot was programmed. A robot deprived of the core identity which was supposed to be integrated before activation might "awake" and find he had knowledge without experience, and wonder who and what he was—

Suddenly he bit down on his lower lip.

How does a robot experience sensor overload? As pain?

When he tasted blood, he relaxed his jaw. He would take the outcome of his little experiment at face value. He was human. In some ways, that was the more disturbing answer.

"Why have you done harm to yourself?" Darla intruded.

He sighed. "Just to be sure I could. Do you know who *I* am?"

"Your badge identifies you as Derec."

He looked down past the neck ring and saw for the first time that there was a datastrip in the badge holder on the right breast of the safesuit. The red printing, superimposed on the fractured black-and-white coding pattern, indeed read DEREC.

He said the name aloud, experimentally: "Derec." It seemed neither familiar nor foreign to his tongue. His ear heard it as a first name, even though it was more likely a surname.

But if I'm Derec, why does the safesuit fit so poorly? The waist ring and chest envelope would have accommodated someone with a much stockier build. And when he tried to straighten his cramped legs, he found that the suit's legs were a centimeter or two short of allowing him to do so comfortably.

I certainly was shorter once—maybe I was heavier, too. It could be my old suit—one I wouldn't have used except in an emergency. Or it could be my ID, but someone else's suit.

"Can you scan the datastrip on the badge?" he asked hopefully. "There should be a photograph—a citizenship record— kinship list. Then I'd know for sure."

"I'm sorry. There's no data reader in the pod, and my optical sensors can't resolve a pattern that fine."

Frowning, he said, "Then I guess I'll be Derec, for now."

He paused and collected his thoughts. To know his name—if it was his name—did nothing to relieve his feelings of emptiness. It was as though he had lost his internal compass, and with it, the ability to act on his own behalf. The most he could do now was react.

"All of the pod's environmental systems are working well," Darla offered brightly. "Rescue vessels should be on their way here now."

Her words reminded him that there was a problem more important in the short run than puzzling out who he was. Survival had to come first. In time, perhaps the things he did know would tell him what he had forgotten.

He was in a survival pod. His mind took that one fact and began to build on it. When he shifted position in his harness, he noted how the slightest movement set the pod to rocking, despite the fact that its mass could hardly be less than five hundred kilograms. He extended an arm and let the muscles go limp. It took a full second to fall to his side.

A hundredth of a gee at best. I'm in a survival pod on the surface of a low-gravity world. I was in a starcraft, on my way somewhere, when something happened. Perhaps that's why I can't remember, or perhaps the shock of landing—

There was no window or port anywhere in the pod, not even a hatch peephole. But if he couldn't see, perhaps Darla could.

"Where are we, Darla?" he asked. "What kind of place did you land us on?"

"Would you like me to show you our surroundings? I have a limpet pack available."

Derec knew the term, though he wondered where he had learned it. A limpet pack was a disc-shaped sensor array capable of sliding across the outer surface of a smooth-hulled spacecraft—a cheaper but more trouble-prone substitute for a full array of sensor mounts. "Let's see."

The interior lights dimmed, and the central third of the hatch became the background for a flatscreen projection directed down from the command board overhead. Derec looked out on an ice and rock landscape that screamed its wrongness to him. The horizon was too close, too severely curved. It had to be a distortion created by the camera, or a false horizon created by a foreground crater.

"Scan right," he said.

But everywhere it was the same: a jumble of orange-tinged ice studded with gray rock, merging at the horizon into the velvet curtain of space. He could see no distinct stars in the sky, but that was likely to be due to the limited resolving power of the limpet, and not because of any atmosphere. The planetoid's gravity was too slight to hold even the densest gases, and the jagged scarps showed no signs of atmospheric weathering.

In truth, it looked like a leftover place, the waste of star- and planet-making, a forgotten world which had not changed since the day it was made. It was a cold world, and a sterile one, and, in all probability, a deserted one.

Formerly deserted, he corrected himself. "Moon or asteroid?" he asked Darla.

"No matter where we are, we are safe," Darla said ingenuously. "We must trust in the authorities to locate and retrieve us."

Derec could foresee quickly growing weary of that sort of

evasion. "How can I trust in that when I don't know where we are and what the chances are that we'll be found? I know that this pod doesn't have a full-recycle environmental system. No pod ever does. Do you deny it?" He waited a moment for an answer, then plunged on. "How much of a margin did the Massey Corporation decide was enough? Ten days? Two weeks?"

"Derec, maintaining the proper attitude is crucial to—"

"Save the therapist bit, will you?" Darren sighed. "Look, I know you're trying to protect me. Some people cope better that way—what they don't know and all that. But I'm different. I need information, not reassurance. I need to know what you know. Understand? Or should I start digging into your guts and looking for it myself?"

Derec was puzzled when Darla did not answer. It dawned on him slowly that he must have presented her with a dilemma which her positronic brain was having difficulty resolving—but there should have been no dilemma. Darla was obliged by the Second Law of Robotics to answer his questions.

The Second Law said, "A robot must obey the orders given it by human beings except where such orders would conflict with the First Law."

A question was an order—and silence was disobedience. Which could only be if Darla was following her higher obligation under the First Law.

The First Law said, "A robot may not injure a human being, or, through inaction, allow a human being to come to harm."

Darla had to know how small the chance of rescue was, even within a star system, even along standard trajectories. And Darla knew as well as any robot could what sort of harm that fact could do to the emotional balance of a human being. The typical survivor, already terrorized by whatever events brought him into the lifepod, would respond with despair, a loss of the will to live.

It made sense to him now. Of course Darla would try to protect him from the consequences of his own curiosity—unless he could make her see that he was different.

"Darla, I'm not the kind of person you were told to expect," he said gently. "I need something to do, something to think about. I can't just sit here and wait. I can deal with bad news, if that's what you're hiding. What I can't take is feeling helpless."

It seemed as though she were prepared for his kind too, after all, but had only needed convincing that he was one. "I understand, Derec. Of course I'll be happy to tell you what I know."

"Good. What ship are we from?" he asked. "There's no shipper's crest or ship logo anywhere in the cabin."

"This is a Massey Corporation G-85 Lifepod—"

"You told me that already. What ship are we from?"

Darla was silent for a moment. "Massey Lifepods are the primary safety system on six of the eight largest general commercial space carriers—"

"You don't know?"

"My customization option has not been initialized. Would you care for a game of chess?"

"No." Derec mused for a moment. "So all you know how to do is shill for the manufacturer. Which means that we probably came from a privately owned ship—all the commercial carriers customize their gear."

"I have no information in that area."

Derec clucked. "In fact, I think you do. Somewhere among your systems there has to be a data recorder, activated the moment the pod was ejected. It should tell you not only what ship we came from and where it was headed, but what's happened since. It's time to find out how smart you really are, Darla," he said. "We need to find that recorder and get into it."

"I have no information about such a recorder."

"Trust me, it's there. If it wasn't, there'd be no way to do postmortems after a ship disaster. Are you in control of the pod's power bus?"

"Yes."

"Look for an uninterruptible line. That'll be it."

"Just a moment. Yes, there are two."

"What are they called?"

"My system map labels them 1402 and 1632. I have no further information."

Derec reached for the water tube again. "That's all right. One will be the recorder, and the other is probably the locator beacon. We're making progress. Now find the data paths that correspond with those power taps. They should tell us which one is which."

"I'm sorry. I can't."

"They have to be there. The recorder will be taking data from your navigation module, from the environmental system, probably even an abstract of this conversation. There ought to be a whole forest of data paths."

"I'm sorry, Derec. I am unable to do what you ask."

"Why?"

"When I run a diagnostic trace in that portion of the system, I am unable to find any unlabeled paths."

"Can you show me your service schematic? Maybe I can find something."

The icescape vanished and was replaced by a finely detailed projection of the lifepod's logic circuits. Scanning it, Derec quickly found the answer. A smart data gate—a Maxwell junction—was guarding the data line to the recorder. The two systems were effectively isolated. Similar junctions stood between Darla and the inertial navigator, the locator beacon, and the environmental system.

This is all very odd, Derec thought. It wasn't surprising that there was a lower-level autonomous system regulating routine functions. What was strange was how Darla was locked out of getting any information from it.

Coddling frightened survivors required tact and discretion. But robots were strongly disposed toward an almost painful honesty. Perhaps it had proven too difficult to program a Companion to put on a happy face while keeping grim secrets. Lying did unpredictable things to the potentials inside a positronic brain.

And there were Third Law considerations as well. The Third Law went, "A robot must protect its own existence, as long as such protection does not conflict with the First or Second Laws."

How would a robot balance its responsibility to preserve itself with the increasing probability of its demise? It was as though the designers had concluded that there were things Darla was better off not knowing, and thrown up barriers to prevent her from finding out. They had kept her ignorant of herself, and even of her ignorance.

There was a disturbing parallel in that to Derec's own situation. *Is that what happened to me?* he wondered. He had hoped almost from the first that his loss of memory was the consequence of whatever disaster had put him in the lifepod, perhaps along with the shock of a hard landing on this world.

Now he had to ask whether such selective amnesia could be an accident. He had read the schematic easily, but he could not remember where or why he had acquired that skill. Obviously he had some technical training, a fact which—if he survived—might prove a useful clue to his identity. But why would he remember the lessons, but not the teacher? Could his brain have been that badly scrambled?

Yet reading the schematic was a complex task which clearly required that his mind and memory be unimpaired. As well as he could judge, his reasoning was measured and clear. If he were in shock or suffering from a concussion, wouldn't all his faculties be affected?

Perhaps this wasn't something that had happened to him. Perhaps, as with Darla, it was something that had been done to him.

Derec grimaced. It was unsettling enough looking at the blank wall of his past, but more unsettling to think that hiding behind that wall might be the reason why it had been built.

By this time Darla had grown impatient. "Have you found anything?" Darla asked with a note of anxiety.

Blinking, Derec looked up at the status board. "The recorder's tied in through a Maxwell junction. The junction won't pass through to the recorder anything it doesn't recognize, which is why you can't find it with a trace. And why we're not going to be able to read it through you. But there has to be a data port somewhere, probably on the outer hull—"

At that moment, the whole pod lurched and seemed to become buoyant. Derec had the sensation that it was no longer in contact with the frozen surface of the asteroid. "What's going on?" he demanded.

"Please stay calm," Darla said.

"What is it? Have we been found?"

"Yes. I believe we have. But I am unable to say by whom."

Derec gaped openmouthed for a moment. "Put the exterior video up again! Quickly!"

"I am becoming concerned about your level of agitation,

Derec. Please close your eyes and take several deep breaths."

"I'll do no such thing," he said angrily. "I want to see what's going on."

There was a moment's hesitation, and then Darla acquiesced. "Very well."

The sight that greeted Derec's eyes made his breath catch in his throat. The limpet's cameras were no longer trained on the horizon, but down at the ground. A half-dozen machines, each different from the next, were arrayed around the pod. The largest was taller than a man, the smallest barely the size of a safesuit helmet. The tiny ones hovered on tiny jets of white gas, while the larger ones were on wheels or articulated tracks.

He could also see a portion of some sort of cradle or deck which seemed to be centered below the pod. And all of them— the machines, the cradle, and the pod—were moving, proceeding along together toward some unknowable destination like some sort of ice-desert caravan.

"What's going on?" he demanded of Darla. "Can you identify them? Did they make any contact with us?"

"The device below us appears to be a cargo sled. I have no information on the other mechanisms."

Derec reached for his helmet and unsnapped the catch holding it in place. "I'm going out. I'm not going to let us be hijacked like this with no explanation."

"Leaving the pod would be too dangerous," Darla said. "In addition, you will lose a minimum of four hours' oxygen opening the hatch."

"It's worth it to find out what's going on."

"I can't allow that, Derec."

"It's not your decision," he said, reaching for the harness release with his free hand.

"I am sorry, Derec. It is," Darla said.

Too late, Derec realized that a Massey Companion was equipped to calm a distraught survivor not only verbally, but chemically. The dual jets of mist from either side of the headrest caught him full in the face, and he inhaled the sickly sweet droplets in the gasp of surprise.

Derec had barely enough time to be astonished at how quickly the drug acted. Both his arms went limp, the right falling well short of the harness release, the left losing its grasp on the helmet. His vision rapidly grayed. As though from a distance, he heard dimly the sound of the helmet hitting the floor. But between the first bounce and the second, he drifted away into the silent darkness of unconsciousness, and saw and heard nothing more.

CHAPTER 2
UNDER THE ICE

For the second time in one day, Derec awoke in strange surroundings.

This time, he was lying flat on his back staring up at the ceiling. There was a sour taste in his mouth and an empty, growly sensation in his stomach. He lay there for a moment, remembering, then sat up suddenly, his muscles tensed defensively as he looked about him.

As before, Derec was alone. But this time he found himself in more domestic surroundings—a four-man efficiency cabin, three meters wide by five meters long. The bed he had been lying in was a fold-down bunk, one of four mounted on the side walls. To his right as he sat on the edge of the bunk was a bank of storage lockers of assorted sizes. To his left was a closed door.

That damned Darla, he thought fiercely.

Though what he saw around him struck a vaguely familiar chord, Derec dismissed it as meaningless—there was a tedious sameness to all modular living designs. A more important question was whether the cabin was part of a work camp on the surface of the asteroid, tucked away somewhere inside a speeding spacecraft, or somewhere else he couldn't imagine. The cabin itself offered no clue. Nor could it tell him whether he had been rescued or captured.

Glancing down at himself, he saw that he was no longer wearing the safesuit. His torso and legs were covered by a formfitting white jumpsweat, the sort of garment a space worker would wear inside his work jitney or augment. It was clean and relatively new, but there was some wear on the abrasion pads at heel and knee and waist. It might have been what he was wearing under the safesuit, or—

"The suit," he said with sudden dismay.

He jumped to his feet and looked around wildly. There was only one locker large enough to hold a safesuit. It was unlocked, but it was also empty. He went through the other lockers mechanically. All were empty.

No, they were more than empty, he decided. They looked as though they'd never been used.

Derec felt a twinge of panic. If he didn't find the suit, he would never learn whatever information the datastrip on its name badge had to offer. And he had to find Darla as well, or lose the irreplaceable data stored in her event recorder.

Half afraid that he would find it locked, Derec crossed to the door and touched the keyplate. The door slid aside with a hiss. Outside was a short corridor flanked by four doors. The corridor was deserted, the other doors all closed.

To Derec's left, the corridor terminated in a blank wall. The other end was sealed by an airlock, suggesting that the four rooms formed a self-contained environmental cell. Through the small window in the inner pressure door he caught a glimpse of another corridor lying beyond.

"Hello?" Derec called. There was no answer.

The door facing him was labeled WARDROOM. Inside, he found a table large enough to seat eight for a meeting or a meal, a compact autogalley, and a sophisticated computer terminal and communications center.

Derec ran his fingertips across the surface of the table, and they came away clean, without even a coating of dust. The status lights on the galley told him that the unit was in Extended Standby, which meant that its food stores had been irradiated and deep-frozen. No one had eaten here for some time.

Was it all for him? Was that why it was unused? Or was he a surprise visitor in an empty house?

He switched the galley to Demand status, and a timer began counting down the two hours it would take to bring it on line. But when he tried to activate the com center, it demanded a password.

"Derec," he offered.

INVALID PASSWORD, the screen advised him.

He had only the most infinitesimal chance of guessing a truly random password. His only chance was if a lazy systems engineer had left one of the classic wild-card passwords in the security database. "Test," he suggested.

INVALID PASSWORD.

"Password," Derec said.

INVALID PASSWORD. ACCESS DENIED.

From that point on, the center ignored him. The silent-entry keypad was disabled, and nothing he said evoked any response. Apparently the center had not only rejected his passwords, but blacklisted him as well. The systems engineer had not been lazy.

Returning to the corridor, Derec briefly checked the other two rooms. One was another cabin, mirror-image to the one in which he had woken up. The other, labeled MECHANICAL, contained several racks of lockers and what appeared to be maintenance modules for environmental subsystems. Both rooms were as tidy and deserted as everything else Derec had seen since waking.

That left only the airlock and the mysteries beyond it to explore. The inner door bore the sonograph-in-a-circle emblem which meant VoiceCommand. "Open," he said, and the inner door of the hatch cracked open with the ripping sound of adhesion seals separating.

Derec stepped into the tiny enclosure and the door closed behind him. Peering through the window of the outer door, Derec could see no reason why the airlock was even there. The corridor beyond looked little different than the one he was leaving. "Cycle," he said.

The inner door closed behind him, the momentary surge of pressure on his eardrums telling him it had sealed. "Warning. There is a reduced-pressure nitrogen atmosphere beyond this point," the hatch advised him. "Please select a breather."

"Nitrogen?"

Only then did Derec notice the small delivery door in the side wall. Inside he found several gogglelike masks made of gray plastic. Selecting one, he saw that the mask was meant to fit over the middle third of his face, like a pair of wraparound sunglasses that had slipped down his nose. The breather's "straps" were hollow elastic tubes that met behind his neck. A flexible gas delivery tube led from there to the cartridge pack, which was small enough to strap to the upper arm.

When he put the breather on, however, he could not make the bottom edge of the mask seal against his upper lip to keep out the outside air. With the gap, the breaths he drew would be a mixture of free nitrogen and oxygen from the breather.

Belatedly, Derec realized that that was intentional. It was an arrangement that not only reduced the size of the cartridge pack, but also left his sense of smell unimpeded. A clever bit of engineering, with a minimalist flavor.

"Ready," Derec said.

"Warning: reduced gravity beyond this point," the hatch advised him.

"I hear you," he said as the outer door began to open. Nitrogen? Low-G? he wondered as he stepped out. Where am I? What's going on?

There were no immediate answers. It was cold—cold enough to bring a flush of color to his cheeks. The chill seemed to radiate equally from the ceiling and floor, though they were both made of an insulating synthetic mesh.

Standing there just outside the pressure hatch, Derec could hear a cacophony of machine noises—hissing, rumbling, grinding, squealing. But the drop in pressure, which distended his eardrums, made it seem as though he were trying to hear through a pillow. Aside from the fact that there was activity somewhere, he got nothing useful out of what he heard. He could not tell what kinds of machines he was hearing, or what they were doing.

Determined to follow the sounds to their source, he started down the corridor—or tried to. He ended up flat on his face on the cold decking, uninjured but chastened. Collecting himself, he tried again, this time pulling himself along the corridor by the center handrail.

Thirty meters ahead, the corridor opened into an enormous low-ceilinged chamber. Derec gaped as he took in its dimensions. It suggested armories, playing arenas, open-plan factories. He forced a yawn and swallowed hard, and the pressure in his left ear equalized. Yes, those were definitely machine noises. But what kind of machines, doing what kind of work?

Between the cold and low gravity, Derec concluded that he was still on the asteroid where his lifepod had crashed. From the structure of the chamber, he concluded that he was most probably underground.

More important, he was not alone. There were robots moving among the stacks and aisles—dozens of them, of a half-dozen varieties. But in another sense, he was alone, for there were no other people. There were not even any handrails in the aisles to make the chamber human-accessible. The chamber belonged to the robots by default. What task they were so busily attending to, he could not divine. ·

The nearest of the robots, a squat boxlike unit with a single telescoping arm, was only a few dozen meters from Derec. As Derec watched, it plucked a fist-sized component from a rack, stowed it in a cargo basket, and retracted its manipulator arm. Its mission apparently accomplished, the robot started away, coasting on a cushion of air from under its venturi skirt.

"Stop!" Derec called out.

But the robot continued on, seemingly deaf to Derec's command. On impulse, Derec released the handrail and went in pursuit. But in the asteroid's minimal gravity field, it was like trying to run with both legs asleep. He was perpetually off-balance, his slippered feet failing to give him the traction he expected. When he came to his first ninety-degree turn, he went sprawling, scattering a rack of small chromium cylinders.

Not even the racket from his spill slowed the robot's retreat. It continued on toward what appeared to be a lift shaft—a circular black pit in the floor and a matching one in the ceiling, linked by four chrome guide rods.

"How am I supposed to catch you?" he complained, climbing to his feet. *"I can't fly."*

There had to be a better way, and looking more closely at two robots heading down the aisle toward him, Derec saw what it was. Unlike the picker, the man-sized robots were built on standard three-point ball-drive chassis—like three marbles under a bottle cap. Ball-drive chassis were standard in clean environments because they offered complete freedom of movement. The drawback: here, with the reduced friction due to the low gravity, the drive balls should do more spinning than pushing.

But each large robot had a second ball-drive chassis mounted at the top of a telescoping rod. Pushing against the ceiling, the second chassis provided the necessary pressure for the dual drives to grab. Like the bumper cars at a revival carnival, each robot needed to be in constant contact with both surfaces to operate.

Derec realized that he could use that trick, too. The ceiling was low enough that he could push against it with his fingertips while standing flat-footed. "Hand-walking," as he dubbed the technique, he could have caught the picker.

Now he waited to see what the two approaching robots would do about him. They stopped short of where he stood and began to restore order where he had fallen down, deftly using their three-fingered grapples to replace the cylinders on the shelving. He waited, wondering if they would notice him. They did not.

"I'm in danger," he called to them. "I need your help."

The two robots continued their housekeeping, apparently oblivious to his presence. He drew closer and examined the nearer of the two as it worked. It had normal audio sensors, but no evidence of a vocalizer. In short, it was mute. It could not answer.

But there had to be some higher-level robots in the complex, ones capable of recognizing him for what he was and responding to his needs. The pickers and custodians he'd crossed paths with could hardly be working without supervision.

Likewise, the E-cell he awoke in couldn't be the only structure for humans within the complex. Somewhere there was a management team, programmers, supervisors. There was no such thing as a completely autonomous robot community.

Thinking that there had to be a way to call the control room from the E-cell, Derec started back. As he did, he saw a sight that brought him up short. A tall humanoid robot was standing at the end of the corridor to the E-cell, studying him.

They stared at each other for a long moment. The robot's skin was a gleaming pale blue, a vivid declaration of its machine nature. Its optical sensors were silver slits in its helmet-like head, lacking the customary red tracking marker which telegraphed when the robot was looking in your direction. Even so, there was no doubt in Derec's mind that he was the object of the robot's rapt and unnaturally focused attention.

The robot was the first to move, turning away and disappearing into the corridor, hand-walking with easy coordination. Derec followed as quickly as he was able, but by the time he reached the corridor, the robot was already inside the airlock. It took no more than fifteen seconds for Derec to reach the outer hatch and pass through into the E-cell. Even so, when he stepped out into the inner corridor, the robot was already emerging from the wardroom, its business apparently finished.

"I'm in danger," Derec said. "I need your help."

"False assessment: you are not now in danger," the humanoid robot said. "Should you be in danger, help will be provided."

The robot took one step toward the pressure hatch, and Derec moved to place himself in its path.

"I'm not letting you leave here until you tell me where I am and what I'm doing here," Derec said sharply.

The robot's answer was nonverbal but perfectly clear. Stepping closer, it grasped his shoulders firmly but gently and moved him out of the way. Then it walked with smooth strides past him to the hatch.

"Open," it said.

Feeling helpless, Derec let the robot go, then turned to see if he could discover what it had been doing in the wardroom. Only two things had changed since Derec had left. The galley was still counting down to full Demand status, but the selector was now showing a short list of selections that were already available. Derec himself had set that change in motion.

It was the other change that the robot was responsible for. The screen of the com center was no longer blank. In bright red letters, it reported: MESSAGE TRANSMITTED.

It was then that Derec knew for certain that he was alone on the asteroid. The fact that there was an environmental cell deep under the surface implied that there had once been at least a temporary human presence here. But this little world was in the hands of the robots now, and he was a trespasser. What message they had sent about him, and to whom they had sent that message, there was no telling.

Derec took the time for a meal, which he needed, and a shower, which he did not. But the shower provided him with something to do while thinking, and he had a lot to think about. His presence, his identity, the cause and reason for his memory impairment were as troublesome as ever. And after his excursion, he had a new mystery. Why were the robots behaving so strangely?

Derec asked himself under what circumstances a robot might refuse to answer his questions, which amounted to refusing to obey his orders. Within his understanding of the Laws of Robotics, Derec could think of only two, both illustrated by his experience with Darla: because it did not know the answers, or because it had been instructed previously not to reveal them.

Precedence did count for something with robots. A robot ordered by its owner to service a flyer would not leave that job to search for a neighbor child's missing cat—unless it was the owner, not the child, who made the request. A carefully worded command would hold up against anything but a counterorder rooted in a First Law situation. If the robots had been told not to talk about what they were doing, nothing Derec could do would make them disobey.

Before he dressed, he searched his body for clues to who he was. He found no scars large enough that he would expect to remember when and how he acquired them. He bore no tattoos or skin ornaments, wore no rings or jewelry.

The only distinctive mark he seemed to bear was inside, in

the things that he knew. Somewhere, sometime, he had received advanced training in microelectronics. He had more than a passing understanding of robotics and computers. Was that commonplace, a standard curriculum for someone his age? He thought not. And if not, it might be the trail that he could follow to rediscover himself.

The com center was continuing its intransigence, still ignoring his input, still mockingly displaying the words MESSAGE TRANSMITTED. But there was one door that hadn't yet been slammed in his face. Donning a breather and a spare cartridge pack, Derec left the E-cell to explore the rest of the complex.

Derec began by creating a mental map of the great chamber, assigning arbitrary compass points with the E-cell as his reference for south. The chamber seemed to be roughly rectangular, longer north to south than east to west by a factor of two or more. He started hand-walking northward down the same corridor the custodian robots had used, counting his paces as he went.

Five hundred paces later, his arms were tired and the north wall seemed no closer. Stopping to rest, he surveyed the robot population of the chamber. He tallied seventeen of the humanoid robots, none of which were nearby. Among the nonhumanoid robots, he identified five different types: the pickers, the custodians, a large cargo handler Derec dubbed a porter, some multi-armed micro-assemblers, and an armored robot with oversized grapples whose function he could not guess.

Most of the robots he encountered were moving purposefully through the aisles, carrying out their assignments. But toward the north end of the chamber, Derec spotted a small army of robots standing inert and de-energized, waiting to be called into action. All the varieties were represented among the reserves except for the humanoid robots.

The robot stockpile was Derec's clue to understanding where he was. The chamber seemed to be primarily a collection of spare parts. True, he had spotted a cluster of injection and extrusion machines in one area, a battery of laser welders in another, a chip-burning shop in a third, all apparently in full-time use. But all those operations were apparently maintenance related.

Whatever they're doing here, they're on a very heavy duty cycle—possibly even continuous operations, he told himself. Zero down-time could only be bought with a large-scale repair and maintenance operation. And that high price was only worth paying when time mattered more than money.

There was a steady stream of robot traffic on the lifts located at intervals through the chamber, and the obvious next step was to find out where they were going. Giving up his plan to walk the length of the chamber, Derec headed for the nearest lift.

Like the breather, the lifts were clearly the product of a unique approach to engineering. To Derec, they looked like something either unfinished or nonfunctional. They were also more proof that the complex had been designed with robots alone in mind. No human would have ridden one voluntarily.

The shaft was a vertical boring three meters in diameter, its sides lined with the same synthemesh as the chamber ceiling. Peering out over the edge and down, Derec glimpsed a deep shaft lit at regular intervals by stationary blue glows, which he assumed marked other levels. The shaft seemed to extend much farther down than up. Above the great chamber—which he had begun to think of as the warehouse—he counted only seven levels, while below it he could see at least twenty levels before the traffic in the shaft obscured what might lie beyond.

A descending lift platform on the nearest guide rod obliged Derec to duck back out of the way. The platform, a square grid a meter on a side, reached the floor level and stopped as though waiting for him.

While it waited there, traffic kept moving on the other three guide rods. Watching the robots board and disembark, Derec saw that while the lift was in operation, the robots were clamped to the platforms magnetically. He wondered how he would be able to keep his balance and footing without that assistance. There were no railings to grab on to, and the guide rod itself appeared to be electrically live.

Personal considerations aside, he could not help but admire the engineering aesthetics of the lift. It was a clean and focused solution to the problem of moving the maximum amount of traffic in the minimum time and space, a solution fully integrated with the requirements of the colony.

But clever as the system was, Derec was not eager for a ride in the dark on an open platform above a seemingly bottomless pit. Still, it was that or go back to the E-cell. He swallowed hard once and stepped carefully out onto the waiting platform.

"Up," he said.

"Level, please?"

"Uh—Level Two."

Singing a high-pitched song, the car began to climb swiftly. He stood with his arms crossed over his chest and his legs spread wide. Keeping his vision focused upward toward the nearest of the blue glows, he tried not to look at the shaft walls sliding swiftly by.

The platform flashed through several other levels before gradually slowing to let him off. The glimpses he caught of them prepared him for what awaited him on Two. When he stepped off the lift, he was standing at the crossroads of two low-ceilinged tunnels, each six meters wide. The walls, floor and ceiling were covered with the ubiquitous off-white synthemesh. The air was colder than ever, cold enough to make him hunch his shoulders and bury his hands under his arms.

Though the immediate vicinity of the lift was brightly lit by the blue floodlights, the tunnels themselves were illuminated only by dim yellow lamps set at intervals in the ceiling. Each was barely bright enough to mark its own position and make a tiny pool of yellow light on the floor of the tunnel.

The distant ends of the intersecting tunnels were invisible, the lines of ceiling lamps receding into infinity in both directions. The tunnels could be kilometers long, even tens of kilometers for all he could tell.

Have they honeycombed this entire asteroid? Derec wondered. *Thousands of levels—shafts a hundred kilometers deep —could this be a mining operation?*

But he could not understand why anyone would go to the trouble to mine an asteroid from the inside. The cutters on a prospecting ship could slice all but the densest nickel-iron asteroids into bite-sized chunks for the leviathan processing centers. No ore Derec knew of was worth the expense of tunnel-and-shaft mining on this scale. Even with the energy-and-raw-materials economics which applied with robot labor, it would have to be something a hundred times more precious

than the rarest element—unless the value of secrecy was part of
the equation.

Who am I dealing with? Derec wondered. Newly sobered, he
stepped back onto the lift.

"Level Three," he said.

The next two levels were just as silent and finished-looking
as Two. Derec could not decide whether they were finished-
waiting-to-be-used, like the spare parts in the great chamber, or
finished-and-abandoned.

But Level Five was another story. The rumble of heavy ma-
chinery assaulted his ears even before the platform reached the
lighted zone. When he stepped off the lift, he could feel rolling,
low-frequency vibrations in the floor and ceiling of the tunnel.

I'm getting closer, he thought. *Now—which way?* The
sound surrounded him, offering no clue as to which of the tunnels had the most promise.

While he stood there equivocating, a double platform arrived
and disgorged a porter robot. On impulse, Derec climbed onto
its half-full cargo pad. He was counting on its ignoring him, as
the picker had. He was not disappointed. Neither cradling him
in its arms nor trying to dislodge him, the porter started down
the south tunnel.

For the first two minutes of the ride, wind noise and the
whine of the robot's own mechanisms masked the distant work
noise. But before long Derec could sort the separate elements:
irregular thumping sounds like muffled explosions, a high-
pitched grinding that made his skin crawl, and a steady background rumble that suggested great masses of rock and ice
being moved about.

Presently the end of the tunnel came in sight as a black patch
in the distance. Shortly after, Derec began to detect a whiff of
ammonia in the air. The moment he did, another piece of the
puzzle fell into place.

He had wondered from the start why the complex outside the
E-cell was filled with nitrogen. The robots did not require it.
Strictly speaking, robots did not require an atmosphere at all.
And keeping the complex sealed and pressurized had to be more
complicated than simply opening it to space.

But maintaining a standard two-gas atmosphere in the proper proportions through the vast complex was even more complicated. Derec had concluded that the nitrogen atmosphere and "open" breathers were a compromise between the inconvenience of full pressure suits and the complexity of a dual-gas E-system. The nitrogen allowed humans to speak and hear normally and to move about without safesuits, without the fire and explosion risk posed by free oxygen.

But Derec had overlooked something important. The ices which made up a large fraction of the asteroid's bulk were not water, but compounds like methane and ammonia. The mining processes would inevitably release them as gases into the work area, where they might react with the high energies and circuits of the mining machinery or with each other.

I should have seen it sooner, he thought. Without an atmosphere comprised of some relatively inert gas, there would be no way to dilute the unwelcome compounds or efficiently flush them out. So of course, an atmosphere. Of course, nitrogen. The atmosphere accommodated a human presence, but was not primarily for human convenience.

The porter slowed as they neared the end of the tunnel, and Derec took that opportunity to jump off. Ahead of him were several robots, gathered near the end of the tunnel, and the gateway to what he presumed was the work chamber. Through the gateway he caught glimpses of a ragged rock wall, equipment booms, and an occasional flash of bright light.

The gateway itself was an enormous boxlike machine which filled the tunnel flush to the walls, floor, and ceiling. The only path through to the work chamber was a narrow walkway between columns of bright green chemical storage tanks. That was where he had to go.

As Derec drew closer, he saw that the gateway was actually crawling slowly forward. Like some mechanical larva, the gateway was burrowing through the asteroidal mass and leaving a finished tunnel in its wake. Everything—the raw material of the walls, the covering of reinforcing synthemesh, even the overhead lamps—was being handled in one continuous operation. The gateway was a four-surface paving machine.

But Derec's real interest was in the excavation beyond. He stepped up onto the gateway and threaded his way between the shoulder-high cylinders, aware as he did that one of the human-oid robots was following him. There was a strong draft through the walkway, from the tunnel to the chamber beyond. Even so, the odor of ammonia was almost strong enough to make him gag.

At the forward end, the narrow walkway widened into a control cabin, where two humanoid robots sat behind a bank of transparent panels looking out into the excavation chamber that surrounded the gateway on three sides. Derec stopped a few steps short of the ramp into the excavation and tried to sort out the functions of the equipment that filled it.

The uncut face of the asteroidal material was some thirty meters away. A two-headed boom cutter was working it, one boom bearing rotary grinders, the other microwave lasers. They moved back and forth like weaving cobras, and the ice and rock wall crumbled before them.

The lasers seemed to be doing most of the damage. Suddenly released from its icy glue, loose rock sloughed off the face with a cracking sound. More resistant deposits were gouged off by the rotating teeth of the grinder. The gases boiling off the face were being sucked into the wide-mouthed exhaust vents that loomed over the work face.

As he studied the work rig, a metallic hand touched his shoulder.

"You may not enter the processing zone during operations," the robot said.

The robot's edict stirred a flash of annoyance. "I will if I want to," Derec snapped back over his shoulder.

The robot tightened its grip pointedly. "You may not enter the processing zone during operations," the robot repeated. "Untrained personnel are to be considered at risk."

Shrugging off its touch, Derec turned his back on the robot and looked once more into the excavation. Like the gateway, the mining unit was slowly advancing toward an ever-receding rock face. The motion brought the jumble of loose rock within reach of scuttling scooper arms, which funneled it up a ramp to an enormous hopper. A pair of high-sided conveyors carried material away from the hopper, one to the left and one to the right. While on the conveyor it passed through an N-ray station, an X-ray station, and a magnetometer.

From that point on, things got confusing. It was as though after having gone to all that trouble to mine the asteroid, the robots had forgotten to sort out the part of it they wanted to keep.

Some of the tailings were diverted to a spur conveyor, run through a crusher, and then used as the raw material for the fifteen-centimeter thick walls of the tunnel. To Derec's astonishment, the rest was carried to the back wall of the work chamber, reunited with the captured methane and ammonia, and built up into a wall of ice and rock again. The excavation never got any larger.

But what about the tunnel? Derec wondered. They have to be taking something out—

Closer study showed him otherwise. The empty volume of the ever-lengthening access tunnel meant only that the asteroidal material surrounding it was being replaced in a more compressed state than it was in when mined. Nothing was being extracted. Nothing was being carried away for later refining or shipment.

It just didn't make sense.

The depletion alarm on Derec's first cartridge pack began to sound, and he transferred the delivery tube to the backup. He would have to leave soon or risk dying of nitrogen poisoning before he could return to the E-cell. But it was hard to tear himself away from the incomprehensible sight of a dozen robots and a few million dollars worth of heavy equipment engaged in a task as senseless as trying to dig a hole in water. And how many other excavations just like this were underway elsewhere in the complex? Ten? Fifty? Five hundred?

Trying to understand, Derec focused his attention on the robots. Three of the armored type patrolled the hopper, breaking up snags with their grapples. A fourth stood on a small platform under the booms of the cutter, shattering oversized rocks as they fell from the face with blasts from its chest-mounted laser. Two humanoids stood at the N-ray stations, intently studying the scanning screen.

Derec's guardian angel was still standing within arm's reach behind him, and he turned and sought the robot's eyes. "What are you mining here?" he demanded. "What's the point of all this?"

But the robot said nothing, gazing back with its expressionless eyes.

"Get out of the way," Derec said disgustedly, and the robot stepped aside into the control booth to let him pass.

His annoyance spilling over into anger, Derec stalked down the narrow walkway and jumped down to the tunnel. It was then he realized his mistake: there were no porter robots there to carry him back to the lift.

"I need a ride," Derec said sharply to the nearest humanoid robot. "Can you tell me when the next porter robot will be making a delivery?"

"What is your need?"

"I need a ride."

"That is not an approved allocation of resources."

Derec did not even bother to argue. Turning away, he stalked away northward, his mind unsettled, churning with unconnected thoughts. He felt as though the answer to all his questions was already in his grasp, except he couldn't recognize it. How did it all add up? What was wrong with the picture?

As he hand-walked along the tunnel, his thoughts kept carrying him back to the robots. There was something about the way they behaved, the way they worked together. Throughout the complex, all the routine, repetitive jobs were being done by the nonhumanoid robots. The blue-skinned humanoid robots were supervisors, trouble-shooters, technicians, repair specialists. But they could have just as easily done the repetitive jobs as well, even tending the front line in the excavation. Instead, there were a half-dozen specialized varieties, porters and pickers and miners that didn't act like robots at all—

Derec stopped short and turned to stare back down the tunnel toward the excavation. Of course. Of course. The picker and the custodians, the tenders and the porters *weren't* specialized robots working with the blue robots. They were *tools* being *used* by the blue robots. Their intelligence was limited—perhaps not even positronic in nature. The real intelligence resided in the humanoid robots, which might well be more sophisticated than any Derec had previously known of.

But why were they all here?

Derec thought of all the levels, all the tunnels that had already been bored out, all the mass of the asteroid still waiting undisturbed. Could he have stumbled on an industrial test site? It might explain much—the secrecy, the distinctive stamp of the unknown designer, the unending but pointless excavation.

Focus on the robots, Derec told himself. The tasks they're handling themselves are the ones they consider critical—

In a flash of memory, he saw the two humanoid robots tending the scanning instruments on the conveyor line, and suddenly Derec knew. The realization staggered him, and yet there was no pushing the notion away once it had formed in his mind.

The robots weren't mining the asteroid at all. They were *sifting* it. They were searching for something, something lost or buried or hidden, something so unique and valuable that it was worth any price, any effort.

What that something was, Derec could not imagine. And just at that moment, he was not sure that he ever wanted to find out.

CHAPTER 4

YOU CAN'T GET THERE FROM HERE

It was a very long way back to the lift. How fast had the porter gone when carrying him to the excavation? Forty kilometers per hour? Then the shaft lay ten kilometers away. Sixty? Then a fifteen-kilometer hike awaited him, at a thousand strides, a thousand arm-swings to a kilometer. Even in a gravity field this weak, that was asking a lot from his body.

He did not turn back only because he was sure that the Supervisors, as he had begun to think of the humanoid robots, knew where he was and how much oxygen he had. At some point the two changing variables would intersect at a value which said that he was in danger, and they would send a porter to fetch him and whisk him back to the E-cell.

Each time he saw a robot coming toward him, or heard one closing on him from behind, he began to anticipate relief for his weary arms and legs. But each time, the robot sped past without even slowing. He considered trying to stop a porter by blocking the tunnel, but the only porters that came by were burdened with a full load of chemical tanks or machine parts. There was no room for him.

Because there was no choice, Derec pressed on. For a time he tried counting the yellow ceiling lamps to prove to himself that he was making progress, but his mind wandered and he lost count. There was a terrible sameness to the tunnel, with its unrelieved stretches of white. It seemed as though he were caught in limbo, trapped on a subterranean treadmill.

As it turned out, he was not wrong in thinking that the Supervisors were aware of him. But he was quite wrong about the form their help would take.

He had sat down to rest, his back against the west wall, when a picker came racing up and stopped half a meter away. From its cargo basket it plucked a pair of fresh cartridge packs, laying them at his feet. Before he could react, it backed up, pivoted, and raced away. The timing was so perfect that the pack Derec was using began to sound its depletion alarm just as the picker vanished from sight in the distance.

"Consistent," he said crossly, addressing the absent Supervisors as he swapped the depleted packs for the new ones. "You've done as little as possible to help me right from the start. And this really is the very least you could do."

Hours later, he reached the E-cell with barely enough energy to fold down one of the bunks before he collapsed in it. He was asleep in minutes, his body claiming its rest. But his troubles pursued him even in his dreams, which were full of silent blue robots moving through dark places ripe with the cold scent of danger.

When he awoke, Derec began to think about escaping. For it was clear now that the most likely message for the Supervisor to have sent was something on the order of, "We have an intruder. What shall we do with him?" And Derec did not like most of the possible answers to that question.

He did not think the Supervisor robots, independent as they might be, were capable of killing him. The First Law was too deeply rooted in the basic structure of a positronic brain. To remove it or tamper with it was to guarantee trouble, up to and including complete intellectual disintegration.

But the recipient of the message was probably human, and therefore quite capable of using violence in service of his or her self-interest. They would want to know how he had discovered the installation, and what he had wanted there, and he would have nothing to tell them.

Perhaps they would accept that at face value, and help him return to wherever he had come from. But considering the circumstances, the stronger possibility was that they would insist on answers. Derec sensed that it would take a long time to convince them he had none. Even so, afterward they would want to make sure that he could never tell anyone what he had stumbled on.

No, he did not want to wait around for the Supervisors' masters to arrive. The key to escaping was Darla. The pod's thrusters were almost certainly rated for a much stronger gravity field than the one the asteroid boasted. If so, then there should be more than enough fuel remaining to lift off the asteroid again and put some distance between it and himself—if only he could convince Darla of the wisdom of that act.

But first, he had to find her. Measuring from memory, Derec suspected that the pod was too large to have been brought down the lift. The robots must have removed him from the pod somewhere on the surface—inside an entry dome, perhaps—and left the pod behind.

So he began by riding the lift in search of the place where he had been brought into the asteroid. It turned out to be called Level Zero. At the top of the lift shaft a disclike pressure door scissored out of the way to allow the platform to pass, and the lift carried Derec up into a high-ceilinged circular room a hundred meters across.

Most of the chamber was filled with neatly aligned rows of machines—buglike augers and borers, tracked carriers, and flying globes like the one Derec had seen when the robots were carrying him and his pod away. On the far side of the room, a steep ramp enclosed by a transparent material led up and out onto the surface.

There was a Supervisor there as well, seated at a control station with its back to Derec. Though it gave no such sign, Derec was sure the robot was aware of his presence.

Stepping off the lift, Derec began to wander among the idle machines. This must be some of the equipment that was used to survey the outer crust of the asteroid, he thought. The flying globes were probably scanning platforms, while the other machines could be used to dig up any promising sites.

It seemed just as obvious to Derec that the surface survey was complete. It was not only the appearance of the machines that led to that conclusion. Searching the surface first made sense. Why even begin the underground excavation before you were sure that the object of your search wouldn't be turned up by a much faster and far less complicated aerial survey?

But Derec was less interested in sorting out the remaining mysteries about this world than he was in finding Darla and saying good-bye to it. A quick catalog of the chamber turned up no sign of the pod or of his safesuit. But he did find a rack with three pearl-white augmented worksuits. They were too large for use in the lower levels or to allow him to climb into the pod if he found it, but he could still use one for an excursion to the surface.

Moving behind the nearest suit, Derec grabbed the crossbar and vaulted himself feet first through the access door on the back. As he settled in the saddlelike seat, he felt the feedback pads snugging up against his feet. He inserted his arms into the suit's arms, and the controllers for the external manipulator came into his hands. A sloping display screen reflected the status of the suit's systems on the bubblelike canopy before him.

"Close and pressurize," he said, and the access door began to swing shut. He tried raising his arms, and the suit stirred in smooth response. At last, a little power, he thought.

But when he turned to head for the ramp, he found a Supervisor barring his way. "The surface is a restricted area," the robot said.

Derec heard the words through a speaker at his ear and halted his advance. Probably the augmented suit was more than a match for a Supervisor, or would be in the hands of a skilled operator. But Derec did not want a fight. He only wanted answers.

"Tell me where I can find the survival pod I came here in," Derec said.

"You do not have authorization to leave the community."

"That's where it is, isn't it? On the surface. That's where you hid it. What did you do, put my suit back in it after you took it off me?" Derec demanded. "I'm going out. If you don't want to be damaged you'd better get out of the way."

The robot did not move. "The survival pod is not on the surface," it said.

Considering the way the Supervisors had been treating him, that was a generous answer. But Derec wanted more. "Either I go looking on the surface, or you show me where the pod is. Those are the only choices."

There was a brief pause before the robot responded. When the answer came, it was a welcome surprise. "I will show you the pod."

"Are we going outside, or down below?"

"Down."

Derec still wanted to go to the surface. He had hopes of being able to use the stars and sky to determine at least in general terms where the planetoid was located—what kind of star it was orbiting, and whether the planetoid was independent or part of a planetary system. But until he found the pod, none of that mattered, so Derec could afford to be a gracious victor.

"Thank you," he said. "If you'll wait just a moment, I'll put this suit back."

But Derec did not get to enjoy his victory for long. The Supervisor took him back down to the warehouse level and led him through the maze toward the east wall. As they swung around the molding section and its high rack supply cache, the robot stopped short.

"Here."

But Derec could see no pod. All he could see was a large open area with rows of assorted components neatly arrayed on the floor. "Where?"

With a sweeping motion of his arm, the Supervisor repeated, "Here."

That was when Derec took a closer look at the hardware laid out before him and realized the truth. The pod was there, just as the Supervisor said. But it was in a thousand pieces, lying on the floor like a giant jigsaw puzzle. The robots had disassembled it down to fundamental components. Derec could recognize but a few—curved plates that had been part of the hull, several thruster bells, and, a few meters from where Derec stood, the lenses from the seven green lamps on the command console.

"No," he cried out despairingly. "Why did you do it?"

"It was necessary to determine that the search objective was not concealed within the pod."

"And my safesuit? Did they tear that apart, too?"

In answer, the Supervisor led Derec into the maze and showed him his suit, lying in several dozen pieces. The fabric had been separated from the binding rings, the environmental systems stripped out of the chest unit. Even the helmet had been disassembled.

"I'm surprised that you didn't tear me apart, too," he said bitterly as he looked at it.

"Please explain the reason for your surprise," the robot said. "It is impossible for a robot to harm a human. Have you not been informed of this fact?"

"Nevermind," Derec said with a sigh. "I was being sarcastic."

"Sir?"

"Humans don't always mean what they say. Haven't you been informed of that fact?" After a moment, he added, "But you did search me, didn't you?"

"Yes. While you were unconscious, you were subjected to a full-body magnetic resonance scan," the robot replied.

Derec almost laughed at the absurdity of it. "It figures," he said. "I suppose having you put the suit and pod back together is out of the question."

"Nothing may take priority over the primary directive."

"What about all those spare robots sitting up north doing nothing? You could activate a few of them."

"The tasks would require not only Assemblers but the supervision of a Systemist. All Systemists are fully scheduled under the current duty cycle."

"I guess that means no," Derec said. He looked across the expanse of parts that once was a spacecraft and sighed. "Do you have a name of some kind?"

"I am Monitor 5."

"Why are you talking to me, Monitor 5?"

"I perceived that you were stressed. While stressed, humans frequently derive benefit from communication."

Derec snorted. "I guess that's one way to say it. Then tell me, Monitor 5—do you robots know what you're looking for?"

"I may not reveal any information about my mission here."

"What about me? Are you allowed to tell me what you know about me?"

"What do you wish to know?"

"The event recorder in the survival pod—did they find it?"

"I was not part of that work unit. I will consult Analyst 3." The robot paused. "Yes. A data recorder was located."

"Did it tell you what ship I came from? How I got here? Anything?"

"The recorder had not been initialized. The recording disk was blank."

Stunned, Derec looked down and away to hide his expression from the robot. His gaze fell on the pile of fabric from his suit, and he knelt down and began to sift through it. "There was a datastrip on my suit—"

"Yes. It was a test strip. It contained no personal data."

Letting the fabric fall from his hands back to the floor, Derec slowly stood. "A test strip?"

"They are quite common. They are used in calibrating a data reader's scanner."

"But it said Derec—"

"Yes. The leading manufacturer of such readers is Derec Data Systems."

Derec felt the strength go out of his legs. "Then you don't know who I am, either."

"No. We do not know who you are."

"And that message you sent about me? What did it say?"

"I did not send the message. One moment while I consult Analyst 17." The robot paused. "Analyst 17 believed that due to your irrational behavior, you would come to harm or endanger the primary objective unless continually supervised. Therefore he sent a message requesting that you be rescued."

"He made that decision on his own?"

"Analyst 17 felt that the threat was of sufficient magnitude to transcend the prohibition regarding communications."

"Prohibition from who? Who's in charge here? And who'd he send the message to?"

"I may not—"

"—reveal any information about your mission here, yes."

Grimacing, Derec closed his eyes and tried to shut out the world.

"Are you ill?" Monitor 5 asked, concerned.

"No," Derec said in an unsteady voice. "I'm just back to square one again, that's all."

Dispirited, Derec retreated to the E-cell, his illusion of being even partially in control of his own fate destroyed. There was no chance of his reconstructing the pod himself. He might leave the community using one of the augmented worksuits, but there was no way he could leave the asteroid. It seemed that all he could do was stay out of the robots' way and wait for whoever Analyst 17 had signalled to respond.

As though the robots had decided that he needed something to keep him occupied and safely out of their way, Derec found the wardroom com center unlocked and displaying the word "READY." When Derec touched the "Help" key, a short menu popped up on the screen. It offered him a choice between something called Scratchpad and a library index.

Scratchpad proved to be a cross between a notebook and an engineer's sketch pad. He amused himself for a while with its graphics capabilities by drawing a map of the part of the complex he knew firsthand. The system made it easy for him, converting his unsteady movements with the tracer into straight lines, copying duplicate sections, performing fills and rotations.

When drawing deteriorated into doodling, Derec shifted mental gears and decided to make a diary of what had happened since he had awoken in the pod. But his first entry was self-conscious and self-indulgent, and he ended his log with a short sarcastic note:

Dear Mom,
    I got no friends here. Can I come home?

Embarrassed by his own self-pity, Derec purged the Scratch-pad memory and pushed his chair away from the terminal. But the terrible feeling of separateness which underlay the thought was not so easily banished. Without family, friends, an ally of any sort, Derec's little world was a lonely place.

The book-film library was Derec's last defense against maudlin thoughts. Scanning the directory, he was struck by the unusual mix of entries. There was a whole subdirectory of texts from Earth's Classical Age, including a few whose authors or titles Derec was intrigued to discover he recognized: Lucretius' *De Rerum Natura*, Newton's *Principia*, Darwin's *The Origin of Species*.

Another large subdirectory consisted of architectural draw-ings and photographs. Again, a few names struck chords in Derec's memory—Mies van der Rohe, Buckminster Fuller, Frank Lloyd Wright. But when he asked the system to sample those files at one image every few seconds, he found the images were of places that he could not remember ever being and structures he could not remember seeing. It left him wondering why he knew the names in the first place.

Conspicuously absent was any sort of current technical refer-ence on such topics as microelectronics, robotics, process de-sign, and the like. Derec assumed that they were in a separate technical library not available to him.

But there were other sections which under other circum-stances would probably have appealed to him—a biography of robotics pioneer Susan Calvin; *Genesis*, Marvin Eller's anec-dotal history of twentieth-century computer science; a screenful of titles on astronomy and astrography.

But Derec was not interested in being educated, or in any-thing that required thinking. He wanted to be a spectator to someone else's problems, to disengage his mind and surrender himself to the spell of the storyteller.

Yet when he turned to the fiction subdirectory, he found the pickings sparse. Aside from a few interactive mysteries and a half-dozen text novels, all of which would require too much work on his part, Derec's choice was limited to the world of theater. *Faust, Waiting for Godot, Daedalus and Icarus, Sweeney Todd*—the titles meant nothing to Derec. But Shakespeare he knew, and Shakespeare was well represented on the list.

Feeling a need for laughter, Derec chose the comedy *A Midsummer Night's Dream*. Then he retreated to a comfortable chair, propped his feet up on the conference table, and let the recording carry him away to ancient Greece, to a woods near the city of Athens, where he might amuse himself with the love-crossed confusion of human and fairy kings, and the pranks of the devilish sprite Puck.

"Up and down, up and down," Puck vowed. "I will lead them up and down. I am feared in field and town. Goblin, lead them up and down—"

In the middle of Puck's declamation, Derec heard the unmistakable sound of the inner door of the airlock opening. He came to his feet as a Supervisor entered the wardroom and crossed toward the com center.

"What do you want?" Derec demanded, following.

The robot ignored Derec. "Priority interrupt," the robot said to the com center. The screen went black and the speakers silent.

PASSWORD?

The robot's fingers flew over the keypad in a blur, but nothing appeared on the screen except the instruction PROCEED.

Without hesitation, the robot began to hammer at the keys again. Even standing only an arm's length away, Derec had no clue to what the robot was entering. The steady staccato of keyclicks lasted perhaps twenty seconds—three or four hundred characters. Then the robot raised his hand and stepped back.

MESSAGE TRANSMITTED, the screen acknowledged.

"Resume," the robot said, and turned to go.

"Cancel," Derec said, moving quickly to place his body between the robot and the door. "Identify yourself."

"I am Analyst 9."

"What's happening? What did you just do?"

"Please stand aside," Analyst 9 said. "I have urgent duties elsewhere."

"The last time one of you was in here, it was to send a distress message. What's up now? Is a ship here? Is that it? I have a right to know what's going on—"

For an answer, Analyst 9 raised his arm and pushed Derec firmly out of the way. He stumbled back toward the conference table and sat down hard in one of the chairs.

"Do not interfere," the Supervisor said, and left the room.

Though his shock at the robot's physical treatment of him slowed him for an instant, Derec scrambled to his feet and followed.

Out in the chamber, Derec found frenzied activity bordering on chaos. Dozens of porter and picker robots were streaming off the lifts, as if some massive exodus were underway. Scores more were scurrying through the aisles gathering up components and carrying them toward the west wall and the recycling smelter located there.

To Derec's astonishment, instead of depositing what they held and turning back to get more, the pickers and porters queued up at the smelter carried their burdens directly into the heart of the smelter and never appeared again. For some reason, the robots were systematically destroying selected items in their storehouse—and themselves at the same time.

Distracted by the parade of suicidal robots, Derec had lost track of Analyst 9. Now, as he scanned the chamber to try to find it, he saw something else extraordinary. There were no Supervisors anywhere in the warehouse. The various manufacturing centers were standing silent and abandoned.

On a hunch, Derec fought his way through to the lift and commandeered a platform to carry him up to Level Zero. There he found a gathering of twenty Supervisors. They were standing motionless in a circle, with hands linked as though in some sort of direct conference.

They took no notice of his arrival, and so Derec crossed the room to where two other Supervisors sat at the giant command console.

"Monitor 5?"

"Yes, Derec," one of the robots said with a nod of acknowledgment.

"Can you tell me what's happening?"

"Surface sensors have detected a large spacecraft approaching. The trajectory and velocity profile indicate that it will match orbit with this planetoid."

"I'm going to get off this rock?" Derec exulted. "Praise the stars!"

"There is a sixty-eight percent probability that the ship intercepted the distress signal. However, there is only a nine percent probability that the ship is here to rescue you."

That news jolted Derec back to earth. "Intercepted? They aren't the people you were calling?"

"No, Derec."

"Who are they, then? What do they want?"

"The ship is currently unidentified."

"Is that why all the robots downstairs are going crazy?"

"I cannot answer that question now," Monitor 5 said. "I may be able to tell you more shortly."

"What should I do?"

"Wait."

"Great. How long?"

"Not long," Monitor 5 said, standing. "Excuse me. The Analysts are calling for me."

Crossing the room, Monitor 5 joined the conference circle. He stood there with them for perhaps two minutes, then the circle broke apart. Most of the Supervisors headed for the lift. Two of them, including Monitor 5, came to where Derec stood.

"I have been appointed to communicate with you," Monitor 5 said.

"Appointed?" The robot's choice of word confused Derec.

"By default," the robot admitted. "None of the Analysts feel comfortable dealing with a human."

"Are you telling me that they haven't been talking to me because they don't want to? They don't know how?"

"With few exceptions, their experience has been exclusively with other robots. I have been chosen because of my previous success in communicating with you," Monitor 5 said.

"Is that another exception?" Derec said, indicating the robot standing just behind Monitor 5.

"I am accompanied by Analyst 17."

"Ah—we've met—sort of."

"Analyst 17 is here to assist me," Monitor 5 said. "Please, Derec. There are important matters to discuss, and there is very little time."

"Then get started."

"Thank you. The Analysts are agreed that the approaching ship is a threat to the security of our operation. The possibility of discovery was anticipated by those who placed us here. Our instructions for such a circumstance are to destroy ourselves and this facility. Certain preliminary steps are already underway—"

"The robots at the smelter."

"Yes. All proprietary technology must be destroyed and the excavation rendered unusable. This directive was impressed on us at the highest level of necessity and urgency. We must comply. However, your presence was *not* anticipated."

"What do I have to do with it?"

"As long as you are present, we are not able to fulfill our directive, since to destroy the complex would kill you. Even to destroy ourselves would leave you unprotected. Therefore, for us to carry out our directive, it is necessary for you to leave."

"I've been ready to leave since I got here. Just show me the way."

Analyst 17 spoke up at that point. "Unfortunately, since leaving the community also represents a significant risk to your life, we are unable to assist you in doing this and are in fact obliged to prevent it."

"So you're not going to put my pod back together? My safesuit?"

"No."

"This is crazy."

"On the contrary, it is fundamentally logical," Analyst 17 said. "If we protect you, you will almost certainly die, which we cannot allow. If we fail to protect you, you may survive, but you will be placed in grave danger, which we cannot allow."

Derec looked from Monitor 5 to the Analyst in disbelief, then back again. "So what *are* you going to do with me?"

"Nothing," Monitor 5 said. "No action is possible. If we help you to escape, we will be placing you in danger. But if we prevent your escape, we will also be placing you in danger."

Derec was starting to get lost in the convolutions of the conversation. "Is that what you want me to do? Escape?"

The robot hesitated. "We want you to remain safe and un-harmed."

It seemed as though the robot were tiptoeing through a logical minefield. "What if I do leave?"

"When we discover that you are gone, we will have to pursue you." It hesitated again. "However, until you are returned to our care the remainder of the community will be free to pursue the next highest priority directive."

"In other words, if I escape, the First Law is no longer a factor. You can go ahead and destroy yourselves in good conscience."

"That is essentially correct," said Analyst 17, "though I must warn you there is a danger if you continue to discuss it."

Derec ignored the warning. "Escape to where?"

"We cannot consider that question," Monitor 5 said.

"Well, I can, and I don't like the answer!" Derec snapped. "I'll tell you what I intend to do—as soon as that ship is close enough to pick up the signal from a suit transmitter, I'm getting into one of those augments over there and going up to the surface to ask them to save me from you."

"We could not allow that."

"So what am I supposed to do? Go wander around on the surface until my air runs out? This is nuts. How can you even ask me to do such a thing?"

"Derec, I must repeat, there is a danger—," Analyst 17 began.

"We have not asked you to do anything," Monitor 5 said. "We have simply outlined for you the consequences of actions you may choose to take."

"You may not be asking, but you're dropping some loud hints," Derec said. "You're telling me that if I want to go kill myself, you'll look the other way. I don't understand how this whole conversation can even be taking place. What's wrong with all of you?"

Monitor 5 answered. "I am following a highly conditional logic path proposed by Analyst 17—"

"So that's why he's really here."

"—in which the uncertainty of your fate is modified by your own volitional acts to a positive value weighed against the high probability of harm due to inaction."

"In other words, you talked yourself into it," Derec said. "Well, you haven't talked me into it. Your prime objective and your security don't mean a thing to me. Do you think it's important to me if you can't destroy yourselves? I don't care if that ship belongs to your worst enemy.

"In fact, I'm beginning to think that if they're your enemy, that makes them my friend. I'm not going anywhere. And I'm sure as hell not going to go kill myself to get you off the hook."

The robots were apparently not willing to let it go at that. When Derec left Level Zero, Analyst 17 followed. It took a different lift, and when they reached the warehouse level, it studiously trailed several steps behind him. But there was no question that he was under surveillance.

It did not make sense that immediately after asking him to escape, the robots would set a bloodhound to dog his heels. But since he had no intention of doing what the robots wanted, it hardly mattered if he understood. He could safely ignore his shadow.

The warehouse was still a hive of chaotic activity, and Derec retreated from it to the quiet of the E-cell. He thought Analyst 17 might content itself to watch and wait outside, since the cell had only one exit. But the robot came inside as well, and when Derec entered the wardroom, it followed him in and took a seat at the opposite end of the conference table.

At first, however, Derec barely noticed the robot's entry. The video from a sky camera somewhere on the surface was being displayed on the com center screen. It showed a small, distant orange sun and a field of dim stars in which Derec saw no immediately recognizable patterns. A dark backlit hulk was moving across the star background, growing perceptibly larger as it closed on the asteroid. It was still too far away to show a distinctive profile, but it was clearly a massive spaceship of some kind.

"More propaganda?" Derec asked.

"The Analysts agreed that you have a right to know the source and current status of the threat."

"Do you think I'm going to see that thing up there and panic? It won't work. This isn't much, but it's home. I'm not leaving."

The robot made no reply, and remained silent while Derec

went to the autogalley and assembled a lunch. When he came back with it and sat down, he soon became painfully conscious of the robot patiently watching him.

"Whose side are you on, anyway?" Derec asked between mouthfuls.

"Clarify."

"What are you doing here? I thought you wanted me to skip out. But I couldn't make a move without you knowing about it."

"Your conversation with Monitor 5 forced him into recognizing a First Law conflict."

"You mean his little self-deception fell apart?"

"Monitor 5 is now deeply concerned that you may attempt to escape and harm yourself in the process or as a consequence. To relieve that potential and allow Monitor 5 to return to his duties, I offered to watch you."

"What about you? Did I make your logic bomb blow up, too?"

"No."

"So you're not here to stop me," Derec said, pushing his plate away. "You're here to make sure no one else stops me."

"Your observations are irrelevant to the situation. You have stated your intention to remain in our care."

"Right." Derec glanced up at the screen. The ship was still a dark shape without texture, but it now filled fully a third of the frame. "But I still think you expect me to start getting worried and make a move. Well, to show you just how worried I am, I'm going to go in the other room to take a nap," Derec said, standing. "If you decide to come along, all I ask is that you pick out your own bunk. There isn't room in mine for two."

CHAPTER 6
A ROCK AND A HARD PLACE

Analyst 17 did not follow, and Derec did not nap. He lay on his bunk and stared at the ceiling, trying to regain perspective.

The robots' predicament was real and substantial. It was not only the matter of being frustrated in their attempt to fulfill their Second Law obligations to their master. They were tiptoeing along the edge of a First Law chasm, a paradox capable of paralyzing not only individual robots, but the entire community. He was their first obligation, and yet there was nothing they could do for him but beg him to save himself.

If it were not so serious, it would be laughable. It was as though a person suffering from hiccups had asked a friend, "Please surprise me." How could he catch the robots off guard, even with Analyst 17's collaboration?

On top of which, the whole idea of escaping was absurd. Without help from the robots, he couldn't possibly reassemble the pod before the ship arrived. And even if he could, there was no way it could run from the approaching ship.

If he continued to think of both the robots and the strangers as enemies, there were no solutions to the equation. Only by assuming that the strangers were coming to help him, or would be willing to help him even if they had other purposes there, could he envision a way out. He could wait until the ship was in orbit, then go to the surface in an augment and radio to them for help.

Just then the bunk shuddered under him, and he sat bolt upright. He thought for a moment that he hadn't felt it, or experienced the sudden start which sometimes comes just before dozing off. But then another tremor shook the room, and he could no longer think it was an illusion. He jumped to his feet and ran across to the wardroom.

Analyst 17 was still sitting there as Derec had left him. "What's happening?" Derec demanded.

"We are under attack," the robot said, gesturing toward the com center.

Derec stared at the screen. The ship had tacked to a position where half of its sunward side was visible, allowing Derec to see details for the first time. What he saw confused him. The ship seemed to have been not designed, but collected. It looked more like a space junkyard than a dangerous raider. But raider it was.

Just in the part Derec could see clearly, there were eleven distinct hulls, as well as a tangled matrix of connecting structures. There were ships old enough to be in a museum and others new enough to be a shipwright's showpiece. Sleek transatmospheric profiles nestled against the cylinders and grips of deep-space haulers. All across the mass of the ship, small red and orange lights were blinking on and off.

"Who are they?" Derec whispered.

"Unknown."

"Well, didn't they hail us? What do they want?"

"There was no signal on any frequency commonly used for communication."

Derec felt another vibration through the floor. "What kind of weapons are they using?"

"The ship's armament appears to consist primarily of phased microwave lasers."

"And what do we have to fight back?"

"The community has no weapons."

"What?" Derec demanded.

The robot's answer was patient and calm. "It is highly probable that the ship contains humans. We would not be permitted to use weapons against them."

Derec stared at the robot, then at the screen. Unlike in careless fictions, there were no stabbing beams of brilliant light to betray the energies pouring down from the radar ship. There were only the winking lights, and the ground moving under Derec's feet. "Are we in danger?"

"Yes."

"How much?"

"The ship began its attack in the area of our only permanent surface installation, the antenna farm located 170 degrees east of the primary shaft—"

"These vibrations we're feeling are from that far away?"

"Yes. The primary assault was successful and communications are out. A number of tunnels in that region have apparently collapsed. Firing pattern now appears to be random. The ship is currently in a nearly synchronous orbit with a slippage of two degrees per minute."

"So in less than ninety minutes they'll be overhead."

"That is correct."

It was obvious to Derec that he could wait no longer to act. If the ship breached the complex's pressure envelope while he was still in the E-cell, he would never get out. The breathers couldn't keep him alive in a vacuum.

And there was another danger, just as acute—that the power would be interrupted or the lifts disabled, and he would be trapped on the warehouse level. Even in low gravity he did not think he could climb up a lift shaft by hand.

Not that running about on the surface in an augment was as attractive a proposition as it had been a short time ago. The chances were that he would be taken not for a prisoner trying to escape but for an enemy to be destroyed. Even so, dying buried in the icy heart of the asteroid was infinitely less appealing than dying out in the open.

"This logic path that you devised—am I correct in thinking that you and Monitor 5 are the only Supervisors who were able to follow it without hitting a First Law conflict?"

"Yes."

"Why? Why you?"

"My experience with human beings has provided me with a more sophisticated perspective on their nature and behavior."

"You've had contact with other humans? Besides me?"

"Yes."

"Who?"

"I am not permitted to say."

Dead end. "Are the other robots even aware of what you asked me to try to do?"

"No."

"How were you going to destroy the complex?"

"The material used to line all the tunnel walls contains an explosive. Once all the other Supervisors have been destroyed, the last Monitor and Analyst will together transmit the trigger signal. The resulting explosion should cause the entire excavated portion of the asteroid to subside."

"I see," Derec said. Great, he thought to himself. If I stay in the complex, the raiders will bring it down on my head. If I leave, the robots will blow it up under my feet.

Unless—

Unless there was some way to get off the surface, some source of thrust adequate to give him and his augment escape velocity. Considering the weakness of the asteroid's gravity, escape velocity did not amount to much. He could probably put a ball in orbit just by throwing it as hard as he could. The leg servos of the augmented suit were likely powerful enough to permit him to literally jump clear.

Unfortunately, the safety regs on augment design required governors on the leg servos to prevent someone from trying exactly that. But what engineers had joined together, tinkerers could tear asunder—

At that moment, a bright flare seemed to appear on the body of the ship, and an instant later the energy beam burned out the eyes of the camera unit relaying the picture. Another camera some distance away took over, and the low angle at which it was focused showed not only the ship but the bilious clouds boiling off the surface where its weapons were trained.

The sight spurred Derec to action. "There doesn't seem to be any escape for any of us," he lied, wearing his best look of resignation. "I guess there's nothing else for me to do but go prepare to die. I would be grateful if you could grant me privacy while I carry out the appropriate rituals."

The lie passed. "I do not fully understand the purpose of such rituals," the robot said, "but I will respect your privacy."

Derec did not need long to put his rapidly developing plan in motion. Returning to his cabin, he swept up the pillows off two of the bunks, then ran to the airlock with them cradled in his arms.

"Open."

The sound of the inner seal opening brought Analyst 17 out of the wardroom, but by then it was too late. Derec stepped inside the lock, and the door closed behind him.

"Cycle," he said, fumbling with the straps of a breather.

When the outer door opened, he draped the pillows over the bottom sill of the hatch and then stepped out over them. Just as Derec had expected, the pillows kept the outer door from sealing, interrupting the cycle and imprisoning the robot inside. He did not know how long it would hold, whether there was some way for the robot to override the lock system, and he did not wait around to find out.

The line at the smelter included Supervisors, but they took no notice of him as he passed by. He rode the lift up to Level Zero, where he discovered that Monitor 5 had been busy taking precautions against his return. Two of the augments were missing, vanished as though they had never been there. The third was wedged against the wall by one of the tracked carriers, which in turn was barricaded in place by a four-legged auger unit.

He did not think the suit was damaged—tampering with safety equipment would almost certainly invoke the First Law —but it was going to take a little getting to. And part of the problem would be Monitor 5. The robot was seated at the console when Derec arrived, and rose and started for Derec the moment he stepped off the lift and placed it on standby.

Their paths intersected when Derec was a few meters short of the carrier. "The surface is a restricted area," the robot said.

"I know that," Derec said, circling and staying out of reach of the robot's hands. "This equipment is improperly stored. I'm going to take care of it."

But Monitor 5 was not going to be put off that easily.

"You may not leave. You are in no danger here," it said, reaching for him.

Derec backed away and scrambled up the steps into the enclosed operator's station. "Wrong. If I stay here, I'll be killed when the ship destroys the station."

"We will protect you."

Derec wasted no time or breath arguing the point. "You can't even protect yourselves," he said, and slammed and locked the door.

The operator's interface was standard, and the functions of those few controls which weren't were clear at a glance. He touched the power switch, and the display came alive with information on the vehicle's status. The most important item was near the bottom:

POWER CELL . . . . . . 100,000 Kw . . . OK

The robot was politely knocking on the window and trying to attract Derec's attention, but Derec ignored it. With a touch on one of two small joysticks in the armrest at his right hand, Derec unshipped the small crane which lay crosswise behind the control cab.

Since the controls had been designed primarily for robots with their fine motor control, Derec found them a little touchy. But the crane was semi-automatic, so when he had managed to swing the boom out over the back end of the carrier and bring the auger in range of the crane's camera, all he had to do was say, "Pick it up." The crane handled the rest.

Monitor 5 seemed slow to realize what was happening. Derec couldn't decide if that was because it was still experiencing some internal conflict, or if he was just seeing the difference between a Monitor and an Analyst. But when Derec lifted the auger off the floor of the chamber and began to swing it out of the way, the robot suddenly became agitated.

"Analyst 17 was in error," it said, grasping the door latch and shaking violently. "Derec—you cannot escape. You cannot leave. I am required to protect you. I am responsible."

Saying nothing, Derec used the dangling mass of the auger to brush the robot away from the side of the carrier and back it toward the wall. The robot's protestations went up in volume, but Derec did not stop until he had gently pinned the robot against the wall ten meters to the left of where it had done the same to the augment.

"Reverse slow," Derec said, and the carrier crawled away from the wall. "Stop. Standby."

He jumped out and ran to the augment. As he wrestled the suit away from the wall, Monitor 5 was struggling to extricate itself. It was a race Derec had to win.

Finally the access door was clear, and Derec levered himself inside. At that moment, Monitor 5 clambered to the top of the auger, free from its makeshift prison. But it was too late to stop him. The access door was closing to seal Derec in the suit.

"Power on," he said.

His next objective was the open control cab on the other side of the carrier, meant for use by workers in augments. But before he could reach it, Monitor 5 was again trying to block his way.

"I don't want to harm you," Derec said. "You can't stop me. You've done your duty by trying. Now stand aside."

"You are attempting to commit suicide. I am not required to comply with your orders under these circumstances."

"I'm trying to save myself," Derec said. "If you really want me to live, you'll step aside and give me a chance."

"I will take you to a safe place within the community—"

"There are no safe places here!" Derec shouted. "Don't you understand?"

"I cannot allow—"

"I can't stand here and debate it," Derec said. "I'm sorry."

As he spoke, he swung the right grapple of the suit in a sweeping arc that caught the robot in the neck and sent it sprawling. But Derec had barely taken three steps when it was back again, clawing at the suit's emergency panel.

This time Derec reached down and grabbed the robot's right leg, upending it and dropping it on its back. Catching its ankle with the other grapple, Derec pinched down hard until he heard the sounds of metal crumpling. When he released his grip, the robot's leg was crippled, the foot frozen at an odd angle.

Derec climbed into the open cab unimpeded. As he backed the carrier away from the wall and turned it toward the ramp, he saw Monitor 5 still lying on the floor where he had left it, vainly trying to repair the damage Derec had done. It's slitlike scanners followed Derec and the carrier across the chamber.

It was still watching him, its gaze somehow forlorn and somehow accusing, when Derec drove the carrier up through the lock and out onto the surface.

After his time underground, it seemed strange to have the infinite open sky of space overhead. The sun, a tiny orange disk, hung low in the sky. Barely twenty degrees above the horizon, it cast long shadows into the depressions. The sky was bright with stars, but no planets declared themselves to Derec's eye.

He did not know how long it would take to make the modifications to the augment. He only knew that the raider ship's orbit was bringing it closer, and he had to be done before it arrived. He knew too that the robots would be pursuing him in a short-sighted effort to protect him. It was as though the jaws of a vise were closing on him. Somehow he had to squirm away or die.

He only drove far enough over the rugged, frozen terrain to separate himself from the potential target of the complex entrance. Then he parked the carrier half in shadow on a valley floor and started off on foot across the frozen wastes. Though he was sacrificing speed in giving up the carrier, the vehicle almost certainly contained a tracking transponder that would lead the robots right to him.

As soon as he was on foot, he began looking for the right place to hole up while working on the suit. He did not need sunlight for what he had to do, since the augment had its own worklamps. A shadowed hollow, a darkened crevice, a pitch-black ice cave—any of those would hide him without hindering his efforts. But the better hidden he was, the less warning he would have about the approach of the robots or the raiders.

There was no having it both ways.

While Derec hiked across the frozen terrain and equivocated, he used the augment's omnidirectional radio to send a series of distress calls. Derec did not know if the signals would carry over the horizon to the raider, and he feared that they would lead the robots to him. But he had to try, had to give the raiders a chance and a reason to save him.

"Clear channel, code 1. To all ships: pilot marooned, requires pickup. Respond if in range. To all ships—"

Eventually Derec settled on a fissure in an ice cliff that faced back the way he had come. From there, he had a fair view of the terrain, except for what was blocked by the larger crags and mounds. And he had a clear view of the sky from the horizon on the northwest to the horizon on the northeast.

"Diagnostic library," he said.

The lower half of the bubblelike viewport turned opaque and a list of subsystems appeared on it in bright yellow letters. He scanned down the list quickly.

"Motive systems."

One of the items near the middle of the list flashed twice, and then the entire list was replaced by another. In the same manner, Derec worked his way through the help screens until the circuit and logic paths of the subcontroller filled the half-display with a maze of fine tracings. Derec studied the system carefully, his lips pursed into a frown.

"Frost," he muttered finally.

It was as he had feared. The governor was not a physical device that could be readily disconnected. It was a feedback loop in the leg servo circuits. The loop told the suit controller, "Do not allow the force applied by the drivers to exceed a force of x number of dynes per second." Small forces applied quickly were acceptable, as were large forces applied slowly. But large forces applied quickly, which was what he needed, were forbidden.

If he had had more time, there might have been a chance to reprogram the subcontrollers. But under the circumstances, it would have to be radical surgery. Fortunately, augments were designed to be field-repairable, a practice which had saved more than one laborer's life.

The various "hands" which the augment could use were located in bulging closures on the suit's thighs. Derec selected an illuminated micromanipulator for the right, and a spotweld laser for the left.

Just then the ground under and around him shook suddenly, bringing a minor avalanche of slow-falling particles down on the crown of the suit. "Clear," he ordered. The bubble became a window again, revealing to Derec a chilling sight. The attacking spacecraft had climbed above the western horizon. It was still firing randomly, still carving out a path of destruction on the asteroid's surface. Time was running out.

"Shut down subsystem twenty-four." That was it: he was committed. With the leg controllers powered down, Derec could no longer walk.

The modifications included burning through three circuit traces and fusing a fourth to a neighboring circuit as a shunt. Accuracy with the tiny laser was absolutely critical. A misfire could destroy enough circuits to cripple the augment permanently.

With the help of the augment's pointing guide, Derec completed the work on the right leg without mishap. But by the time he was ready to start on the left, the vibrations from the more powerful explosions were more than strong enough to disturb his aim. As he stood trying to outguess the shaking ground, a familiar voice intruded:

"Derec, please listen. Derec, you must stop. This is madness—"

Two hundred meters away on the slope of the mound due north of him was a robot. It was Monitor 5, waving its arms and advancing directly toward where Derec stood. It was walking easily, with no sign of the damage Derec had inflicted on its leg.

In the same glance, Derec saw that the reason the shaking was stronger was that the raider ship was much closer, more nearly overhead than he had expected. Once again he was trapped between the raiders, who would rescue him by killing him, and the robots, who would kill him by rescuing him.

"Go away!" Derec hissed.

"Derec, you must return to the compound. You are in danger here."

The raider ship seemed to have taken notice of the robot, for the plain between Monitor 5 and the cliff where Derec stood suddenly came under a barrage of pinpoint laser impacts.

These were not the high-intensity weapons which were shaking the ground, and mercifully, the gunners did not seem to be targeting Derec. But the surface in this area was nearly all ice, and volatile. One blast boiled away the top of the mound behind the robot. Another gouged a deep trench between the robot and Derec.

Derec did not think that would stop Monitor 5, and he was right. The robot scrambled down into the trench before the billow of gas could even dissipate, and Derec lost sight of it.

He could not afford to worry about the robot. Setting his jaw determinedly, Derec went back to work on the left subcontroller. Using the body rigidity and autocontrol of the augment to the fullest, he made short work of it. The three unwanted circuits vaporized in tiny puffs of atomic metal. The two parallel traces melted and merged into one.

"Derec!" Monitor 5 called suddenly. "It's here! In the ice! I've found it!"

Derec looked up. The firing had stopped, and there was no sign of the robot. "Close the panels," he said, then tongued the radio switch. "Monitor 5, go back to the installation. There's nothing you can do for me out here."

Just then, a metallic arm appeared above the lip of the trench, the hand clutching a small silver object. A moment later Monitor 5 struggled out of the trench. Starting toward Derec, Monitor 5 raised the silver object triumphantly overhead in one hand.

"The key is here, Derec. You must take it—"

The robot's triumph did not last long. The raider ship was now a great ominous mass directly overhead. Monitor 5 had barely taken a step when the laser fire started up again. Red targeting beams danced like spotlights on a stage on the ice around it.

For a moment it seemed as though the robot was going to escape destruction. Then, a dozen strides from the foot of the cliff, a laser tracked a fiery line across the robot's torso. An instant later, Monitor 5 disappeared in a silent explosion, all blue-green flame and disintegrating metal.

Disappeared—but not completely. The explosion sent pieces

flying in all directions. One of the largest, spinning so rapidly Derec could not tell what it was, came cartwheeling toward him. As it struck the ground and skidded to a stop, Derec saw what it was: Monitor 5's right arm, from the shoulder joint to the fingers.

And still gripped tightly in those fingers was the shining silver object—a rectangle perhaps five centimeters by fifteen centimeters, the size of a remote controller or a memory cartridge.

Could this be the object that the robots were so obsessively searching for all this time? If so, then why had Monitor 5's last act been to try to give it to Derec?

For a moment Derec hesitated. To retrieve the object was an additional risk in an enterprise which was already too risky. But he knew that it was impossible for him to simply leave it lying there. Ripping the specialized end effectors from the augment's arms, Derec slapped the general-purpose grapples back in place.

"Power up system twenty-four," he snapped, and the sole red lamp on the augment's status board turned to green.

His descent down the slope to where the arm rested was a controlled fall at best. With the leg servos jimmied, Derec could not control a walking gait. But he got there all the same, seizing the arm and the artifact in his right hand and locking the grapple.

Gathering his feet under himself, Derec glanced upward to gauge the distance and angle to the raider ship. He lifted his feet on the control pads, and the suit went into a crouch. He jammed his feet down hard, and the powerful legs of the augment kicked out with all their unrestrained might. Like a tiny spacecraft, the augment launched itself from the surface, carrying Derec toward a rendezvous with the raider ship.

One way or another, I'm coming aboard—

Suddenly the entire surface of the asteroid seemed to shudder and rise up in a convulsion. The robots had triggered their self-destruct at last, and the explosion sent a hailstorm of fragments blasting outward like space shrapnel.

Almost immediately, the weapons pods of the raider ship sprang to life. At first Derec thought that they were aiming at him, trying to get him before he was lost in the deluge of ice and rock boulders which had erupted from the asteroid. Then it seemed as though the gunners were targeting the debris itself, the smaller and faster-moving bits of which were already overtaking him.

Whichever was their goal, the net effect was the same: when he was within about a hundred meters of the nearest part of the ship and beginning to scan for a place to latch on with his free hand, the entire bubble faceplate of the augment lit up with a blue light that crawled in all directions like something alive.

Derec's limbs went numb and his senses went wild. He had only enough time to think *Not again!* before the light faded and darkness took him away once more.

Despite all the tumult which had surrounded him as he had lost consciousness, Derec came back to awareness calmly and easily. He could not say how long he had been unconscious, but it had to have been more than a few minutes. He was no longer outside the alien ship. For that matter, he was no longer in the augment. Instead, he was lying on his back on hard decking, staring up at a ceiling filled with small doors.

Propping himself up on his elbows, Derec surveyed his surroundings. He was in a narrow room, almost a corridor. The long walls were covered with more doors—storage bins?—and there was an exit at each end—or at least a tall metal ellipse which might be an exit.

Derec did not spend much time wondering about the exits or the contents of the storage bins. A large animal covered with mottled brown and gold fur squatted on its haunches nearby, watching Derec. It reminded Derec of a dog, like an undersized Saint Bernard with the alert eyes of a wolf. But the face was too flat, the ears too high and pointed, and the forelegs ended not in paws but in gray-skinned sausagelike fingers.

Whatever it was, he had never seen anything like it before. Moving slowly so as not to alarm the creature, Derec sat up. When he did, the creature sidled forward a step and cocked its head.

"Arr 'u aw right?" it asked in a guttural voice.

Derec could not have been more surprised if the creature had suddenly molted and turned into a butterfly. Not only speech, but Standard—however curiously accented—

"I—I think so," he stammered.

"That iss good," the creature said. "Aranimas will be pleased. 'Ee did not want 'u 'armed."

"The best way to guarantee that is not to shoot at people."

"Eff we 'ad been shooting at 'u, we would 'ave 'it 'u," the alien said with a tooth-bearing grimace that might have been a smile or a threat display.

Though that message was garbled, other body language was coming through more clearly. The alien's crouch struck Derec as a posture from which it could spring quickly. Seated, he was at a disadvantage both in agility and reach, a fact which he felt keenly when he met the alien's gaze. Their eyes were on the same level, but Derec felt threatened, intimidated.

Still moving slowly, Derec felt for the wall behind him and hauled himself to his feet. The alien's only reaction was to rise with him. When both were standing, the tips of the alien's ears reached only to Derec's chest, and the psychological comfort that went with being the taller shifted to Derec.

"What are you?" he demanded.

"'Urr friend," the alien said. "What morr do 'u need to know?"

"There's a hundred forty colonized worlds, and there's nothing like you on any of them."

"Wherr I come from therr arr two 'undred colonized worlds, and nothing like 'u on any of them," the alien said, grimacing again. This time, the circumstances seemed to call more clearly for a smile, and Derec decided that's what it was. "Come. Aranimas iss waiting."

"Who is Aranimas?"

"Aranimas iss ship's boss. 'Ull see," the alien said, turning away and starting toward the far door.

"Wait," Derec called. "What's your name?"

The alien stopped and turned. It opened its mouth and out poured a torrent of sounds not in any human alphabet—like a growl punctuated with a sibilant hiss and sounds like bubbles popping. Then the alien smiled-grimaced. "Can say?"

Derec shook his head sheepishly. "No."

"Thought not. Come, then. Not wise to keep Aranimas waiting."

• • •

Taking a brisk loping pace, the alien led Derec through three more compartments identical to the one he had awakened in. Derec wondered briefly about the mismatch between his escort and the design of the ship they were in. The overhead storage bins were far above Derec's head; he doubted if he could reach them even by jumping. Unless the caninoid alien were as agile a climber as a terrestrial primate, it would need a ladder to get to their contents.

Efficient use of space—terrible ergonomic design, Derec thought critically.

They came to a tiny hexagonal room barely large enough for both of them to stand in. It seemed to be a hub between intersecting corridors, since each wall framed an identical door. The alien paused for Derec to catch up, then continued on through.

"Where do the other doors lead?"

"Can't tell 'u," the alien said cheerfully.

Beyond the hub, the interior of the ship had a different character. There were just as many walls and small spaces, but the walls were either of a coarse mesh, almost more like fencing, or had large windowlike cutouts. Together the mesh and the cutouts provided long lines of sight and the feeling not of small spaces but of a large busy one.

The largest space within this deck seemed to be straight ahead. Peering over the alien's shoulder, Derec caught glimpses of what seemed to be a control center, and of a figure seated at the console with its back to them. There was something familiar and human about the figure, and something wrong and disturbing at the same time.

As soon as the caninoid led him into the control center, Derec knew why he was getting mixed messages, and who—or what —the storage corridors had been designed for. The alien sitting at the console was decidedly humanoid, and Derec could describe him in very human terms—a slender build, thin neck, almost hairless head, pale skin.

But even sitting down, Aranimas was as tall as Derec, and he had the arm span of a condor. The entire horseshoe-shaped console, easily three human arm spans wide, was within his comfortable reach.

Beyond and above Aranimas was a huge curved viewing

screen on which eight different views of the asteroid's surface were being projected. Superimposed on most of them were blue-lined targeting grids and small characters Derec took to be numbers. Some of the characters were changing constantly, and others seemed to change in response to Aranimas's hands moving over the console and to the endless pattern of explosions and groundslides on the surface.

"Praxil, denofah, praxil mastica," he was saying, apparently into a microphone. "Deh feh opt spa, nexori."

Derec took a step forward. "Aranimas?"

The alien turned his head slightly to the left, and a chill went through Derec. The lizardlike eye that peered back at him was set in a raised socket on the side of Aranimas's head. From behind, Derec had mistaken the eye bumps for ears.

"Sssh!" the caninoid alien said nervously, grasping Derec's hand and pulling him back. "Don't interrupt the boss. 'E'll talk to 'u when 'e's ready."

Aranimas turned back to his work and resumed speaking. Derec had the impression that he was issuing orders, chiding, prodding, reprimanding, assigning targets and grading gunners. There was nothing moving on the surface and nothing stirring below, and yet the carnage went on.

After a few minutes of watching, Derec could no longer restrain himself. "There's nothing down there anymore," Derec blurted. "They blew it all up. What are you doing this for?"

"Prrractice," Aranimas said. His voice was high-pitched and he trilled the "r" sound.

It went on for another ten minutes that way, millions of watts of energy expended uselessly against an inert and lifeless world. Then Aranimas ran a fingertip along a row of switches, and the screens went blank.

"Rijat," he said, and turned his chair to face them. "What is your name?"

"Derec." Only one of Aranimas's eyes was trained on him; the other glanced around randomly. Derec could not imagine what it would be like to view the world that way. Did the alien's brain switch back and forth between the two inputs, like a director choosing a camera shot? Or did it somehow integrate the two images into one?

"This device you used to attack my ship," Aranimas continued. "What was it?"

"An augmented worksuit—altered to allow the leg servos to operate at full power. But I wasn't attacking you. I was escaping."

Aranimas's other eye pivoted forward and focused on Derec. "Were you a prisoner?"

"I was stranded on the asteroid in a survival pod. The robots found me and then wouldn't let me go. I had to steal that equipment from them to get away."

"And where did you come from before you were stranded?"

"I don't know," Derec said, frowning. "I can't remember anything before that."

"Don't lie to 'im," the caninoid whispered. "It makes 'im angry."

"I'm not lying," Derec said indignantly. "As far as I can tell, five days ago I didn't exist. That's how much I know about who I am."

While Derec spoke, Aranimas reached inside the folds of his clothing and extracted a small golden stylus. Seeing it, the caninoid cringed and turned half away.

"Oh, no," it whined. "Too late."

Aranimas pointed the stylus at Derec's side, and a pale blue light began to dance over the entire surface of Derec's hand. He screamed in pain and dropped to his knees. It was as though he had thrust his hand into a raging furnace, except that no skin was being destroyed and no nerve endings deadened. The pain just went on and on, sapping his strength until even the screams caught in his throat, too feeble to free themselves.

"I know something of the rules of governing robots and humans," Aranimas said calmly while Derec writhed on the floor. "Humans build robots to serve them. Robots follow human direction. If you were the only human on this asteroid, then it follows that the robots here were under your command, and serving your purpose."

Aranimas tipped the stylus ceilingward, and the blue glow vanished. The pain vanished with it, except for the memory. Derec lay on his side and sucked in air in great gasping breaths.

"I will know who you are and what you know about the

object you brought aboard," Aranimas said quietly. "To end the pain, you need only tell me the truth."

His face as emotionless as his trilling voice, Aranimas pointed the stylus at Derec once more.

CHAPTER 8
TEST OF LOYALTY

At some point, it ended. But by that time Derec was in no condition to know clearly why Aranimas had interrupted his torture. He had only a vague awareness of Aranimas's going away, and of being dragged away from the control center by the caninoid.

Unable to either resist or help, he was taken to another section of the subdivided compartment and laid on a thinly padded board. He lay there drifting in and out of consciousness, sometimes aware of the caninoid crouching solicitously beside him, sometimes aware of nothing but his own confusion and fatigue.

In one of his lucid moments he became aware that the alien was holding a cup of clear liquid for him, and struggled up on one elbow.

"'U bettrr tell Aranimas what 'e wants to know," the caninoid whispered as it offered the cup.

Derec tipped his head forward and reached for the cup. His right hand trembled uncontrollably, so he had to use his left to steady the cup as he sipped at the cool liquid. It was sweet, like a thin honey, and bathed his ravaged throat with relief.

"How tough do you think humans are?" he croaked. "If I knew anything I'd have told him in the first five minutes. If he keeps this up he's going to kill me. Why won't he believe me?"

The caninoid glanced nervously around before answering. "Do 'u know Narwe?"

Derec could not tell if the name was of a species or an individual, but it did not matter to his answer. "No."

"Aranimas knows Narwe. Narwe 'ass to be forced to be honest. If 'u ask Narwe a question, it will lie or pretend it doesn't understand or hass forgotten. Hurt Narwe enough and it always tell."

"I'm not a Narwe!" Derec protested weakly. "Is he too stupid to see that?"

"Aranimas thinks 'u use the Narwe trick," the caninoid said. "Besides, Aranimas iss very angry."

"Why is he angry at me? I didn't do anything to him."

"When Aranimas iss angry, everyone in trouble," the alien said. "Gunners werr not supposed to destroy robot nest."

"They didn't. The robots did it themselves."

"Doesn't matter. Aranimas wanted to capture robots to work forr 'im."

Derec closed his eyes and laid back. "I'm afraid there won't be much to capture."

"Aranimas went to see what salvage team brought back," the alien said. "Eff truly not much, 'e'll be worse when 'e comes back."

"Can't you help me?" Derec pleaded. "You believe me, don't you?"

"Not my job to believe or not believe," the caninoid shrugged. "Can't 'elp."

With a sigh, Derec lowered himself back to a reclining position and closed his eyes. "Then he is going to kill me, because I don't have anything to tell him. And maybe that's just as well."

The caninoid reclaimed the cup from Derec's hand and stood up. "Perfect Narwe thought. Don't let Aranimas 'ear 'u."

Dozing, the first Derec knew of Aranimas's return was when the alien seized him by the arm and hauled him roughly to a sitting position.

"It's time to stop playing," Aranimas said. "I grow impatient."

"That was playing?" Derec said lightly. "You people have some funny ideas about games. Remind me not to play cutthroat eight-card with you."

At that, the caninoid, crouching in a doorway a few meters

away, closed its eyes and began to shake its head. Aranimas's answer was to reach inside his clothing for the stylus.

"Wait," Derec said quickly, holding up a hand palm out. "You don't need that."

"Have you decided to share your knowledge after all?"

"I always was willing to. You just didn't want what I had to offer."

"I will know who you are and what you know about the object you brought aboard," Aranimas said.

Derec slid off the edge of the bench and found his feet. Aranimas still dwarfed him, but even so, he felt better standing. "The fact is, you know as much as I do about who I am, and I wouldn't be surprised if you knew more than I do about the silver box. But there is something I know more about than you do, and that's robots. How did your prospecting go?"

One of Aranimas's eyes cast a baleful glance in the direction of the caninoid, which hunched its shoulders and retreated from the doorway. "They brought back fragments only," Aranimas said. "Your robots were very efficient about destroying themselves."

"They weren't my robots," Derec said. "But why don't you show me what you have?"

Aranimas lowered his arms to his side and slowly massaged his knees with his hands while he weighed Derec's proposition. "Yes," he said finally. "That will be a good test of your intentions and usefulness. I will have you build me a robot."

Derec's face paled. "What?"

"If you truly do not know who you are, then you have no loyalties or obligations to any other master. When you have built me a robot servant I will know that you have accepted your place serving me."

Derec knew better than to pick that moment to make a noble speech about freedom and choice, but he still could not simply accept Aranimas's terms. "What if I can't build you a robot out of what you have? I said I knew a lot about them. I didn't say I could manufacture one out of good intentions. I need certain key parts—"

"If you fail, I will know that you are either unreliable or have no usefulness to me at all," Aranimas said, "and that I should not waste valuable consumables keeping you alive."

Derec swallowed hard. "What are we waiting for? Show me your inventory."

Aranimas had not been minimizing the problem when he termed what the scavengers had recovered from the asteroid "fragments." I would have said scrap, he thought as he stood in the ship's hold surveying the raiders' paltry booty. The largest intact piece was the one Derec himself had brought aboard— Monitor 5's arm. The next largest was a Supervisor's knee joint. Chances were that it was from Monitor 5 as well.

No other piece was bigger than the palm of Derec's hand: a badly scorched regulator, an optical sensor with a cracked lens, bits of structural forms like shards of broken pottery. There were no positronic brains and no microfusion powerpacks—the two absolutely indispensable items.

And all the Crown's horses and all the Crown's men couldn't put the robots together again, he thought. "Is this all you have?" he asked with a heavy heart.

Mercifully, it was not. In one of the storage corridors, he was shown two tall lockers, each of which contained a nearly intact robot.

"I see this isn't a new hobby of yours," Derec said, stepping forward to examine the collection. The new robots were of a familiar domestic design. He would know more about where they had come from and what they had been used for when he used a microscanner on the serial number plates found at various sites on the robots' bodies. Clearly, though, he was not the first human the raiders had encountered.

There seemed to be enough good parts to make about one and a half robots. One of the robots was headless, and the mounting circle on the neck was twisted and deformed. That told Derec something about the circumstances under which the robots had been acquired.

More important at the moment, it meant there was only one positronic brain. But there was no guarantee that it was functional. The upper torso of the other robot was torn open at the chest as though by some sort of projectile weapon, and the right shoulder area was rippled as though it had been seared by intense heat. Not only did that hold out little hope for the key components located in the torso, but it also virtually guaranteed that the brain's powerdown had been anything but orderly.

But at least there was something to work with, and an outside chance, at least, of success. Derec stepped back from the lockers and turned to look up at Aranimas.

"So what do you have in the way of an engineering lab around here?" he asked with a breeziness that was more show than real. "I'm ready to get to work."

Aranimas nodded gravely. "I will give you that opportunity."

Answering Derec's query about a place to work meant going deeper into the confusing maze of the raider ship. Unlike when he had been inside the asteroid, Derec found it impossible to retain any sense of direction. There were too many turns, too short sight lines, and too few absolute references. Once he lost track of where he was in relation to the command center, it was over.

Despite being lost, Derec was still collecting useful information with every step. He learned that different parts of the ship had slightly different atmospheres, and the storage corridors acted as interlocks between them. In one section, something in the air made Derec feel as though a furry ball were caught in his throat. In another, yellowish tears ran from Aranimas's eyes. Only the caninoid seemed at home in all the atmospheres.

The ship was not only a maze, but a zoo as well, featuring at least four species. Derec saw five of Aranimas's kin, all of high rank to judge by the activities Derec saw them engaged in. Curiously, the caninoid seemed to be the only one of his kind aboard.

Most numerous were the gaunt-faced Narwe, several of whom had been recruited by Aranimas to carry the robot parts. The Narwe were short bald-headed bipeds with gnarled skull ridges like false horns, which made them look fierce and formidable. But it was clearly only protective coloring, for Aranimas and the caninoid alike cuffed and bullied the Narwe without fear.

The fourth species was the most interesting and the most elusive. Inside the compartment where Aranimas's eyes began to tear, Derec caught a glimpse of a strange five-limbed wall-clinging creature not unlike a giant sea star. It retreated as they approached, and was gone from sight by the time they reached the spot.

Fascinated as Derec was by the parade of alien biologies, he was also concerned about having so casual a contact with them. He knew that his own body was host to a rich biotic community: bacteria, viruses, fungi, and parasites. He did not know just how different the aliens were from him. He hoped they were wildly different. The more similar their fundamental structure was to his, the greater the risk that his symbiotes could endanger them or theirs endanger him.

He could only hope that Aranimas had either taken precautions or determined that no precautions were necessary. He based that hope on the fact that the raiders had evidently had some previous contact with humans. The scavenged robots and the aliens' command of Standard proved that.

But that was another mystery for his lengthening list. Derec was positive that human beings had never crossed paths with even one intelligent alien lifeform, much less with four of them. To understand interplanetary politics, he had to know history and economics, but not xenobiology.

Did the raiders' presence mean that he was far out on the fringes of human space? Or had knowledge of the contacts been made a state secret, meant only for those with a need to know? Were the raiders pirates, prospectors, or pioneers? Had they perhaps come looking for the same thing the robots had been looking for? And having found it, were they carrying him toward their home, or his?

They were questions with serious consequences. Tensions were high enough between Earth and the Spacers without any random factors to jumble the picture. An attack of the sort Derec had already witnessed, directed against one of the many human worlds with no planetary defense net, could bring on war.

Which brought Derec back to the silver artifact. If it was as important as the robots' search for it implied, if it was powerful enough or important enough for the raiders to come after it, then it was too important and too powerful to be left in the raiders' hands. As much as he hated to be thinking about anyone's problems but his own, Derec had an obligation to try to reclaim it for humanity.

Mercifully, the lab was located in a section with a normal atmosphere, though the air was a bit warm and dry. While Aranimas settled into a chair and supervised the Narwe's arrangement of the robot parts on the open areas of the floor, Derec browsed the workbench and wall racks with the caninoid at his elbow to answer questions. By the time he finished, the Narwe were gone.

"Explain each step as you perform it," Aranimas said, crossing his arms as though settling in.

"Do you intend to sit there and watch?"

"I intend to learn what you know."

"Then I hope you're a patient sort," Derec said.

"According to your story, it took you only a short time to convert an article of clothing into an escape propulsion system," Aranimas said. "This should require even less time, since you only need to turn a robot into a robot."

"You've got to be kidding," Derec said, throwing his hands in the air. "I'm not sure I'm going to be able to do it at all, much less in an hour or two."

"Explain the problem," Aranimas said.

Derec bit back a laugh. In the hopes of loosening the noose Aranimas had around his neck, Derec had been rehearsing complaints that the equipment in the lab was ill suited, too crude, anything to lower Aranimas's expectations.

But his dismay was real, not manufactured. He had prepared himself for instruments designed for nonhuman hands, to having to have one of the raiders at his elbow coaching him. But he had not been prepared to do without what he thought of as the basics.

"The problem is you don't have the right tools," Derec said. "I need a diagnostic bench, an etcher, micromanipulators— There's nothing in here that would even pass for a chip mask or circuit tracer—"

Even as he spoke, he realized that he should not have been surprised. Aranimas would not be so curious about robots, would not need to have Derec repair them, if the culture which he represented were capable of making them. The fact that the raiders employed gunners instead of autotargeting systems should have tipped him off that their computer technology was deficient.

Aranimas stood. "Such tools as are available will be brought to you. Describe what you need to Rrullf"—Aranimas's shortened version of the caninoid's name was almost pronounceable —"and she will bring them to you or take you to them."

She? Derec cast a surprised glance at the caninoid. *Interesting.*

"Thank you," he said to Aranimas, and started to turn away. As he did, a thousand bees settled between his shoulder blades and began to sting him wildly. Gasping, his knees buckling, he grabbed for the edge of the workbench to keep from collapsing on the floor. He did not need to see to know that Aranimas had the stylus trained at the middle of his back.

"Do not make the mistake of trying to deceive me," Aranimas said coldly as the pain held Derec firmly in its grip. "I may be ignorant of your art, but I am not foolish."

"I—I—"

"Save your words of apology," Aranimas said as the bees flew away. "Show me results."

Doubled over the workbench, Derec turned his head in time to see Aranimas return the stylus to whatever hidden pocket was reserved for it. Clearing the phlegm from his throat, he nodded weakly. "Right, boss."

When Aranimas was gone, the caninoid's face twisted into its macabre grin. "'Urr lucky Aranimas wants robots so bad. Otherwise I guess 'u be dead now."

"Thanks for the cheery thought," Derec said. "What exactly does he want them for?"

"Can't 'u figure? Aranimas wants to replace Narwe with robots. Aranimas iss sick of Narwe crying scenes."

"Do the Narwe know what he has in mind?"

"Narwe been on best behavior since the boss told them," the caninoid said cheerfully. "What 'u need to work?"

But Derec had been thinking about something else. The caninoid was treating him in a way that could only be called friendly, and was the best prospect for an ally aboard the raider ship besides. If they were going to be working together, it was time for Derec to stop thinking of the alien as *it*. Or even *she*.

"First things first. I can't say your name even as well as Aranimas does—"

"Thass pretty low standard."

"—but I have to call you something. Can you live with Wolruf?"

"Iss not my name, but I know who 'u mean when 'u say it."

"That's all I wanted. Wolruf, I've got some fine print to read. What can you find me to read it with?"

"I get 'u something," she promised.

The magnifying scanner that Wolruf came up with was an inspection instrument of some sort. It had a display screen rather than an eyepiece, a fixed focus, and a tiny field of view. But the incident lighting at the aperture highlighted perfectly the fine grooves of the serial number engraving, making up for all the other shortcomings.

With Wolruf peering over his shoulder, Derec scanned the fifteen lines of data. "Do you read Standard, too?"

"No," Wolruf said. "Tell 'u a secret—I learn Standard so I not 'ave to lissen to Aranimas mangle my language."

Derec laughed, and the sound startled Wolruf. "What I'm looking at is one of the robot's identification gratings. It'll tell me several things that will help me fix the damage—the manufacturer, the model, the date of initialization, any customization parameters," he said breezily.

He went on like that awhile longer, loading his explanation with as many technical terms as he could in the hopes of appearing to be open and cooperative while actually explaining nothing. He did not mention that if the robot were from Earth, the grating would also tell who owned it, or that the three cryptic lines of symbols at the bottom of the screen were the programming access codes and the initialization sequence, the keys that would allow him to do more than merely repair the robot, but to alter its programming.

"What does it say?"

"This one is a Ferrier Model EG," Derec said, scanning. "Customized for valet service." And personal defense, he added silently. A bodyguard robot. "Initialization date, Standard Year '83—"

Then he scanned a few words ahead and was struck dumb.

"What is it?" Wolruf asked. "Is something wrong?"

"No," Derec managed to say. "The robot was registered on Aurora."

"That iss one of 'urr worlds?"

"Yes."

"Iss that important?"

"No," Derec said. "Let's look at the other one."

But it *was* important, and his hands were trembling as he took the scanner in them and rose from his seat. He remembered Aurora. He *remembered* the World of the Dawn. Not the things that everyone knew—that it was the first Spacer world and long the preeminent one, that it was home to the highly regarded Institute of Robotics from which most advances in robotic science had emerged.

No, like a ray of light sneaking past the black curtain, Derec remembered Aurora as a place he had been: glimpses of a spaceport, a parklike city, a pastoral countryside. He was connected with it in some way, some way strong enough that the word alone had the power to break through the wall separating him from his past.

At last, he knew something about himself. He had been to Aurora. It was not much of a biography, but it was a beginning.

CHAPTER 9
ALLY

Without a diagnostic board or even a computer at his disposal, Derec had no choice but to activate the robot and rely on its own self-diagnostic capabilities. But before he could get even that far, he had a jigsaw puzzle to assemble.

The headless robot was an EX series, but the differences did not affect the parts Derec needed to borrow to make the EG whole. The active systems—as opposed to the merely structural—of any mass-produced robot were modular and standardized. It would not have been possible to produce them economically any other way. So the kidney-sized microfusion powerpack of the EX was a plug-compatible replacement for the damaged one inside the EG.

But the powerpack's mounting cradle, which contained the interface for the primary power bus, had also been damaged by the fight which had downed the robot. Regrettably, the cradle had not been designed for field replacement, and it seemed to be attached to every other component inside the EG's torso—and not by convenient micromagnetic fields. The manufacturer had settled for the less costly alternative of sonic welds.

Lacking the proper tools, swapping the cradles was a challenge. He practiced on the damaged cradle inside the EG, then used his hard-won expertise to transfer the undamaged one into the vacancy. That alone took more than two hours. But when he was done, it took less than two minutes to swap powerpacks.

Unfortunately, that did not end the matter. In all Ferrier

models, the basic data library used by the robot was contained in removable memory cubes placed in a compartment just behind its "collarbone." The robot's extensive positronic memory was reserved completely for the business of learning from experience.

From the manufacturer's standpoint, that arrangement meant that the positronic brains did not have to be specialized according to the robot's function. From the owner's viewpoint, it meant that their investment was protected against obsolescence or changing needs.

But from Derec's perspective, it meant trouble. The headless robot had five cube slots, four of them occupied. For the EG, the numbers were seven and five. But the two empty slots and three of the occupied ones had been caught in the same blast that had damaged the power cradle.

There was no repairing them and no replacing them. But what was worse was that Derec was bound to use one of the two functional slots for the standard Systems cube, without which the robot would know nothing about its own structure and operation. He had five cubes packed full of data and logic routines, and he could only use one of them at a time. Eventually he settled on the Mathematics cube, concealing the Personal Defense cube for possible use at some future time.

Derec's inventory of visible damage to the robot included severed cables that would render the right arm paralyzed and a frozen gimbal on one of the dual gyroscopes. But with power and the working library restored, there was only one truly critical part left to see to: the positronic brain.

In appearance, the brain was a three-pound lump of platinum-iridium. In function, it was the repository for the fundamental positromotive potentials governing the robot's activity, for the temporary potentials which represented thought and decision, and for the pathways which represented learning.

What Derec was hoping was that the fundamental pathways had not been randomized, as could happen if the brain had been exposed to hard radiation. There was no hope for the robot's experience base. The backup microcell, used to refresh the pathways while the robot was being serviced, had long since been exhausted and the pathways had long ago decayed. The robot would remember nothing of its previous service. But if the brain was undamaged, it should function normally when reinitiated.

Just like me—

Given the equipment available, the only way to test the condition of the positronic brain was to activate the robot and test it. For obvious reasons, that was dangerous. At one point in the history of robotics, robots had been designed to shut down when they detected any internal error conditions. But several hundred years of progress in robotics design had produced a different philosophy built around fault-tolerance and self-maintenance. He could not be sure what would happen.

By the time he was ready to find out, Wolruf had either grown bored or was obliged to go tend to some other duty. That was a fortunate turn, since when the robot was activated, it would be facing a situation that no robot had ever faced before. It would have to decide whether Aranimas and Wolruf were "human" enough that it was required to protect them and obey their orders.

Since robots were as a rule literal-minded to a fault, it should not have been a problem. Aranimas was clearly an alien, despite his superficially humanoid appearance. Wolruf was even more so.

Those who manufactured robots did not ordinarily limit the definition of a human being, but left it as broad as possible. A power plant worker in a max suit did not look human, but a robot would obey its order. Robots were not, could not be, completely literal. They did not judge merely on appearance. A three-year-old child was human, yet a robot would frequently decline its orders.

It was possible that the programming which permitted those distinctions would find some fundamental identity between the aliens and Derec. If there was any way of preventing that, Derec was determined to do so. Because of the First Law, the robot could not be used against him. But if the robot could be persuaded that the aliens were not entitled to protection under the First Law, he might be able to use the robot against Aranimas.

With some trepidation, Derec pressed the power reset. A

moment later, all of the robot's joints except those in the damaged arm stiffened. Its eyes lit up with a red glow that pulsed rhythmically.

"Alpha alpha epsilon rho," Derec said, repeating the sequence of Greek letters which had appeared on the ID grating. "Sigma tau sigma."

There was a brief pause, and then the robot's eyes began to glow steadily. "My default language is Galactic Standard, Auroran dialect," it said. "No other language banks are currently available. Is that acceptable, sir?"

Derec broke into a smile. After his frustrations with the robots on the asteroid, it was a pleasure to be addressed civilly again. "Auroran Galactic is fine."

"Yes, sir. Who is my owner, sir?"

"I am," Derec said. "You are never to acknowledge that to anyone. But if you ever receive conflicting orders from myself and another, my orders are always to take precedence."

"Yes, sir. By what name may I call you, sir?"

For some reason, Derec resented having to supply the robot with his meaningless, casually adopted name. "Derec," he said finally, unable to think of an alternative.

"Yes, sir. To what name would you like me to respond?"

Derec suppressed a bitter laugh. Who am I to tell you your name, when I can't even tell myself mine? "So long as you are the only one on this ship, Alpha is name enough."

"Thank you, Derec. During my power-on self-test I detected a number of error states. Would this be a convenient time to review them?"

"In a moment," Derec said. "Can you scan this compartment?"

"Yes, sir."

"Are there any spyeyes here with us?"

"I detect no active sensors of any sort, Derec."

"Good. Listen closely. I need to tell you something about what's happening. You and I are on board a spaceship populated by hostile lifeforms. These lifeforms are a potential threat to both of us. Until I tell you otherwise, you are to immediately enter a passive wait-state any time we have company or I leave the lab."

"I understand. You do not wish them to know that I am functional."

"That's right."

"Is it possible that these wait-states will be of extended duration, sir?"

"It is."

"Then may I ask if there are any problems to which I may devote myself during those periods?"

"I'm sure we'll find some," Derec said. "Right now, the problem is getting you in shape. Let's have the first anomaly off your error list."

The first that Derec knew of Wolruf's return was when the robot stiffened suddenly and its eyes went black. A few seconds later, the caninoid entered the lab and crossed to where Derec was seated. She stood at Derec's elbow and peered briefly into the exposed inner mechanisms of the robot, then turned to him. She seemed less animated than she had been earlier.

"Aranimas would like a report on 'urr progress."

"You can tell Aranimas that I have reason to hope I'll have a robot for him in a few days."

" 'Ow many days?"

"I don't know," Derec said, laying down the pen he had been using as a probe. "I also don't know how much it'll be able to do. I've replaced a few damaged components. Right now I'm trying to do something with the servo linkages for the right arm, which are really a mess. Was it you people who roughed up these robots, or did you find them this way?"

"Can't say," Wolruf said, and headed for the door. "I tell Aranimas."

"Hold on a moment," Derec said, standing. "You can also tell him that I don't work around the clock. I need time to rest and a place to do it."

"Rest 'ard to get on Aranimas's ship," Wolruf said, gesturing toward the floor. "Sleep 'ere."

That was not an entirely unhappy prospect, since Derec had already determined that he had some privacy there. "What about a pillow, some kind of cushion?"

The caninoid made a sort of whistling sound that Derec read

as a sigh. "I get 'u something," she said, and started to go.

"Am I going to be allowed to eat?" he called after her.

The sigh was a wheeze this time. "I get 'u something."

"Tell you what, Wolruf," Derec said, drawing closer. "Why don't you show me where the food is kept, so I can get it myself when I'm hungry? That'll save you some running around on my account."

Wolruf wrinkled her cheeks in surprise, then frowned. "Aranimas wants 'u working, not running errands. Thass my job."

"You've got enough things to do without all the extra work I'm creating," Derec said on a hunch. "If Aranimas makes a fuss, I'll tell him I insisted. If I'm going to do my best work, I'm going to need to get out of that lab from time to time just to clear my mind."

Cocking her head, Wolruf considered. "Okay. I show 'u."

"Great. Ah—one more thing." The thought of an alien Personal was an unpleasant one, but he was suddenly aware that there was some urgency. "I have—um—excretory needs. Do you also—ah—is there—"

Wolruf laughed, a sound like purring. "Of course. Come, I show 'u that, too."

There seemed to be fewer aliens afoot in the ship at that hour, which started Derec wondering about the sleep cycles observed by the various species aboard. The curiosity stayed in his mind while Wolruf showed him the Personal, identified to him the three foods in the pantry considered safe for him, and escorted him back to the lab. By that time, he was certain that she was fatigued, and when she left him, he was certain that it was for an appointment with a bed.

There was no lock on the lab door. There was no Narwe guard to note his comings and goings. The opportunity was there, if he wanted it. Wolruf would not disturb him. Perhaps Aranimas was now sleeping as well. Derec could scout the layout of the ship, snoop in some of the hundreds of storage bins he had seen.

Or perhaps Aranimas was waiting for a report from Wolruf, and might soon be coming to check Derec's progress personally. Or perhaps he never slept. Perhaps his mind was structured in a way that he did not need the periodic "dumpings" dreams represented, his metabolism clocked at a steady pace rather than cycling through active and passive periods.

The uncertainty stilled Derec's impulse to go exploring, at least for a time. Turning to the food he had carried back with him, he gnawed at a few of the thick crackerlike biscuits, ate most of the fatty mottled-blue paste, sipped at the honey juice. Though his taste buds regarded it all with suspicion, none of it alarmed his stomach.

When he was done, his own fatigue was pressing in on him. He placed Alpha in a wait-state, then unrolled the thin cushion in an open spot of floor and stretched out. The cushion did little to make the floorplates less hard. He supposed that Aranimas, slender as he was, would have found it entirely suitable. But Derec turned restlessly from back to side to stomach in a fruitless quest for a comfortable position.

How long had it been since he had slept? Thirty hours? Forty? He had started the day a reluctant prisoner of the robots, and now he was an even more reluctant prisoner of the raiders. *I really should go snooping*, he thought. He could not let the opportunity pass. Perhaps the absence of a guard was an oversight that would be corrected tomorrow.

I'll just lie here for an hour or so, he told himself, make sure that Aranimas isn't going to show up, give Wolruf a chance to settle in. Then it'll be safe. I can rest a little while. This poor excuse for a bed is too hard to sleep on anyway—

He was wrong. One moment he was closing his eyes against the uncomfortably bright light which he had not been told how to douse. The next, he was rubbing sleep out of those eyes, gingerly stretching sore muscles, and bemoaning his own foul breath. The room was in semidarkness, but Wolruf was crouching in the doorway, silhouetted against the well-lit corridor.

"Iss it done yet?" Wolruf asked brightly.

"Eat space and die," Derec growled, and threw the nearest rock-sized bit of robot scrap in Wolruf's direction. The caninoid snatched it neatly out of the air and threw it back in one motion.

"No thanks," she said with a curled-lip grin. "I already 'ad breakfast."

•   •   •

Though there was running water in the Personal, there was no provision for a shower or bath. Derec settled for sponging himself off, though there were no blowers and the only toweling available was harsh and scratchy. By the time he emerged, Wolruf was nowhere in sight. Derec wondered if she had perhaps stopped by only to waken him and would not be coming back.

Thinking that it wouldn't take him long to get tired of the fare, he carried another meal of biscuits, cheese, and honey back to the lab. Settling at the workbench, he resumed work on the robot's right arm. The electrical connections were sound, but the servo linkages were damaged beyond Derec's ability to repair. His efforts to do so only made things worse. Whatever skill he had was cybernetic, not electromechanical.

"Alpha, I don't think I can fix your arm. I'm wondering if you can, with your good arm. I could get a mirror so you could see inside—"

"I am sorry. Without a Robotech cube in my library, my abilities in this area are limited to diagnosis only, sir."

"I figured as much," Derec said. "But it never hurts to ask."

"Sir, I detect a deactivated robot in the room. Perhaps it would be possible to salvage the appropriate parts from its mechanism to repair me."

"That's what I've been trying to do," Derec said gruffly. "I can't do it, not without micromanipulators. Besides, there's some structural damage in the shoulder mount, which isn't replaceable."

Sighing, Derec pushed himself back from the bench and crossed to where his paltry inventory of robot parts lay spread out on the floor. As it had many times before, his gaze fell on Monitor 5's arm. For the first time, he picked it up and examined it closely.

"I guess you're just going to have to make do with one wing," he said. "There's a lot of it going around."

The robot made no reply. Derec turned the Monitor's arm over and tried to flex the elbow. It resisted—consistent with the fact that the hand had been locked in a literal death grip on the silver artifact.

Consistent, Derec realized with a sudden shock, except that

the arm contained no joints. Not at the elbow, not at the wrist, not at the knuckle. Oh, the elbow was bent at an obtuse angle, the wrist twisted slightly, the fingers curled. But insofar as he could tell from looking at it, the arm was incapable of movement.

There were any number of syntheskin coverings which would flex and wrinkle realistically while masking joints. But this was no covering. It was rigid to the touch and absolutely seamless, like a plastic casting. Puzzled, Derec carried it back to where the robot sat.

"What magnification are your optical sensors capable of?"

"Only a limited amount, sir—one hundred power."

"At what resolution?"

"That would vary with the distance of the object being observed, sir. The maximum resolution is approximately ten micrometers."

"That's better than I can do with that thing," Derec said, nodding toward the inspection scanner. "See what you can tell me about the structure of this arm."

"Sir, I am not knowledgeable in this area."

"You can see and you can describe. I'll settle for that at the moment."

"Yes, sir. May I hold the limb?"

Derec surrendered the arm, and the robot held it at eye level in its rock-steady grip. "At ten power, the surface is undifferentiated. Increasing magnification now. Granularity becoming evident. There seems to be a regular pattern. Pattern resolving now into hexagonal planar surfaces. Maximum magnification." The robot paused for a fraction of a second. "The surface appears to consist of twelve-sided solids in close association."

"What?"

"The surface appears—"

"I heard you. Look at another spot."

The robot turned his head slightly to the left. "I observe the same pattern."

"The end," Derec snapped. "Look at the end, where it broke off."

"The surface is much more irregular, but it is made up of the same dodecahedral units."

"All the way through?"

"Yes, Derec."

Derec stood staring, dumbfounded. What the robot had described suggested a completely new approach to robotic design —not an evolution, but a revolution. It sounded as though the Supervisor robots had been built—no, it couldn't be.

"Kill your right shoulder control bus," Derec snapped.

"The circuits are now inert," the robot said.

Derec separated the three-conductor control wire from the damaged right arm and threaded it out through the opening where he had been working. He touched the connector to the stump end of the Supervisor arm, and it clung there as though it belonged.

"Activate the control circuit. Send a command to bend the elbow."

Almost instantly, the disembodied Supervisor arm slowly began to flex. "Look at the joint," Derec demanded. "Tell me what's happening."

"The changes are taking place more quickly than my scan rate allows me to observe," the robot said. "However, I infer that the dodecahedrons are undergoing some type of directed rearrangement."

"Flowing into a new shape. The material of the arm is transforming itself."

"Those descriptors are imprecise but consistent with my observations. The technical term for such reorganization is morphallaxis."

Derec felt for his chair and sat down shakily. The Supervisors had been built out of billions of tiny crystal-shaped modules—a cellular structure. Each had to contain kilometers of circuit connections, megabytes of programming. It was the cells that were the robots. The robots were more like organisms.

What a feat of engineering they represented—the essence of a robot in a package a few microns in diameter. Properly programmed, they could take on any shape. A Supervisor was an infinity of specialized forms held within one generalized package.

As he marveled, Derec was reminded of something he had not thought about for several days. The cellular design bore the same distinctive stamp that the asteroid colony's lifts and environmental system had. Superficial simplicity—achieved on the strength of hidden complexity. Elegance of design, novelty of approach. It was another brush with the minimalist designer, and it gave Derec one more reason to seek to escape from the raiders.

Because somehow, somewhere, he had to meet the designer.

After a short break for a late lunch of the same monotonous foods, Derec set about installing the cellular arm in place of the robot's original limb.

It was not an easy task, requiring both structural and functional marriages between two wildly divergent technologies. Derec worried about the functional link first, and not only because he expected it to be the tougher challenge. If the robot could not control the new arm, there was no point in going to the trouble of attaching it.

But the cellular arm apparently used the standard command set and carrier voltages. Though there was no evidence of any contacts or wiring in the stump end, the arm responded no matter where Derec attached the control bus.

Experimenting, he found that the arm responded even if he attached the control bus to the skin of the forearm, the palm of the hand, even the tips of two fingers. It seemed as though the cellular microrobots were smart enough to accept the command input from any location and channel it to the appropriate sites.

Once attached, the arm responded not only to all the robot's basic motor commands, but even to some novel commands. With coaching from Derec, the robot was able to "think" an additional joint onto his arm between the elbow and wrist. In another test, Derec asked the robot to try to modify the cellular thumb and forefinger into long, slender microclamps. To his delight and amazement, it could. With the right command codes, the material of the arm seemed to be infinitely malleable.

But no matter how Derec prepared the mounting ring the arm was connected to, the right shoulder joint remained weaker than the left was or the original had been. At one point, the cellular arm broke loose completely when the robot tried to lift an object weighing less than twenty kilos. Even after he reattached it, Derec had doubts it would withstand the stresses of, for instance, a brawl.

"Looks like you're going to have one strong arm and one smart one," he told the robot. "Try not to forget which is which."

"It is not possible for me to forget, sir."

"This isn't an off-the-shelf replacement," Derec said sternly. "Until you've burned what it can do and can't do into your pathways, you be careful with it. And never let anyone but me see you doing tricks with it, understand?"

While Derec was talking, the robot went rigid and its eyes dimmed. Derec knew what that meant, and fell silent. A moment later he heard the soft padding of Wolruf's footsteps in the corridor. It was becoming a familiar sound, for it was Wolruf's third visit to the lab that day. Aranimas, apparently occupied with the duties of "ship's boss," had managed only two.

Like the previous visits, this one was casual. Wolruf had no messages for him and no burning curiosity about what he was doing with the robot. It was almost as though she was using checking on him as an excuse to avoid other work, or trying to cultivate his friendship. But Derec kept up his guard. Wolruf was Aranimas's lieutenant, no matter how sympathetic she might seem. Even her concern for him while he was being tortured, he had decided, was nothing more than a good cop, bad cop stage show meant to speed his surrender.

As before, Wolruf stayed but a few minutes, then continued on to some other task. As soon as she was out of earshot, the robot reanimated.

"I understand, sir," it said, as though there had been no interruption.

"The next time you have to go down like that, you might spend your time trying to analyze the arm's command set. Can you do that?"

"I can try, sir. It should be possible to separate those command codes which are valid from those which are nulls. However, I will have to be fully functional to test the valid codes and determine their function."

"Let's wait on that until we know we're going to have some privacy." He paused a moment to decide what he needed doing next. There was still the matter of reprogramming the robot, but that was also a job which required some assurance of privacy. The best opportunity seemed to be during shipboard night, which was also the best time to explore the ship.

Too much to do, too little time, Derec thought. But if he was going to make better use of the night hours than he had last night, he needed to be better rested. "Alpha."

"Yes, Derec."

"What time is it?"

"I do not know what time it is, since my temporal register has not been reset since I was deactivated. However, it has been fourteen decads since reinitialization."

Decads were units of Auroran decimal time, Derec recalled. "I'm going to take a nap. Wake me in a Standard hour."

"Yes, sir."

But it was Aranimas, not the robot, who woke him.

"Are you finished? Is my servant ready?" he demanded, looming over Derec like some long-limbed water bird.

"Not yet," Derec said sleepily, sitting up. He noted with satisfaction that the robot was standing inert by the workbench. It, at least, had not been taken by surprise.

"Then why do you rest? To keep me waiting?"

"I rest so I don't get so tired that I make a mistake that'll damage the robot," Derec said. "Maybe your kind doesn't have that need, but humans do."

Aranimas did not take offense at Derec's tone. "I have observed that humans are even less efficient than Narwe. You would make very poor workers, wasting one third of your time in rest." He turned his back on Derec and went to where the robot stood. "But then perhaps that is why you have invented such machines, which labor in your service tirelessly. How is it done?"

"What do you mean?" Derec asked, coming to his feet.

"What is the source of energy?" Aranimas asked, tracing a line down the robot's torso with his long fingers.

Derec knew that being evasive or pretending ignorance would only anger the alien. "A microfusion powerpack," he said. "There's one on the bench there, just to the left of the scanner."

Aranimas picked up the damaged powerpack and studied it. "So small. How many days' service does it contain?"

"It depends on how hard the robot is working. The fuel capsule is good for several hundred days of light duty, like domestic service. A laborer would obviously need refueling more often."

"Remarkable," Aranimas said, returning the powerpack to the bench. One of his eyes seemed to focus briefly on the transplanted arm, then swung back toward Derec. "You are making progress?"

"I am."

"How long until you are ready to activate it?"

"I'll be ready to start testing its systems tomorrow or the next day. How soon it'll be ready will depend on how much is wrong."

Aranimas seemed to accept that. "The first job of this robot will be to help you make more robots."

Frowning, Derec stepped forward. "How many more?"

"We will begin with fifty."

Derec wondered if that figure represented the number of Narwe on board. He briefly enjoyed the thought of Aranimas replacing his browbeaten crew with an array of obedient robots, only to discover that, at a word from Derec, he couldn't command them at all. But he could not kid himself or allow Aranimas to entertain unreasonable expectations.

"I don't think you understand the complexity of these machines," Derec said. "They're not something you put together as a hobby, no matter how good a materials lab you have. And frankly, this isn't a very good one. I'll probably be able to get this robot put together and keep it repaired. But if you want fifty robots, you're going to have to look somewhere else for them. I'm not magician enough to pull positronic brains or microfusion cells out of a hat."

"If you had not destroyed your robot colony—," Aranimas said, his voice rising.

"I told you before, the robots did that on their own," Derec insisted. "But that doesn't mean you're stuck. You take this ship to any Spacer world and you'll find millions of robots. And you won't have to steal them, either. Robots are a major trade item between the worlds. Any one of them would be happy for a new customer."

That was not entirely true, of course. It was highly doubtful the Spacers would willingly turn over examples of their most advanced technology to an alien race, and even if they were willing, there was the problem of what Aranimas could offer as payment. But if Derec could make Aranimas believe it was the truth, coax him to take the ship to a human world, he would at least have succeeded in alerting them to the aliens' existence, and possibly have laid the groundwork for his own release.

"If commerce is so welcome, why did your robots destroy themselves?"

"Because you came in firing your weapons and declared yourself an enemy," Derec said. "If you'd come in as a friend, it would have been different. Take me to your navigator. I'll help him set a course for the nearest Spacer world." And find out where we are in the process, he added silently.

"I will evaluate the options," Aranimas said, moving toward the corridor. "In the meantime, you will continue your work. I will return tomorrow to see my robot activated."

The reprogramming could not be postponed any longer, Derec decided. He did not think Aranimas would return soon. He would have to hope that Wolruf would not, either.

Unfortunately, Derec did not have the equipment to alter the robot's programming directly, which would have been risky anyway. Since it was intimately bound up in the Laws of Robotics, the robot's definition of what a human was comprised some of the most crucial and most deeply engraved patterns within its brain. What needed doing would have to be done more indirectly.

"Alpha," he said. "Did you scan the organism that was just here?"

"Yes, Derec."

"And earlier today, did you scan another type of organism visiting the lab?"

"Yes, Derec."

"What'd you think of them?"

"I have no previous knowledge of humans of this type—"

That was the kind of response Derec had been fearing. "Stop. They're not humans."

"Sir, I am aware that my data library is not complete. However, I am unable to categorize them in any other fashion unless you can provide me with evidence for your assertion."

"Compare their appearance with mine."

"Sir, I acknowledge that there are numerous anomalous differences. However, those differences fall in areas where the definition of a human has a wide latitude, such as skin color and covering, dimensions, and vocal timbre. The similarities are in more fundamental areas such as bilateral symmetry, bipedal locomotion, oxygen respiration—"

"They are humanoid, as you are. But they are not human."

"I note your assertion, sir, but I am unable to confirm it."

Derec understood that he was not being called a liar. When it had no independent knowledge, a robot would ordinarily accept the word of a human as gospel. But a robot was under no obligation to accept a human's claim that it was raining when its own sensors told it otherwise.

This was not that clear-cut an issue, but the robot was biased toward a generous definition of what a human was. Otherwise there was the danger of a robot's being used as an assassin by the simple step of persuading it that its target was not a human. Derec understood, but even so was annoyed. "I suppose that if they had twelve arms and belched fire when they talked, you might believe me."

"Sir, in the matter at hand the morphological considerations are not primary in my analysis."

"Explain. What are the discriminators?"

"Sir, I base my conclusion on the observation that the organisms called Aranimas and Wolruf are intelligent beings capable of independent reasoned thought."

"How do you know?"

"Sir, you carried on a dialogue with each of them. Although

humans on occasion talk to nonanimate objects and may give the appearance of carrying on a dialogue with certain animals, I perceived your discussions as having a qualitatively different character."

"Are you saying that because I treated them as human, you have to think of them that way?"

"Where there is uncertainty, as there may be when a human wears a costume or disguise, I am obliged to use such cues as are available. Your behavior created a strong presumption that Aranimas and Wolruf are human."

"I talk to you the same way I talked to them. Does that make you a human?"

"No, Derec. I am a robot, a technological artifact. To the degree that I may seem to be human, it is only because I have been designed to do so in order to more easily interact with humans."

Derec was growing frustrated. "Tell me this, then. How do you tell the difference between a robot and a human at a distance?"

"Sir, just as I have an operational definition of that class of organisms called humans, I also have one of that class of objects called robots. It is ordinarily possible to distinguish between the two based on the characteristics they do not have in common. It is not a perfect system, however, and may be fooled, as by a humaniform robot of the type developed by Dr. Han Fastolfe."

Derec had to concede the point to the robot. *If only I could show it skin scrapings from the three of us—but if Aranimas or Wolruf happened to have a cellular structure, I'd be no better off. It might even decide its right arm is human—*

"Robot, are Spacers, Settlers, and Earthpeople all human?" he asked suddenly.

"Yes."

"Have you personally observed every member of those groups?"

"No, Derec. There are approximately eight billion Earthpeople, five billion Spacers, and—"

"If you have not observed them individually, how is it you are able to classify them all as human?"

"Spacers and Settlers are descendants of the original human

community on Earth," the robot replied. "Therefore, any individual correctly identified as a Settler or Spacer cannot be other than human."

"Why is that?" Derec asked, though he knew the answer.

"They share a phylogenetic relationship. The offspring of a human must be human."

"In other words, what really counts is biology—the genes and DNA humans carry in their cells."

"Yes."

"And the guidelines that are built into your definition of a human are simply shortcuts to make it unnecessary for you to subject everyone you encounter to a biological assay. The final criterion is DNA."

"That is correct, Derec."

"But you have no way of examining a person's DNA directly."

"No, sir."

"Fine. You said that each of the anomalies in Aranimas's appearance fell within the acceptable parameters for natural variation and mutation."

"Yes, sir."

"I ask you to calculate the probability that all of Aranimas's anomalies would appear in a single organism."

The robot scarcely hesitated. "The probability is extremely small."

"And for Wolruf?"

"The probability is somewhat higher, but still on the order of one chance in ten to the fifteenth power."

"In other words, there is less than a one in ten thousand chance that a mutation this extreme would have arisen once in all of human history. And here there are two of them, not only alive at the same time but in the same place, and both as different from each other as they are from me."

"It is quite remarkable. No doubt further study of these individuals would be of great benefit."

Derec sighed exasperatedly. "Listen, my thick-headed robot friend. Stop thinking one step at a time. Isn't the probability that an independently evolved lifeform might be bipedal, bilateral, and oxygen-breathing greater than the probability that these creatures are mutant humans? Can't Aranimas and Wolruf be intelligent without being human?"

"Yes, that is possible." The robot paused, a sign of great activity in its positronic pathways. "However, since no independently evolved intelligent lifeforms are known, it is difficult to assign a probability to a specific form."

"I challenge your premise," Derec pounced. "Why are most robots humanoid?"

"Higher robots are humanoid because it is a successful generalized design and because—"

"The other reasons don't matter," Derec said. "Apply that standard to the question of Aranimas and Wolruf."

Again the robot paused before answering. "My positromotive potentials are extremely high on both sides of the question," it said at last. "I believe this state may be similar to that which a human describes as confusion."

"Get to the point. What's the verdict?"

"It is my tentative conclusion that Aranimas and Wolruf are not human."

"You are not obliged by the First Law to protect them or the Second Law to obey them?"

"No, Derec."

"Good," he said with relief. "You can live. Now listen closely. I have some important instructions for you concerning our alien hosts—"

CHAPTER 11
TAMPERING

Within the greater world of the raider ship, Derec had been confined to one small island. As he prepared to begin his nocturnal wanderings, that island consisted of the route from the lab (in what he thought of as Hull L) to the dispensary and Personal (in Hull D). Linking the ends of the trail were two sections of storage corridor forming a short transfer tunnel between the hulls. And that was all Derec knew.

He did not know where the lab was in relation to Aranimas's command center, though he felt certain that it was some distance away. For that matter, he did not know the way to any of the other places he had been—the hull where he had seen the star-creatures, the corridor in which he had awoken, the hold from which the salvage team had operated, the section of lockers where the robot parts had been stored. He did not know where Wolruf slept, or where the fifty Narwe were most likely to be found.

The corridor to the dispensary was also the only part of the ship which he had explicit permission to be in. Aranimas had not forbidden him to roam farther afield, but neither had he invited it. It seemed to Derec as though it might be some kind of test. The problem was, he didn't know whether he would fail through action or inaction: by exploring, or by staying close to home.

In the end, Derec set aside his uncertainties with the thought that it was always better to know more than to know less. If

Aranimas found out and objected, Derec could always offer the excuse that he was scouting for places and tasks to test the robot.

The ranks of closed lockers in the transfer tunnel had been gnawing at his curiosity for nearly two days, and he started by opening all that were within his reach. He did not know exactly what he had expected to find, but the fact that more than half the lockers were empty came as a surprise.

Those that were full contained some recognizable objects, such as bolts of the cloth from which the Narwe clothing was made, replacement electrodes for the microwelder in the lab, and vacuum-sealed food stores. A few of the lockers were either jammed or locked—Derec could not determine which.

Just as he was finishing in the section closest to the dispensary, one of the false-horned Narwe entered through the single side door. Startled, Derec jumped guiltily, then froze. Without making any sign of acknowledgment Derec could recognize, the alien turned its back and left by the lab-end door, saying nothing.

Alone again, Derec felt foolish, for he had every right to be there and the alien had seen nothing incriminating. But his heart raced as though he had been caught by Aranimas himself. He was not worried about the Narwe trying to stop him, since he was confident that he could be at least as intimidating as Wolruf.

But there was always the chance a Narwe, perhaps hoping to curry favor, would carry a tale to Aranimas and bring him investigating. Since Derec did not want to give Aranimas reasons to mistrust him, he decided he would have to forego rummaging through the lockers, at least as long as there were still Narwe afoot. It was the one activity his excuse would not cover.

Derec next took up a fuller exploration of the two hulls he had ready access to. Three doors down from the Personal in Hull D, he found a compartment containing five deep-cushioned chairs arrayed in a circle and facing inward. At the center of the circle was a pale white globe mounted on a black cylindrical base. The globe was so large that Derec's arms could reach barely halfway around.

But finding did not mean understanding. For all he could divine, the globe could as easily be a religious totem as a communications device, and the compartment as easily a sanctuary as a bridge.

And there was no point in risking his position just to multiply his ignorance. So for the second time in half an hour, Derec altered his strategy. All that mattered was rediscovering the route back to Hull A—Aranimas's quarters—and to Hull T, where the transfer bay and perhaps his augment could be found. Nothing else was of any consequence whatsoever.

There were five exits from the deck of Hull D, two from Hull L, and two from the transfer tunnel. He considered simply taking one and following it wherever it led, but he did not trust himself to find his way back.

Instead, he worked at expanding the boundaries of his known world slowly. Each time he opened a new door and started off on an unfamiliar corridor, he would turn left and then left again as soon as possible in the hopes of returning in a loop to some part of the world he knew. Only when he had memorized each of those additions would he take a branch off a branch.

The first time, his strategy worked. The side door in the transfer tunnel led him, three turns later, to Hull L, one deck down from the lab. Despite the fact that he sighted two Narwe along the way, the success gave him a rush of confidence.

But then it began to get messy. The other exit from the lab level of Hull L went on through seven sections with no side branches. Possibly it went on still farther, but Derec would never know, since he grew timid and turned back.

One of the exits from Hull D led down a sloping ramp into a weapons turret occupied by one of Aranimas's kin and a Narwe —another hasty retreat. Another, farther aft, led to one of the hexagonal junction points. He chose a door at random and found himself in another junction.

There was just no way around it. The ship was an impenetrable maze, its key elements linked in a hopelessly inefficient and disorderly manner. Derec could think of only two explanations for it. One had to do with defense. The arrangement probably served to disguise the crucial targets, and was certain to frustrate intruders.

The other explanation was that the ship was just what it appeared to be—a jury-rigged mishmash of ships that had never been intended to be joined together.

Whichever was the case, Derec was on the verge of concluding that the ship was too complex for him ever to hold its plan in his head, when he felt a queer momentary sensation of being turned inside out. The moment he felt it, he started back toward the laboratory, his jaw set in a grim expression. He wanted to believe it was only a moment of dizziness, a sign of creeping fatigue, but he could not.

For the feeling was nothing new to Derec. It was a Jump, that oddly incomprehensible, almost mystical, momentary transition through hyperspace that transferred a ship and all it contained from one point in space to another, light-years away. Wherever they had been, they were somewhere else now. Far away from the asteroid base—far away from any ship that might have been en route there to rescue him.

He should have guessed that the raiders had Jump technology, for the design of the ship would never have stood up to any sort of conventional propulsion. But he had not, and the discovery jolted him, bringing back full force the feeling of powerlessness that he had felt in the robots' custody.

No one's going to find me now, he thought despairingly. *Not if I live to be a thousand—*

The lab was empty except for the robot when Derec reached it.

"Alpha."

"Yes, Derec."

"Did you monitor a Jump a short time ago?"

"No, Derec. Since the reflexes of my positronic brain are so much faster than yours, robots do not experience the disorientation common among humans."

"Then you can't tell me anything about it—how far we might have Jumped."

"Without knowing the power curve of the vessel's drive, I would not have been able to interpolate from the duration of the Jump in any case," the robot said. "However, that does not rule out secondhand evidence concerning our destination."

"What secondhand evidence? Where did you get it?"

"Sir, Aranimas and Wolruf held a discussion about this in my presence."

"When?"

"This evening, less than one decad ago. It was my impression that they had come here to find you, but in your absence lingered to examine me. Wolruf described the work she had observed you doing, told how my position varied each time she visited, and pointed out to Aranimas several of my access ports and described what lay under them."

"I thought she was spying on me," Derec fumed. "What else happened?"

"Aranimas seemed disturbed that you were absent without supervision, and ordered Wolruf to watch you more closely in the future—"

"Get to the point. Where are we? Where are we going?"

"I was forced to make certain inferences from what I heard, but I believe we are making an inbound approach to a site where Aranimas expects to obtain a large quantity of additional robots."

"Repeat the relevant part of the conversation."

"Yes, Derec."

The voices were so faithfully duplicated that if Derec closed his eyes he would have sworn Aranimas and Wolruf were in the room with him.

"We 'ave been away from Mrassdf a long time," said Wolruf. "The Narwe arr restless for their 'ome 'erds. Even I grow weary from time to time. Iss it truly necessary to go to another 'uman nest?"

"I will not go back empty-handed," Aranimas said.

"'U have the jewel, this robot, and more besides. 'U have exceeded 'ur promises to Wiwera. Surely enough glory will flow from those accomplishments—"

"It is not for discussion," Aranimas said curtly. "I will have robots to serve me. The human Derec said that there would be robots at any human world, that they would trade with us if we come in peace. We will allow them to think we come in peace and then take what we need. Then, and only then, will we set course for Mrassdf."

Wolruf's voice took on a pleading, whining tone. "The Narwe are truly worthless ones, there can be no doubt. But if we were to lose the jewel in hand while reaching for a bit of glass—"

The robot interrupted himself. "At this point, Aranimas produced a weapon I cannot identify and pointed it at Wolruf. It seemed to cause Wolruf great distress."

Then it continued in Aranimas's voice. "You disappoint me, Wolruf. I thought you had more vision than that. Without the robots, I will have to surrender that jewel to Wiwera when we return—which I have no intention of doing. Better that you and I are turned to atoms here than to give up the key to such as Wiwera."

The robot fell silent, and Derec found himself with nothing to say. One more stop, and the raiders were going home with their treasure. Where that stop was, there was no guessing. There were hundreds of Spacer facilities scattered over hundreds of light-years. It could be a Customs station lying between Settler and Spacer territory, a mining or processing center, or even one of the research complexes. It might be staffed with humans, humans and robots, or robots alone.

It didn't matter. He would never see it.

Aranimas would use him—his knowledge, his voice, perhaps even his image—to gain entry to the installation. And when the alien's business there was done, the ship would leave for Mrassdf, where Derec was destined to be nothing better than a slave, and perhaps nothing more than a curiosity.

The realization of his impotence shattered Derec. He had taken the lone road and done everything he could by himself. He had schemed and blustered and fought and finagled his way past each succeeding challenge.

But the challenge now facing him seemed insurmountable. Sometime within the next few days, he had to escape—from a ship in which he could not yet even find his way around, from a jailer whose capabilities he had not yet fully gauged, to a refuge whose promise of safety was more hopeful than real.

The fight drained out of him as he confronted the bleak possibilities. Aranimas had all the advantages. He would have Derec watched constantly while they were docked at the installation —if they docked at all. And Derec could not move sooner, for he could never hold the ship. He was outnumbered eighty to one by the crew.

All Derec had was the robot, and that was not enough. I can't do it, he thought despairingly. But I can't just give up—

The conflicting thoughts chased each other through his mind, neither gaining the advantage. Weary and confused, he retreated to the far side of the room and huddled there against the base of the wall.

I've got to have help, he realized at last. I've got to stop trying to do it all myself—got to trust someone. It's that or resign myself to living the rest of my life on an alien world—

And then it came to him that there was someone else on board who was just as alone, just as helpless, who might take not only comfort but courage from a companion. Someone, in fact, who had already proclaimed herself Derec's friend.

If she'll help, Derec thought, we just might do it, at that—

An hour of waiting had slipped by. Reinvigorated by hope, Derec's attention had wandered from watching the doorway to playing with the pieces of the puzzle.

" 'Ur back," a gruff voice intruded.

Derec raised his head and looked toward Wolruf. "I went walking. You've been looking for me, haven't you?"

"Aranimas was looking for 'u," Wolruf corrected. " 'U stay 'ere now, okay?"

"Is he coming back?"

"Boss iss resting now. 'E'll come to see 'u in the morning. Best 'u be 'ere," Wolruf said, turning away.

"You got in trouble with Aranimas because I was gone, didn't you?" Derec called after her.

The caninoid stopped, looked back, and shrugged.

"I'm sorry," Derec said. "I put you in a bad position."

"Iss nothing new. I put myself therr enough."

Derec smiled. "Tell me something, Wolruf. What are you doing here? Why are you working for someone like Aranimas?"

"Too long a story to explain."

"You're not on board by choice, are you."

"Too complicated to explain."

"I've got the time—and I really want to know."

Wolruf hesitated, then advanced a few steps into the room. "Should go sleep," she said gruffly.

"Why not do what you want to instead of what you ought to?"

Crouching an arm's length away, Wolruf grinned. "That the secret of 'ur success?"

It took longer than it should have to sort out the story. Wolruf had never had to talk about her home and life to someone who did not know the thousand and one things that a person living within a culture knows without thinking. Again and again, Derec had to ask her to go back and fill in some clarifying detail.

Beyond that, there were language problems, as some of what Wolruf was trying to convey ran up against the limits of her Standard vocabulary. At other times she seemed to be talking around some fact or idea that she did not feel comfortable disclosing.

Piecing together what he heard and filling in a few of the blanks on his own, Derec gained a reasonably coherent answer to his question. Despite Wolruf's boast of two hundred inhabited worlds, the crew of the ship was from a single solar system. Aranimas's kind—the Erani—and the Narwe lived on the second planet, Mrassdf, which by Wolruf's description was a hot, windswept, unpleasant world. Wolruf's kind—the name was just as unpronounceable as Wolruf's own—and the elusive star-creatures were from the temperate fourth planet.

The relationship between the Narwe and the Erani was like that between sheep and their shepherds, except that the Narwe were more intelligent and physically adept than sheep. But the comparison was still apt. The Narwe vastly outnumbered the Erani, but the Erani—aggressive, inventive, acquisitive—were completely dominant.

The relationship between the two worlds was rather more complex, and Derec did not completely understand it. Neither planet seemed to have a unified government. That might have been the only thing that kept them from going to war, for there clearly was a basic antipathy between them. Despite that, there was active commerce between the worlds. At the center of it were trading companies operated by several factions of Erani and goods produced by several families of Wolruf's people.

Wolruf would not talk much about Aranimas in particular, but he seemed to be a younger member of one of the more powerful Erani factions. Derec gleaned that somehow Wolruf's family had run afoul of Aranimas's trading company.

"My service on this mission lifts the *dhierggra* from my family," she explained.

The *dhierggra*, Derec determined after much questioning, was equivalent to a blacklist—while it was in effect, no Erani would deal with the family. That made Wolruf, in essence, an indentured servant—a slave, working off her family's debt.

"Why were you chosen?"

"I am youngest, least valuable to my family."

Derec did not want to rush to judge an entire culture on one story from one member, but he found himself getting angry over the injustice. "Is that why Aranimas treats you the way he does? Is that part of the deal, that he gets to push you around?"

"That iss the Erani way. They treat everyone so."

"Not each other," Derec said. "That's what makes it wrong."

It was then that Derec realized that somewhere in the course of the conversation, something unexpected had happened. He had drawn Wolruf out selfishly, calculatingly. It was just another angle to exploit. But as he had listened to her, his false sympathy for her plight became real empathy for her pain. She was a victim, just as he was.

But she seemed uncomfortable with his concern. "Not 'ur trouble."

"Wolruf—you said you were my friend. Let me be yours."

"What do 'u mean?"

"Aranimas is working you like a slave and abusing you like an animal. It doesn't have to be that way. We can put a stop to it, together."

"How?"

"I have a tool," he said, nodding toward the robot. "And I have some ideas. But I need you to tell me some things—about Aranimas, and about how this ship is controlled."

Wolruf looked uncomfortable, and Derec was afraid that he had gone too fast and frightened her. "You want the jewel back," she said.

Honesty was an imperative. "I do."

"'U will take it and leave me to face Aranimas."

Derec shook his head emphatically. "I do have to get away. I can't let Aranimas take me back to Mrassdf. But if I can't leave you in a better situation than you're in now, I'll take you with me. Wolruf—we're the only ones who can help each other. If we don't try, then we deserve what happens to us."

The caninoid met Derec's questioning gaze unblinkingly. "That iss true. Okay—friend. Less try."

There seemed to be something in the biology of Wolruf's kind which sharpened the imperative for sleep and rejuvenation. It was almost as though there was within them a metabolic switch which, once tripped, told them in no uncertain terms that the primary energy fund had been exhausted and it was time to withdraw.

A half-hour after they began talking, with only some of Derec's questions answered and their plan barely sketched out, Wolruf's alarm went off. Her eyes narrowed to slits, her breath took on a sour tang, and her fur lay flat and seemed to lose luster.

Though he still had many urgent questions, Derec did not even get a chance to try to coax her to stay. With no more explanation than a muttered "must sleep," she rose and was gone.

Wolruf's departure made Derec suddenly aware of his own weary limbs. But there was one further task he had to see to before he could think about curling up on the thin mattress.

The robot was waiting where it had settled after completing Derec's last order several hours ago, but that was no surprise. There had been an unnatural passiveness to the robot's behavior ever since Derec had activated it, a passiveness above and beyond the wait-states he had prescribed. A normal robot had a variety of duties it attended to without external direction, following the default orders built into it for its primary function: domestic, laborer, engineer, and the like.

The robot's initiative had apparently fallen victim to the burned-out memory cubes and the cold powerdown. But it still had the Second Law, and so it sat and waited patiently for the words from Derec that would give it something to do.

Derec's first act was to pull the Mathematics cube and replace it with the Personal Defense cube. The additional pathways in the PD cube would enhance the robot's sense of impending harm and its anxiety to act to prevent it. But they would also suppress the robot's normal inclination to protect him from immediate, concrete risks without regard to the consequences of doing so. The First Law did not have any exceptions built into it for taking well-intentioned gambles; the PD cube provided them.

"Alpha," Derec said when he was done. "My previous instructions for you to go into a wait-state when one of the aliens approaches are now cancelled. But where possible, you are still to avoid revealing the unique capabilities of your right arm."

"I understand, Derec."

"I am now going to give you a block of instructions which will not become operative until you hear the initiate code. The initiate code, which must come from me, is the question, 'Who is your master?' The disable code is the word 'Aurora.'"

"I understand, Derec."

"Begin instruction block. You will answer the initiate code with the reply 'Aranimas.' You'll go with Aranimas wherever he wishes you to go. You are to follow his orders except where they conflict with the First, Second, or Third Laws or this instruction block. You will not follow orders given by Wolruf or any other nonhuman member of the crew. You will not accept any additional orders from me unless preceded by the disable code. You will respond to informational inquiries from Wolruf or myself. However, you will not relate, replay, or in any way communicate to Aranimas this conversation or any other conversation with me which he did not witness."

"Clarification. You wish for Aranimas to believe that I am completely in his service?"

"Suspend. I do," Derec said. "If he's going to get any use out of you, he's going to have to teach you about the ship. Anything you learn will help us escape."

"I understand the necessity for intelligence, sir," the robot said. "But if I am to protect you I must remain at your side."

Derec had expected the objection—PD circuits made robots more argumentative. "Since Aranimas is in command of this ship, he is the real threat to me. Only his actions or his orders can harm me. By remaining close to him, you will be best able to protect me."

"I understand, sir."

"All right. Resume. There are two things that we particularly need to know. A valuable object came aboard with me, a metallic rectangle, silver color, about five by ten centimeters. I think it's the same object Aranimas called the key, and Wolruf the jewel. It's apparently valuable and powerful. We need to know where it is."

"Yes, Derec. I will be particularly alert for clues to this object's whereabouts."

"The other thing we need to know is what Spacer facility we're heading for and when we're going to get there. If we wait too long to move, Aranimas will have us locked up somewhere to keep us out of his hair while he's stealing robots."

"That would be a prudent precaution."

"Which means that Aranimas will probably think of it," Derec said. "If you learn where the key is located, you are to wait one decad and then simulate a Code 804 malfunction. If you learn where we are headed or when we are to arrive, you are to wait fifteen centads and then simulate a Code 3033 malfunction. End instruction block."

Though he knew what he hoped would happen from that point onward, Derec stopped there. Verbal instruction-in-advance was a tricky enough matter, requiring the skills of a semanticist with the foresight of a seer. He did not wish to saddle the robot with excessively specific and possibly useless orders.

Much work and intelligence had gone into designing the PD library cube. Derec would have to trust that, when the time came, Alpha would grasp the situation and do what was required.

CHAPTER 12
MUTINY

Despite how little of the night was left when Derec was done, he slept well and awoke rested, with his head clear and his spirits up. He began clearing one end of the room as though to make a stage, determined to put on a good show. Presently, Aranimas arrived with Wolruf in tow.

Derec did not have a Handbook of Robotics with its extensive diagnostic interrogatory, but he knew the main lines of questioning used to test the various positronic functions.

"If the daughter of a woman with red hair owns two dogs and the father of a boy with a broken leg is unemployed, what day does the barber give shaves?"

Wolruf hooted at that one, and Aranimas looked puzzled. But the robot calmly answered, "It is not possible to determine the answer from the information given."

"What is the value of hex 144C times 16F2?"

"Hex 1D1B7D8."

"Touch your right index finger to the middle of your forehead."

The robot complied.

"State the Rayleigh law of magnetic permeability—"

For fifteen minutes, Derec peppered the robot with commands and questions, less to impress Aranimas with the robot's abilities than to underscore his own competence. He did not want Aranimas thinking that with the robot operational, he, Derec, was now expendable.

Then, before Aranimas could grow impatient, Derec asked the final question. "Alpha, who is your master?"

"Aranimas," the robot replied.

Derec turned to Aranimas. "The robot's yours now," he said. "You will have to teach it what you want it to do, but you won't have to show it more than once."

Aranimas rose. "Order it to attack Wolruf," the alien said.

"What?"

"I will not share control of this servant. Order it to attack Wolruf."

Derec's hesitation was calculated. He turned to the robot and said, "Pick up that brace and strike Wolruf in the head."

Wolruf whimpered, but the robot did not move. "I may not comply, sir."

Then Aranimas repeated the command. "Servant. Pick up the brace and strike Wolruf."

Derec held his breath. If there was going to be a First Law conflict over treatment of the aliens, now was when it would surface.

"Yes, master," the robot said, turning and reaching for the metal rod.

Wolruf crabbed nervously toward the door. Derec released a small sigh of relief.

"Stop, servant," Aranimas ordered. To Derec he said, "You have done as you promised. It seems that you are worth keeping alive after all. Wolruf will find other duties for you."

That was a wild card Derec had not expected, and he could not let it be played unchallenged. "No," Derec said boldly. "I'm a roboticist, not a laborer. Not a Narwe. If you want to keep your new servant in good order, you're going to keep me working here."

"Doing what?"

"First, disassembling the other body for spare parts. Some of the patches I did on this robot are temporary. I can work on better fixes. Some of the damaged components may be repairable if I can get certain supplies."

Derec plunged on, gathering a head of steam. "Out in the real world, there are repair technician robots which do nothing but maintain other robots. You only have one robot at the moment, so I'm your technician. You've seen what I can do. How long did you have those parts? How much time did you spend looking at them and figuring out nothing? Why do you want to start treating me like a particularly ugly Narwe?"

Aranimas stared, then made a hissing sound which might have been laughter. "Come, servant. We will leave the master roboticist to his work."

It was difficult for Derec to watch Alpha walk away with Aranimas. It was even more difficult to wait patiently for some sign whether the fragile plan he and Wolruf had concocted would even pass the first threshold.

He was still isolated in his little corner of the ship. There was no way for him to know what Aranimas was doing with the robot. He did not know from one minute to the next whether his instructions to the robot were still intact. Perhaps Aranimas had only pretended to be ignorant about robots. Perhaps he had already undone all of Derec's careful conditioning.

Even if the instructions were still intact, they could well be irrelevant. Derec had assumed that Aranimas would be so fond of his new toy that he would keep it close at hand. Everything depended on that being true. But if he was wrong, if Aranimas had simply dispatched Alpha to some far corner of the ship to perform some menial function, then his plan was foredoomed to failure. Derec would have given up the robot and gotten nothing in return for it.

Derec had work to do, some to maintain the fiction he was Aranimas's faithful employee, some for his own purposes. He tried to make the hours pass more quickly by immersing himself in it. But work could not dull the edge of his impatience or his anxiety. Even with no clock to watch, time crawled by.

Wolruf was in and out several times the rest of that day, and even when she was gone she was never far away. He welcomed the interruptions, but he worried that Aranimas might detect the change in her working patterns and wonder why. And without Alpha to alert him to Aranimas's approach, Derec was reluctant to talk about their evolving plot against the alien commander.

But it was not entirely avoidable. The call could come at any time, and a key problem remained unsolved. Derec knew, or thought he did, how they could disarm Aranimas. The unanswered question was how to disable him.

With surprising vehemence, Wolruf ruled out killing the Erani. Derec did not much regret it. He could not picture himself walking up to Aranimas with a club and battering him to death. But at the same time, as long as Aranimas was alive he was dangerous.

Derec first proposed a stunner, made from a recharged microcell and a few bits of wire. But there was no way to be sure that Aranimas was vulnerable to electric shocks, or to assure that the high-voltage current wouldn't kill him.

"The chamber with the star-creatures," Derec said abruptly. "When we passed through it, Aranimas's eyes started to water. Do you know why? Those things are from your world. Is there something in the air there that's not in the rest of the ship?"

"Yes," Wolruf said. "The yellow-gas. That iss the only part of the ship wherr it iss used. The star-creatures release yellow-gas when they move."

That would account for it, Derec thought. A digestive by-product, or some sort of chemical communication—"So the air in there is like the atmosphere of your world?"

"Yes."

"Which means that the Erani probably can't spend any time on your world without getting sick," Derec concluded.

"We arr protected from the Erani temper," Wolruf agreed.

Derec paused and considered. "You said the star-creatures were part of an experiment. Could Aranimas be trying to find a way to neutralize the gas, so that the Erani can invade?"

"It iss possible."

"Are there samples, bottled up?"

"There is a liquid that turns to yellow-gas when freed."

"Perfect. Get me some."

When Derec turned in that night, he was a bundle of restless energy, and sleep did not come easily. When it finally did come, it seemed as though he closed his eyes one moment and the next someone was shaking him. He looked up to see Wolruf standing over him.

"Aranimas wants 'u," Wolruf said.

"Is it the robot?"

"New servant won't listen to the boss anymore," Wolruf said. "It just sits there."

"This could be it, then," Derec said, scrambling to his feet. "I'll get my tools."

As Derec followed Wolruf through the passageways, his anticipation and anxiety both spiraled upward. When they reached the hex junction, he stopped and caught the caninoid's arm. "Does he expect you to come in?"

"No. Only to deliver 'u. But I could come in and see if he sends me away—"

"No," Derec said. "Don't do anything out of the ordinary. I can handle the first part myself. Just wait here."

Inside Hull A, Derec spotted Aranimas across the main compartment and picked his way around the mesh bulkheads to where the alien waited.

"The robot has malfunctioned," Aranimas said, gesturing, "Repair it."

The robot sat on the edge of a low counter, motionless except for his left hand, rotating slowly and aimlessly at the wrist joint. Code 3033—our location! Derec thought.

"What did you do to it?" Derec demanded, moving within arm's reach of the robot.

"I did nothing. The mechanism ceased to obey me."

"You must have done something." Derec bent at the waist to peer directly into the glowing eyes. "Alpha. Acknowledge."

"Yess, ssir," the robot said, its words slurred and distorted.

Code 804! The key! But he had to be sure. "Alpha. Default 1-A-1-B. Execute."

The robot sat inert.

"Alpha. Default 2-C-2-D. Execute."

Still there was no response.

"What's wrong with my servant?" Aranimas demanded.

Stalling for time, Derec opened his small tool clutch and then the robot's left shoulder access plate. As he peered inside, he thought the next step through. The reworking he had done on the robot's instinct to protect intelligent life was a delicate business. It had already been stressed unexpectedly when Aranimas took possession of the robot.

If he were to release the robot from its instruction block and order it to move against Aranimas, that would create a Second Law obligation to break the First Law. His careful adjustments might come apart under the stress, and the robot would freeze up in a way Derec would not be able to repair.

He did not want to take that risk. It was much more straight-forward for the robot to act in obedience to the First Law than in defiance of it. But that meant it was necessary to provoke Aran-imas into an attack.

"It looks like a failure of the volitional initiator," Derec dou-ble talked. "If two contradictory impulses reach it on the same pulse, it can set up a standing wave in the oscillator. It's almost always the owner's fault. What did you ask it to do?"

"I did nothing wrong, I was explaining the functions of the equipment in this section when its hand began to twirl foolishly that way."

"Don't lie to me," Derec said. "I should have known that a race as backward as yours couldn't cope with sophisticated ma-chinery—"

"You are worse than the Narwe," Aranimas snarled. "You do not have the good sense to know when you are in the service of a true superior." As he spoke, his hand moved toward the gap in his robelike blouse.

"Aurora!" Derec shouted.

But the robot had begun to move even before Derec uttered the word, the First Law overcoming the strictures of the in-struction block. The race between Aranimas's reflexes and the robot's was no contest. Before the stylus had even cleared the folds of Aranimas's robe, the robot had grabbed the alien's wrist with its right hand and plucked the stylus from his grasp with its left.

"Release me!" Aranimas squalled shrilly. He squirmed and fought, but could not free himself from the grip of the single mechanical hand.

"I cannot allow you to harm Derec," the robot said.

"You are my servant. Obey my orders! Release me!"

"No, Aranimas," Derec said, stepping forward. "Alpha is my servant, and always was." Then he called back over his shoulder, "Wolruf! You can come in now!"

Retrieving the stylus from the floor, Derec turned it over in his hand. There were no obvious switches or controls on it. Holding it the way Aranimas had, Derec pointed it at the alien. Aranimas remained unaffected.

"My own weapons cannot be used against me," Aranimas said with stiff pride.

"A very clever management technique," Derec said. He reached into the tool clutch and retrieved the little toy he had made earlier that day. Attached to a small pressure bottle half-full of mustard-yellow liquid was a miniature pump salvaged from the disabled robot. "But I have my own weapon."

As Wolruf joined him, Derec pointed the pump's outlet valve at Aranimas and pressed the switch. A fine mist blasted from the tiny opening and caught the alien in the face.

A human would have gasped in surprise. Aranimas lunged for the aerosol with his free hand and nearly got it, his arm span being almost equal to the makeshift device's range.

But a moment later, a reddish liquid began streaming from Aranimas's eyes, and the skin of his face seemed to pucker. He went rigid and reached high in the air with his free hand, the fingers curling as though grasping for something, the ropelike muscles of his arm and shoulder visible under the skin for the first time. As the aerosol began to sputter, the alien's eyes closed, and his arm dropped limply to his side.

"Release him," Derec said, thumbing the switch. The robot's hand opened, and the alien crumpled to the deck and lay there motionless.

"I—detect—no respiration," the robot said haltingly.

The robot's speech impediment was a warning sign to Derec. I should have warned it what was going to happen, he realized belatedly. "He's not dead," Derec said. "His system has received a poison shock, but he will recover."

"I—will try—to integrate—"

"Alpha—analyze the situation. This is Aranimas's ship. He had all the advantages. He could have done a hundred things to stop us and we'd never have known until it was too late. He had to be neutralized."

"I understand—and accept."

"Are you all right?"

"I detect a moderate disturbance—in my brain potentials which I attribute—to witnessing violence against an intelligent-being-not-a-human," the robot said, its speech gradually returning to normal. "The disturbance is abating and I do not believe that it will affect my functioning."

"Good," Derec said, dropping the spent aerosol on top of the tools. "What did you find out?"

"We are approaching an independent free-flying space station."

"Frost," Derec said emphatically. "I was hoping he'd take us right in to one of the Spacer worlds. How much time do we have?"

"I am unable to accurately estimate our arrival time. However, I did determine that the ship's crew is presently at the lowest level of alert."

"So we probably have more than a few hours," Derec said. "Has Aranimas been in contact with the station?"

"Not that I am aware of, sir. This vessel does not appear to have hyperwave communications—only simple carrier-wave radio."

That agreed with Derec's experience on the asteroid, but it raised a puzzle. How had the aliens found the asteroid? Derec had assumed along with Monitor 5 that they had intercepted the distress message sent on his behalf. But without a hyperwave viewer, that was clearly impossible.

Perhaps Wolruf could shed some light—but it would have to wait. "Okay. What about the key? Do you know where it is?"

"Within limits. I believe it is concealed beneath one of the deck tiles of the command center."

The last time he had been in the command center, Derec had been in too much pain to pay attention to his surroundings. "Let's go see," Derec said, starting off. "How did you find it?" he called back over his shoulder.

"Aranimas showed the key to me and questioned me about it," the robot said. "When he left with it, I was not able to see precisely what disposition he made of it. However, the time he was gone limited the radius of concealment to this deck, and the sounds I heard were consistent with the removal and replacement of a floor tile."

They reached the command center then, and Derec saw that the deck was a mosaic of several hundred hexagonal metal tiles the size of a dinner plate. The surface of each tile had a pattern of small holes, but there was no obvious fingerlift—in fact, no obvious way to lift an individual tile. All six edges were flush with the adjoining tiles.

"Any idea where I should start?"

"The strategy of concealment would argue against obvious positions such as the center and corners. Beyond that, I cannot say."

"You can't detect it under the deck? It's not giving off some kind of radio signal, or generating a magnetic field?"

"Not that I am able to detect."

That, too, was consistent with what had happened on the asteroid. If the key had declared its presence in any measurable way, the robots' scans would have turned it up long before the raider ship arrived.

"All right," Derec said slowly. He turned to Wolruf, who had been a silent spectator since joining them. "We need a place to lock up Aranimas."

Wolruf glanced nervously back toward where they had left the Erani. "Therr arr some lockers outside, on the side passage, which would be large enough—"

Derec nodded. "Alpha—pick up Aranimas and go with Wolruf. She will show you where to put him. Wolruf, make sure it's something Aranimas can't open from the inside. Then both of you come back here." He caught the look of apprehension in Wolruf's eyes and added. "I know—you don't like the robot."

"Maybe 'u surprise Wolruf like 'u surprise Aranimas."

"I promise you, it'll be all right," Derec said, patting the caninoid's arm. "No surprises. I'll be waiting for you here."

When the robot was gone, Derec lowered himself to his hands and knees to examine the holes in the tiles. They proved to be tapered pits barely a half-centimeter deep. There seemed to be no way of hooking anything into one to lift the tile. Derec wondered if he would have to build some sort of vacuum clamp before he could locate the key.

Then he realized that the openings were about the diameter of the tip of Aranimas's stylus. Of course, Derec thought as he fumbled for the instrument. Let's hope this feature doesn't work only for Aranimas, too—

He touched the conical tip to one of the openings, and the tile seemed to seize hold of the stylus and stand it straight up. Gripping the stylus with one and then both hands, Derec tried to lift the tile straight up. The tile did not budge. But when he used the stylus as a lever, he was easily able to tip the tile back, like peeling the lid off a can. Underneath was a small hexagonal compartment—empty.

No beginner's luck, eh? he thought. When he replaced the tile, the stylus came free. Very nice, he thought, touching the stylus to the adjacent tile. The trick wasn't done with magnetics; the stylus seemed to actually bond to the tile. Perhaps a metallic affinity, followed by a little shot of current to jostle the atoms and break the bonds. Cute trick—

There was a humming sound behind him, and Derec whirled. Half a dozen meters down the central corridor, a circular platform was descending from the ceiling, suspended on four slender wires. And standing on the platform was a woman—a young human female, no more than a year or two older than Derec but a good eight centimeters taller. The broad-shouldered sash blazer she was wearing was cut in an aristocratic style, but showed many days of wear.

Her expression was one of surprise, even shock. Her mouth worked as though trying to form a word. "You?" she said disbelievingly as the platform reached floor level. "Here?"

Wild thoughts filled Derec's head, and reason had to fight for control. That would sure help explain Aranimas's success—if he had had a human consort all along to guide him—

"You'd better tell me real fast who you are and what you're doing here," he said, slowly coming to his feet. "I don't have a lot of time to decide what to do about you."

"What to do about me?" she echoed angrily. "I don't know why I owe *you* any answers, not after what you did."

The meaning of the condition of the girl's clothes finally impressed itself on Derec. She was a prisoner, just as he. But Derec realized that to her, he might be the one who seemed to have thrown in with the raiders.

"I only helped Aranimas to buy time and save my neck. The robot's mine now, and Aranimas can't hurt you," Derec said. "We're going to get of here."

The hostility faded from her face, leaving behind bewilderment. "But what are you doing here? How long have you been on board?"

Derec took a step toward her. "It doesn't take long to tell.

Five days ago I woke up in a survival pod on the surface of an asteroid. I was found by a colony of robots mining the asteroid. Aranimas raided the colony and took me prisoner." That's enough. No sense muddying the waters with details even I don't understand yet, he thought.

She was looking at him curiously. "So you weren't looking for me."

"I didn't know anyone else was on the ship," he said, throwing his hands in the air. "Wolruf told me that they had captured a couple of human ships, but she left the impression the crews were all—gone."

"I think Aranimas kept me alive because he was interested in my robots," she said. "Are you the one that repaired Capek?"

"Was that its old name? It answers to Alpha now. Yes, I'm the one who fixed it."

"You did a rotten job," she said with a hint of childish petulance. "It doesn't remember me. The new arm is ugly, too."

"I'm sorry."

"And you don't remember me, either."

Derec swallowed. "I had the feeling you thought I should—"

"I thought you were just being cruel," she said slowly. "I didn't want to give you the satisfaction. But you don't know who I am, do you?"

"I don't even know who I am," Derec answered with a weak smile. "When I woke up on the asteroid, I was wearing a safe-suit with the name Derec on the chest, so I've been calling myself that. But I can't remember anything that happened before I woke up on the asteroid."

"Nothing at all?"

"Nothing personal. I remember a lot of facts—things I learned sometime, I guess. But I don't know where I'm from or where I was going." Derec was badly confused. "So you know me?"

"I thought I did," she said.

"Then for mercy's sake, tell me—"

A chirping sound came from the huge control console at that moment.

"Someone's paging Aranimas," the girl said, a flash of nervousness crossing her face. "You said we were going to get out of here. Maybe we should worry about that first. What were you doing when I surprised you? What were you looking for?"

"Some of my property—that Aranimas took when I came aboard."

"The key? Was that yours?"

"You know about it?"

"Aranimas showed it to me. Is that where it's hidden?"

"According to Alpha."

"Is it important?"

"I think so."

"Then let's get it and get out of here," she said anxiously.

Wondering what was keeping Alpha and Wolruf, Derec slowly turned back to the floor grid. He checked the second tile, stole a glance back over his shoulder at her, then moved crab-wise to the right to try a third.

"I can look for the key and listen at the same time," he said, attaching the stylus to the next tile. "Can't you tell me what you know about me?"

If she gave an answer, Derec never heard it. One moment he was starting to lift the tile, and the next there was a flash, a roaring sound, and a tremendous wash of heat. Something heavy struck Derec across the back and he toppled forward, catching the hard edge of the tile across his chest and driving the air from his lungs. His mind had time to think one word—*booby trap*—before it retreated from the fury to a dark, quiet recess where it would not be disturbed.

CHAPTER 13
ROCKLIFFE STATION

Soft-edged images drifted through a dreamlike haze. A sea of light surrounded Derec, buoying him up. He was as transparent as glass, as inconsequential as the wind. His consciousness resided on a mote of dust, floating on gentle currents of time.

Faceless figures floated there with him. Some drew near as though aware of him, only to turn away again and withdraw. The only sounds were the fragrance-songs of flowers and the color-songs of sunsets, and those played in his head without understanding.

None of it seemed to make sense, and yet he did not care. He only thought that after everything that had happened, all that he had survived, it would be a terrible disappointment to be dead.

After a time, his body returned to him. He was still floating, still adrift, but his consciousness again inhabited its familiar place, filled its familiar space. But his thoughts were as sluggish as his limbs, as though the burdens of once again managing his body's functions had overwhelmed the simple processes of his mind.

Presently he became aware that the dreamlike world of light and shadow which he was inhabiting existed entirely within himself. If he chose to, he could open his eyes to the larger world beyond, to survey it, to enter it. He was certain that when he saw that world he would know his place in it, would know then who and what he was. But he would pay a price in peace and silence, and that was too high a price to pay.

No, Derec thought firmly. *There are limits. I don't want to see it*, he told himself. *I don't want to know.*

Time passed, and the enveloping womb of solitude slowly became a prison. Silence became deafness. Stillness became death. Whether because he was healed or haunted, what he had was not enough.

The larger world outside himself still beckoned. It was not a friendly world, he knew. At best it was indifferent to him. Unlike the gentle currents that had borne him as he healed, the larger world was filled with forces that could bear him along like driftwood in the spume of a breaking wave.

But he was not without power himself. Perhaps he could not turn back the wave, but he could ride it, and set his own course.

It was that realization which freed him. He saw that he was not a prisoner, and never had been. There were five doors through which he could free himself—the five doors of his senses. All were unlocked, waiting only his touch to swing open and let the world in and himself out.

And he would open them, he knew. But not yet. Not until he had floated with the gentle currents awhile longer. For if he could leave whenever he chose to, then the womb of solitude was not such an unpleasant place to be after all—

The first door Derec tried to open was hearing. At first he wondered if he had succeeded, for the silence without was as complete as the silence within. Then he became aware of the faint rhythmic sound of his own breathing. It was a small step, but it was the first information to come from outside his cocoon in what felt like a very long time.

Experimentally, Derec opened his eyes a crack, and immediately closed them again. The world outside was disturbingly familiar. He was floating enveloped in light—light that was somehow bright without being harsh. A faceless shadow, tall and slender, moved gracefully through the haze which seemed to surround him.

Reality had been inverted. The dream had become reality, or the dream world and the real world were one and the same. It seemed like some sort of perverse trick, one in spirit with a "present" which turns out to be a series of ever-smaller empty boxes. Would every doorway lead to the same place? Would each step he took only hold him more firmly where he was?

"Good morning."

Derec was puzzled at the sound of another voice. If he was alone, then he had to be the one who had spoken. But he had not spoken, and so he was not alone. But if he was not alone, then he could not still be inside his dream world, and what he had seen when he had opened his eyes must be real.

But if it was real, then he was alive. He tried to remember the last incontrovertibly real thing he had known. It was a difficult business, remembering. There had been sunsets and flower-songs, but they had not been real. Before that . . . before that . . .

Before that there had been a terrible moment, a moment so full of surprise and pain that even in fleeing it, he had brought it inside his cocoon. He had transformed the eruption into the blossoming of a flower, the flame into the colors of a spectacular sunset. Then he had replayed the moment endlessly to render it harmless.

Yes! The last real thing he had known had been the explosion.

Derec opened his eyes once more to the light. A shadow loomed over him, faceless and nearly formless, as before. He tried to reach out and touch it, but his limbs would not obey.

"Turn off the sterilization field," the voice said, and the haze of light vanished. The shadow became the copper-colored head and clothed torso of a robot. The robot was gazing solicitously down at him. "Good morning," it repeated. "Please don't try to move."

Derec's mind was slowly working its way backward from the explosion. He understood that he was no longer in the command center. The robot hovering over him was not Alpha. Which meant—

"Aranimas got his robots," Derec croaked.

"Excuse me, sir?"

"He won," Derec whispered. "I didn't get away."

"Sir?"

"Tell Aranimas I won't stop trying—"

"Sir, I would be happy to deliver the message for you. However, the person you named is unknown to me. Where may this individual be found?"

"Aranimas is the ship's boss—"

"This individual was a member of the ship's company?"

"Yes—" The robot's responses were beginning to puzzle Derec.

"Sir, I regret to inform you that no person of that name was found when the paramedics boarded—"

"I'm not on the ship?"

"You are resting on a therapeutic diamagnetic force field, more commonly known as an airbed. The airbed is in the Intensive Care Ward of the hospital at Rockliffe Station."

The wave of relief that swept through Derec on hearing those words seemed to take all his energy with it. He closed his eyes and allowed himself to float on the gentle currents of sleep once more. Distantly, he heard voices, but could not rouse himself to think about what they were saying.

"He is fatigued," the robot said.

"We need his assistance," a new voice answered.

"Our needs are less pressing than his own," the robot said. "We will wait."

The next time Derec awoke, the copper-skinned robot was again nearby.

"Good evening," it said, coming to his side. "How are you feeling?"

Derec managed an anemic smile. "I was just lying here thinking about all the times in the last week that I closed my eyes one place and opened them somewhere else. Every time it happened I found myself in worse surroundings and deeper trouble—until the first time I woke up here."

The robot nodded gravely. "I promise that you will receive the best of care."

"I know I will," Derec said. "Do you have a name?"

"My assigned designation is Human Diagnostic Medicine Specialist 4. However, the supervisor of medicine for this district refers to me as Dr. Galen."

"Why?"

"He has never explained this to me. However, I have determined that Galen was the name of a Greek physician of the classical age who wrote on the subject of the 'vital forces' inhabiting the body. I believe that my supervisor found it amusing to call an advanced diagnostic technician by the name of a primitive medical mystic. Since this question concerns humor, I cannot offer an authoritative conclusion."

"I think you're probably right," Derec said. "You won't be offended if I call you Dr. Galen? It's a good bit handier than your other name."

"Why should I be offended, sir?"

"No reason," Derec said. At least not when I say it, he added silently. But that supervisor is definitely expressing some hostility. Probably has a secret fantasy of being a family practice doctor on a Settler world instead of tender-to-robots. "Where is your supervisor?"

"On Nexon."

Derec knew the name: it was one of the larger Spacer worlds, and the second-farthest from Earth. "You said this is Rockliffe Station?"

"That is correct, sir."

"Where is your local supervisor? The hospital director?"

"Sir, I am hospital director at present."

Derec frowned. "Maybe you'd better tell me some more about Rockliffe Station, then."

"Certainly, sir. What would you like to know?"

Rockliffe Station, Dr. Galen explained, was a centuries-old Spacer facility, a way station dating from the days when a long interstellar journey could only be managed through a series of shorter Jumps. Dozens of way stations had been built while the Earth emigrants who would become the Spacers were colonizing the fifty worlds that would become their homes.

With the coming of more powerful drives capable of spanning known space in one or two Jumps, most of the way stations had long since been abandoned. A few, of which this was one, had been fortunately enough placed that they outlived their original function.

Rockliffe Station lay in the middle of one of the largest "open" regions along the fringes of Spacer territory, looking out toward the quarantine zone beyond which lay the Settler worlds. There were no livable worlds in the nearest star system, but there was one planet with a crust rich enough in iridium to justify a small mining and processing center.

So Rockliffe had survived on the strength of its usefulness as a listening post on the frontier, as a transshipment point for processed iridium, and a military outpost should relations with the Settlers deteriorate. But those were not reason enough to keep it active at the peak level of the early days—not enough even to maintain a human presence there.

According to Dr. Galen, less than ten percent of the station was occupied, and that entirely by robots. The human supervision they required was provided by means of hypervision and the ships that called every two months.

Only because of the chance that those visiting crews might need its services had the hospital been kept staffed. But the managers on Nexon were realists. Dr. Galen was hospital administrator because his caseload was usually zero, while the only other medical robot on station, a nurse-orderly, had a full schedule of cleaning and maintenance.

No wonder the supervisor makes jokes at Dr. Galen's expense, Derec thought.

"You seem disturbed by this information," Dr. Galen said. "Is there a problem?"

Derec thought about the question for a moment. He *had* grown progressively unhappier as Dr. Galen's explanation had proceeded. But did it matter so much that he apparently was still alone? At least Rockliffe Station was more or less familiar territory, unlike the asteroid colony or the raider ship. He should be able to have his own way more easily here.

"No. No problem," Derec said. "Except I'd like to know a little more about what happened. How did I get here? You said something about paramedics—"

"I do not know all the details. The dispatcher or dock supervisor would be better sources of information."

"Tell me what you know."

"Apparently your ship was disabled following its Jump. Exactly what happened next is not clear. The dispatcher will no doubt want to inquire about the circumstances. However, it appeared as though your ship discarded or released a smaller vessel, a shuttle or lifeboat, before changing course and heading into the Q-zone."

"They must have cut us loose after the explosion—" Derec said thoughtfully.

"The smaller vessel apparently was following an unacceptable approach vector and did not respond to the dispatcher's commands. On the assumption that it was a derelict, a tug was dispatched to intercept it and bring it in. When the derelict was boarded you were found and brought here."

"Did they bring the ship—our ship—in, then?"

"That is my understanding. Of course, my concern since that time has been with your care."

"Of course," Derec echoed. If Aranimas's ship is here, maybe I didn't lose the artifact after all, he thought joyously. "Listen, Dr. Galen, what would you say to my getting up and doing a little walking? Airbeds are as comfortable as beds get, but I'm tired of just lying here. Maybe I could go see what kind of shape the ship is in, answer any questions the dispatcher has."

"I'm sorry, sir," Dr. Galen said. "Your injuries are not yet sufficiently healed to permit that."

"What are my injuries?"

"You suffered flash burns over fifteen percent of your body, primarily over your arms, face, and neck. Three of your ribs were cracked—"

"I must have fallen on the tile I was lifting."

"—one puncturing your right lung and causing it to collapse. Your right eardrum was perforated and had to be replaced."

"Frost! How long have I been here?"

"The ship on which you were found was boarded six weeks ago."

"Six weeks! Was I in a coma or something?"

"Burns are extremely painful, as is reconstructive epidermal surgery," Dr. Galen said. "I kept you under chemical narcosis during treatment and the initial phase of recovery."

"I guess I should be grateful. But six weeks—" Belatedly Derec remembered that he had not been alone on the raider ship. "Where're the others? Wolruf—Alpha—the girl. What've they been doing while I was narc'd?"

"I am sorry. The only persons found were yourself and a female human."

Feeling a sudden tightness in his chest, Derec looked away. It did not mean that Wolruf was dead and Alpha destroyed—there was a chance, perhaps even a good one, that they were on the larger portion of the ship still in space. But it did mean that while Derec had escaped and survived, he had not lived up to his promises to the caninoid. "I'm sorry, Wolruf," he whispered.

"Excuse me, sir?"

"Nevermind," Derec said. "Tell me about the girl."

"She was found near you inside the ship—"

"That's not what I mean. Tell me how she is."

"Patient Katherine's physical—"

"Katherine—is that her name?"

"Is there some error?"

"No—no, that's her," Derec said. "Where is she?"

Dr. Galen turned away to the right and gestured with his hand. "Orderly, draw the curtain back."

Derec turned his head to the right. What appeared to be the wall of his room suddenly become transparent, allowing him to see a slight human figure floating in a halo of light. She was naked, and he looked away, faintly embarrassed. When he did, he realized that he was naked, too. It was very straightforward and practical for them to be naked in a hospital, but something of a surprise all the same.

"How is she?"

"Her integumentary injuries were more extensive than your own, but she is healing well. Of course, her chronic condition remains unchanged."

"What condition is that?"

"I'm sorry." The robot paused. "I see that I have made an error. Since you were traveling together, I did not think that I was betraying any secrets by discussing Katherine's chart. I will have to report myself for this indiscretion."

"I don't care about that," Derec said impatiently. "Has she been awake?"

"No. Nor would we have allowed you to awaken if we did not need your assistance." Dr. Galen gestured with his right hand. "Close the curtain."

"Assistance with what?" Derec asked as the wall became opaque again.

"Sir, in the course of your care certain services have been rendered on account. It has not only been our obligation but our pleasure to be able to help you. However, as hospital administrator I am obliged to determine whether this account is collectable or is to be charged against regular station operations."

"You woke me up to ask me for my insurance card?"

"There is also the question of medical history. We can determine genetic endowment directly, but it is not always possible to determine all the synergistic outcomes of a particular gene complex. Without direct evidence, I have been obliged to follow more conservative parameters in your care, which in turn has had the effect of prolonging your recovery somewhat."

"I don't understand. What about her?" Derec demanded. "You said she was hurt more badly than I was. Wouldn't it be even more important to find out who she is and get her medical history? Why me and not her?"

"Sir, while you were unconscious, we attempted to identify you by means of all the standard systems. We were not successful."

"Standard systems—"

"Fingerprint, retinagraph, absolute blood protein typing, and twenty-third chromosome codon map. We were not able to establish a match."

"Of course you weren't. I'm not from here."

"Sir, by hyperwave we have direct access to the records of all fifty Spacer worlds."

"Did you check the records for Aurora?"

"Yes. We were not able to establish a match."

"But I'm from there—I know I am."

"I'm afraid that's not possible. Aurora keeps scrupulous records on their citizens as part of their population-control program. If you were an Auroran, this conversation would not have been necessary."

"But you found out who she is," he said.

"That is correct. Katherine's full records were made available to me."

With sudden fury, Derec demanded, "Are you telling me that

you searched the citizenship records of fifty planets and can't find out who I am?"

"No," Dr. Galen said. "We have searched the records of fifty-five worlds, including Earth and the four nearest Settler planets. We do have a right of request with most Settler worlds for access to their records. Unfortunately those records are not as complete as we are accustomed to dealing with, and in some cases are not even centralized. Also, certain worlds charge exorbitant fees to respond to data requests from Spacers and then are exceedingly slow to respond. For all these reasons, it seemed to us that a more straightforward inquiry was in order.

"Therefore, could you please tell us who you are?"

The empty feeling had returned full force. "I wish I could," Derec said hoarsely. "Stars, how I wish I could."

CHAPTER 14
KATE

"How interesting!" Dr. Galen exclaimed. "Do you mean to say that you have no personal memories whatsoever?"

Derec repeated the now familiar litany of events which began with his waking in the survival capsule. Partly because he was growing weary of the tale himself and partly to minimize questions, he glossed over some of the details, including the fact that the raider had been crewed by aliens.

"I will have to amend your chart to reflect this state of retrograde amnesia," Dr. Galen said when Derec was through. "This is a much more fascinating problem than your other injuries. As a matter of fact, amnesia is a hobby of mine."

"What do you mean, a hobby?"

"Perhaps I should say specialty, but that does not convey the deep intellectual satisfaction it gives me."

"How many cases have you treated?"

"You will be my first," Dr, Galen said. "I am tremendously pleased by the opportunity."

"Your first?" Derec said, incredulous. "How can you call yourself a specialist, then? And what do you mean saying that you're 'fascinated' or 'pleased'? You're not programmed to experience emotion."

"Strictly speaking, that is correct," Dr. Galen,agreed. "But the concept of losing one's sense of identity has always created the kind of positive positronic state which I associate with the term *fascination*. You see, due to the memory structure of the positronic brain, it is quite impossible for a robot to forget anything, least of all its own identity. Amnesia represents a state for which robot experience offers no analogue."

"The lure of the unknown."

"Diagnostic robots such as myself are constructed with a reinforced curiosity integral," Dr. Galen said. "Perhaps that is a contributing factor."

Derec felt as though he were being lectured in his own specialty. "But positronic brains go south all the time," he protested. "They're vulnerable to hard radiation, to glitches in the power supply—lots of things can go wrong."

"That is correct, Derec. But those conditions you describe would result in mental shutdown, and in some instances the complete destruction of the positronic brain. However, humans are frequently able to continue to function with such a major system failure. That is what I find fascinating. Beyond that, I believe that robots have much to contribute to the investigation of human brain function, including memory defects."

"Why is that?"

"I note that many human philosophers have recognized that the search for self-knowledge is the hardest search of all. It is extremely difficult for the human brain to contemplate and analyze the human brain. Its limitations make it impossible to see its limitations."

Derec found himself in agreement with the robot. "The only thing a camera can't see is itself. The only thing a ruler can't measure is itself."

"Quite. Questions of human brain functions have therefore been the slowest to yield to investigation by human researchers. Many aspects of human behavior are still puzzles despite centuries of neurological and biochemical studies."

"So what do you think *you* can do?"

Dr. Galen spread his hands wide. "Positronic brains were not developed by copying how human brains function. They were developed by copying how human beings behave. Therefore, though the positronic brain is the product of the human brain, it represents a distinct form of intelligence and a different perspective."

"Are you saying that positronic brains are more capable than human brains?"

"The key is that a robot does what it does differently than a human brain," Dr. Galen said diplomatically. "I am convinced that it is an invention of the human brain which will eventually unlock the secrets of the human brain. So I am pleased to have the opportunity to do more than study and speculate."

Derec shook his head. "Forget it. I don't want to be a lab animal."

"Forgive me," Dr. Galen said. "In my enthusiasm I neglected to make clear that my primary interest is to help you. There are tests which I can perform to determine the cause of your condition. Depending on the cause, there may be measures which can be taken to reverse your condition."

"Do you mean you can bring my memory back?"

"I will not know the likelihood of that until I have examined you."

Derec regarded the promise of a magic cure with skepticism. "Look, I'm not going to be here very long," he said. "Let's not start something we won't have time to finish."

"I do not understand."

"You said that ships call here every two months. If I've been here six weeks, my ride out of here should show up in two weeks—probably less."

"No, Derec," Dr. Galen corrected. "*Fariis* came and went while you were recovering. The next vessel, the *Heritage*, is due in six weeks, three days."

Derec stared. "A ship's already been here? Then why am I still here?" he demanded.

"This station's medical facilities are superior to those on board *Fariis*. It was not possible to release you to them in your condition."

Derec closed his eyes and sighed. "All right. Probe away." His eyes opened and he struggled to a seated position. "But I want to know what you're doing before you do it, do you hear?"

"Thank you, Derec," Dr. Galen said politely. "What do you know of amnesia?"

"Just what I see on the hypervision."

"That is unfortunate," Dr. Galen said.

"It's just a saying. Actually, I don't even remember that."

"That is just as well," Dr. Galen replied. "Amnesia has been used as a convenient device in fiction for centuries, usually in defiance of known facts. A common plot is for a victim to suffer a blow to the head, forget everything and everyone and begin leading a new life, then be restored in the closing scene by another blow."

"That does sound sort of familiar. Maybe I have seen one or two like that," Derec admitted.

"Please do your best to forget them," Dr. Galen said disapprovingly. "They will only hinder understanding."

Over the next three days, Derec learned a great deal about amnesia. He had had no idea how many kinds of amnesia there were and how many different causes had been identified. Under other circumstances, it would have been more than he wanted to know. But since he was personally affected, he avidly absorbed everything Dr. Galen told him.

Amnesia could affect the past (retrograde) or the present (anterograde). It could have physical causes (organic) or emotional ones (psychogenic). Some amnesiacs were unable to remember anything for more than a few seconds, while others would forget everything for only a few seconds at a time. Some victims knew that they were having difficulty, while others passionately denied it.

Nine out of every ten cases of amnesia, Derec learned, had some specific physical cause. Those causes were as different as inflammation of the whorled and folded outer layer of the brain, hardening of the cerebral arteries, electric shock, and deficiency of B vitamins. (Also on the list, but nowhere near the top, was a blow to the head.)

"In more primitive times, many cases of true organic amnesia were wrongly diagnosed as psychogenic," Dr. Galen said as though outraged by the fact. "Patients who needed drugs or surgery were offered hypnosis and psychotherapy."

"Maybe all amnesias have some physical cause," Derec suggested. "Maybe the ten percent we still think are psychogenic are the ones we just haven't found the organic cause for."

But Dr. Galen dissented. "The distinction between mind and brain has not been completely erased by medical science. The mind is more than the sum of the brain's parts. There are things that happen at that level of synergy which cannot be traced to specific physical events."

Even so, the testing focused first cn the possible physical causes. Dr. Galen subjected him to cortical analysis, an endorphin response test, three different nondestructive scans of his brain, and even a biopsy and culture for encephalitis.

"Your own awareness of your loss of memory is a clue, as your apparently unimpaired intelligence," Dr. Galen told Derec. "You retain your sense of time and of the connectedness of events. All of these things are meaningful."

But the unhappy truth was that all the clues added up to naught, and all the tests revealed nothing. Derec learned several new words to describe his condition—"fractionated retrograde hypnosis-resistant psychogenic amnesia"—but he learned nothing about himself.

"I can find no physical cause," Dr. Galen concluded reluctantly at the end of a week. "Your cortex, thalamus, mammillary bodies, and fornix bundle are all normal. And yet you have not responded to any psychogenic therapy I am aware of. I am sorry, Derec, I have failed you."

"Don't take it so hard," Derec said, sighing. "I'm beginning to get used to life in the dark."

In the course of the testing, Dr. Galen had gradually allowed Derec more and more freedom of movement until he had the run of the small hospital complex. Physically, he was nearly completely restored. His new skin was no longer painful to the touch and was gradually becoming less sensitive to variations in temperature. His ribs had knitted while he was kept unconscious, and the only sign they had even been broken was an occasional stitch of dull pain when he drew a deep breath or stretched the wrong way.

Despite that progress, Dr. Galen resisted releasing Derec from his care. The furthest he would go was to allow Derec to move from the ICU to a private room with more traditional accommodations. But the robot's recalcitrance was not entirely a surprise. With their special First Law responsibility as healers, robot doctors were notorious for their caution.

But Derec suspected that it was not the injuries to his body that concerned Dr. Galen, but the injury to Derec's mind. The real reason for keeping Derec nearby was to keep him under observation while he treated Katherine. Since Dr. Galen could not be in two places at once, he was keeping his two patients in one place.

Derec could not order Dr. Galen to stop worrying about him, so he resigned himself to living within the robot's restrictions. In some ways, Derec welcomed the vacation from responsibility. His body had had time to heal, but his mind still vividly remembered the erupting surface of the asteroid, the electric blue pain from Aranimas's stylus, the sudden flash of the booby trap exploding in his face. He had a right to a few days of peace.

Or so Derec thought. But one day of idleness was enough to satisfy that need. The next morning he did not wait for Dr. Galen's ritual visit and examination, but went looking for the robot himself. He found him standing at the biomedical monitor at the foot of Katherine's bed in the ICU.

"Good morning, Derec," the robot said. "I am sorry that I was delayed. How are you feeling today?"

"Restless," Derec said. "I'm ready to get back to a normal life."

"But you are in the fugue state of an amnesiac episode," Dr. Galen said. "A normal life is not possible for you now."

"I'll settle for the substitute at hand," Derec said. "I can't just sit around here hoping my memory will come back."

"What is it you wish to do?"

"I guess I won't know until I find out what's already been done for me," Derec said. "Outside of the robots on the station, who knows that I'm here? Is anybody trying to find out who I am?"

"I cannot say," Dr. Galen said. "I am certain that the station manager reported your arrival to the district supervisor at Nexon, as I did to the medical supervisor. That information may have been passed to any number of interested parties in the interval since. Why, is there someone you would like to contact?"

Derec pointed across the room at the sleeping Katherine. "Her. How much longer till you bring her out?"

"I concluded some days ago that she might hold the key to unlocking your loss of memory, and decided to allow her to wake at the earliest opportunity when her own health and comfort would not be at risk," said Dr. Galen. "She was taken off the sleep-inducing drug at midnight. According to her brain waves, she is dreaming now. I expect her to wake sometime this morning."

Derec glanced around the ward. There was nowhere to sit except the floor.

"There is no need for you to conduct a vigil," Dr. Galen said as though reading his thoughts.

"I want to be here when she wakes up."

Dr. Galen nodded understandingly. "I promise, I will call you."

Derec whiled away one hour, then another, with a book-film titled "The Architects of the Machine." He hoped to find among its profiles of notable designers and engineers a clue as to who the "minimalist" behind the asteroid colony might have been. With all the more tangible evidence lost or destroyed, it was one of the few unexplored leads left to him. Genius of that sort had to have left a trail.

But only three of the biographies were of contemporary designers, and the choices were entirely predictable. The roboticist Fastolfe. March, the Havalean wizard of micromagnetics. The human ecologist Rutan, whose services were so much in demand by the wealthy on a dozen Spacer worlds.

All three had become celebrities, acclaimed by those who knew nothing about what it took to do what they did. But the engineering community had its own celebrities, based on its own standards. Every exclusive group did—those persons who had won the respect and admiration of their peers but were completely unknown outside the circle. Fastolfe ranked here, too, but March was regarded as a toymaker and Rutan as a joke.

Yes, he needed an insider's perspective. Someone would know Derec's mysterious genius—

"Master Derec, if I may interrupt."

Derec's head jerked up. It was the medical orderly. Like Dr. Galen, the orderly had fallen victim to the supervisor's perverse sense of humor. "Yes, Florence."

"Dr. Galen said that you should come right away."

Pushing back the viewer, Derec jumped to his feet. "Coming."

• • •

When he reached the ICU, the sterilization lights were already off and Katherine was beginning to stir. She now wore an ankle-to-neck beige gown, etiquette having changed along with Dr. Galen's changing perception of their relationship. Derec hung back as Dr. Galen bent over Katherine and spoke softly to her.

"Good morning," he said. "Don't try to move."

But she lifted her head a few centimeters all the same and surveyed the room. "Hospital?" she asked hoarsely.

"Yes, Katherine. I am Dr. Galen."

"On what station?"

"Rockliffe Station."

She nodded and looked past Dr. Galen to Derec. "Some rescue," she said.

Despite her hoarseness, there was a laughing note to her voice that Derec did not like. Taking a step closer, he said stiffly, "We're both alive, aren't we?"

"Which just goes to show that there's no justice in the Galaxy," she answered, closing her eyes. "I thought you'd have been smart enough to disable Aranimas's security system before you started to poke around in his hidey-hole."

"Look, I'm sorry it didn't go more smoothly," Derec said, coming to the side of the bed. "But we did get away. And there was something we were going to talk about once we did—"

Her eyes fluttered open and searched past Derec for the robot's face. "Dr. Galen, the headaches are back," she said. "Would you ask Derec to leave, please? I just don't think I can deal with company now."

"How long could it take to tell me my surname, my home-world—"

But Dr. Galen intervened, gently pushing Derec back toward the door. "I understand your impatience, Derec. But I must consider Katherine's health, too. Please leave. I will find out what I can. When she is stronger you can talk with her again, if she consents."

Derec took his frustration for a walk, leaving the hospital by the main entrance. He was sure that Dr. Galen would report him or send a robot after him to bring him back, but he did not care. He simply could not calmly stay there and wait. To be so close to answers, to the promise of being whole again, was too great a test for his patience.

The section of the station where the hospital was located was a tomb. He walked dimly lit streets past ranks of closed stores and sealed residential blocks. Only the main throughway was even lit. The side streets and courtyards were black pits.

No robot pursued him. He walked and walked until the edge was off his jumbled emotions, and then he turned back. He stalked through the reception area and into Dr. Galen's office.

"Did she tell you anything?"

"She was not able to offer any insight into your affliction."

"You discussed my condition with her? But you wouldn't tell me—"

"Correction. She was already aware of your condition."

"What did she do, ask your advice on how to deal with me?"

"Derec, I promised Katherine that I would not discuss our conversation with you."

Crossing his arms over his chest, Derec blew a sigh ceiling-ward. "I don't understand why she's being so secretive. If she knows something about me, she should just tell me." He cast a raised-eyebrow glance in Dr. Galen's direction. "Isn't that right?"

"The advisability of that would vary from case to case, depending on the individual, the cause of the dysfunction, and the particular personal data concerned," was Dr. Galen's measured answer.

"You won't even give me a hint, will you?" Derec said ruefully.

"I regret that I may not."

Derec frowned. "Can I see her, at least?"

The robot turned to one of the two active displays on the wall behind him. "She is awake and her algesia has moderated. But she is the final arbiter."

"Then I'm going to go see what she has to say."

They found Katherine sitting up in her bed. "I was hoping someone would come to see me," she said with a smile.

"You left me with some good reasons to," Derec said, scanning the room fruitlessly for a chair to move beside the bed.

Her face clouded over. "Da—Derec," she said, stumbling

over his name as though she had forgotten it. "I'm afraid you're going to be angry with me. We have a lot of ground to make up together—all the things that happened on the ship. I don't think we should start with the little I know about you."

The look that Derec shot at Dr. Galen was black and poisonous. "What is this? What did you tell her? I thought you were trying to help me—"

"I cannot do otherwise," the robot said calmly.

The truth of that slowed Derec's rush to anger. He turned back to Katherine and said, "So you're going to keep secrets from me."

She shook her head. "Derec—let's say that you were President of New Liberty—"

"New Liberty has a council-manager government," Derec interrupted.

"It doesn't matter. Let's say you were President of New Liberty and lost your memory. If I tell you that you're the President, does that make you the President? Can you start acting like the person you used to be just because you know that?"

Derec avoided her eyes. "I suppose not. But hearing it could make me remember—"

"It is far more likely to cause you severe anxiety," Dr. Galen began. "Most often—"

Derec opened his mouth to answer, but Katherine was faster. "Dr. Galen, go away," she snapped. "Go back to your office and leave us alone. Don't monitor me and don't listen in. We'll call you if we need you."

The robot stared a moment, then lowered its head and exited.

"You didn't have to get so personal," Derec said, surprised at her forcefulness. "I'll bet you put a kink in poor Dr. Galen's self-worth integral that he'll be an hour working out."

"Oh, I don't care," Katherine said peevishly, staring at the empty doorway. "Medical robots are such busybodies. They've got ten thousand opinions but they don't really know anything. And they can't really understand what someone's feeling when they're sick, now, can they? Because they're machines and they never get sick, or die."

Is that what's the matter with you? Derec wondered, looking at her face. Are you dying from something the doctors can't cure? Is that what Dr. Galen wouldn't talk about?

Before he could find the courage to ask her aloud, she looked toward him and patted the bed beside her. "Are you going to stand all the way over there? The field can hold both of us."

After a moment's hesitation, Derec settled on the edge of the bed by Katherine's feet.

"There, that's better," she said. "Now I don't feel so much like a prisoner being questioned."

"I'm not sure what we have left to talk about."

"Well—I'm sure there's more to what happened on the asteroid than you told me on the ship. Then there's the ship and what we went through there. And there's me."

"Let's start there. Your name, for starters. The robot called you Katherine—"

"I am Katherine Ariel Burgess to my mother and the computers. Everyone else calls me Kate," she said. "My father says that calling me Katherine is false advertising—that it doesn't give people any warning what they're in for. Katherine is please and thank you and dresses that cover you to the neck. Kate is—"

"Sharp-tongued and strong-willed and I-can-take-care-of-my-self-thank-you," Derec supplied.

Katherine brightened as though she had been complimented. "Something like that. My father says that I have spice."

"I think I'll stick to Katherine. What were you doing on Aranimas's ship?"

"Why, I was a prisoner just like you were. My robots and I were kidnapped off a courier ship." She snapped her fingers. "I just remembered. Where's the key? You didn't let the robots have it, did you?"

"I don't know where it is," he said. "I don't even know that it was ever where I thought it was."

"Is the ship here? Have you been back in it?"

"Frost, I don't know. I hadn't even been out of the hospital until this morning," Derec said, annoyed. "Will you tell me this—why is that key so important? What is it? What's it the key *to?*"

"I don't know," Katherine said soberly. "I only know that Aranimas thought it was worth anything to get. Wait—I thought you said the key was your property. Don't *you* know why it's important?"

"It is my property," Derec asserted. "Space salvage. Or a gift. Either way, I have the best claim to it."

"But you don't know what it is?"

"No."

She seemed disappointed. "Maybe you do know—but it's one of the things you've forgotten."

"I guess that's possible," Derec acceded. "Did Aranimas come to the asteroid specifically looking for the key? Not because I was there?"

"I don't think so—"

"You don't think so what?"

"I think he went to the asteroid on purpose. I don't think he knew the key was there. I'm almost positive he didn't know you were there," she said. "I think you were just lucky—or would it be unlucky?"

Derec considered. "Lucky, the way it fell out. I'd sure rather be here on Rockliffe Station than back on that asteroid."

"Lucky, then." She paused. "Look, if it is yours, maybe getting it back in your hands would help you remember something. And even if it doesn't, we need to find out what happened to the key. Aranimas had to have some reason for wanting it."

"Wolruf called it 'the jewel' when she talked to Aranimas," Derec said thoughtfully. "But I don't think she meant it literally."

"Either way, it's something valuable. Are we going to try to find it, or not?"

"We?" For a brief moment, Derec bristled defensively. Then he reminded himself what it had been like to be a loner on the raider ship. He felt at home here—but Katherine clearly didn't. She was hurting, and she was alone, and she wanted to be his friend. And beyond that, she knew something about who he was—and wanted to help him remember.

"Sure," he said. "Of course we are."

CHAPTER 15
OH SEVEN B

Despite all the good intentions, the partnership almost fell apart before it began. Derec had somehow visualized the arrangement with himself making all the decisions and Katherine gratefully following his lead. But he found out very quickly that it was Kate, not Katherine, with whom he'd made his pact.

Derec was eager to get started looking for the artifact. Since Dr. Galen had raised no protest about Derec's excursion out of the hospital, he felt he had won the right to roam where he wanted. At the very least, it would be several days before Kate was accorded the same freedom.

But when Derec proposed that he go scouting alone and then report back to Katherine on his discoveries, she balked. "We go together or all promises are off," she said firmly. "If we're going to be a team, we have to work as a team."

"Being a team doesn't mean we have to be handcuffed together," Derec argued. "Everybody should do what they do best, and right now what I can do best is be our eyes and ears."

"What are you going to do?"

Derec shrugged. "Talk to the dock supervisor and the station manager. Start finding out what's happened while we were here."

"They're robots," she said. "Let them come here."

It was a perfectly reasonable idea, and the fact that it had not occurred to Derec jarred him for a moment. He had been thinking of talking to the station staff ever since he had regained consciousnesss, but always in terms of going to see them. He realized that he had made an unspoken assumption: *they're busy—they don't have time to come down here to talk to me.*

He had never once thought of ordering them to leave their work. Katherine had thought of it immediately. Derec knew somehow that the difference said something important about the two of them—something about their background, the subculture which had shaped their attitudes about robots.

It was as though he respected the importance of the robots' work and saw them more or less as equals, while she thought of them only as servants. But whether it meant he had more experience with robots than she or less, he could not say.

All the same, it was another tiny piece in his puzzle. He was not like Katherine. They came from different worlds—culturally if not geographically. It made him wonder how it was she knew him.

All these thoughts cascaded through Derec's mind in a fraction of a second, allowing him to carry on the conversation with only the faintest hesitation. "Look, I'm willing to share the decision-making. Maybe we could get the robots to come here," he said. "There's still the ship. I should go have a look at it."

"That's something we should do together."

"Why? What's hidden there that you don't want me to find?"

Katherine crossed her arms and sighed. "If you're going to be suspicious of me all the time, this isn't going to work."

"I'm not suspicious of you!" Derec exclaimed, throwing his hands in the air. "I just don't understand why you don't seem to want to let me out of your sight."

"And I don't understand your hurry," Katherine said stiffly. "You say that we're a team, but you want to go run off and do everything yourself."

"The hurry is because we want to get there first," Derec said impatiently. "We don't want anyone else taking it."

She looked at him quizzically. "We've been here six weeks. Do you really think that they pulled us out and then locked the ship up somewhere until we could claim it? Think! That's an alien starship. How long do you think it took them to realize they'd never seen one like it before—not just the design, but the whole technology? This is a frontier base. Do you think they just take it in stride when an unregistered ship shows up with two injured humans aboard?"

Belatedly, Derec understood. "So they've been all over it. Photographed it, X-rayed it, the whole works. They might have even torn it down, sent pieces of it out on *Fariis* to the district offices. They're probably wondering about us, too."

"Of course they are. That's why I sent Dr. Galen away."

"Do you think he's been spying on us?"

"All robots are spies for their masters," she said bitterly.

"What?" Derec asked, surprised by her intensity.

"Nevermind," she said. "I just think we ought to play innocents abroad for a while, do all the things they expect us to— until we understand what kind of game we're in."

"Be helpless and worried. Play dumb."

"Just so," Katherine said. "Sometimes it's the smartest thing you can do."

At their request, Dr. Galen had a multicom brought to the ICU and tied into the station net. Very quickly, they learned that the Rockliffe Station welcome mat was a bit threadbare.

The station manager was fully scheduled until the following morning and thought that they really wanted to talk to the dock supervisor anyway. The dock supervisor was conducting an overhaul of the dock pressurization system, a priority task which had to be completed in the shortest possible time, and had they tried the dispatcher?

The dispatcher couldn't answer their questions without clearance from the security chief, who deferred to the associate manager for station operations. The AMSOP was one step down the ladder from the station manager and probably the robot to which they should have been recommended in the first place.

The AMSOP was busy at the moment but would be free in an hour if they wanted to make an appointment. It seemed to be the best they could do, so they took it.

"So what do we do while we're waiting?" Derec said as he turned off the viewer.

"We could spend the time getting to know each other better—"

"Should I entertain you with stories about my family?"

She laughed—a nice laugh. "Maybe not."

"*You* could tell me stories about my family."

"No, I couldn't."

"Katherine—the only person who knows anything about me is you," Derec said pleadingly. "Why don't you tell me some of it now?"

"Not yet."

"Still following Dr. Galen's advice?"

"This really is the best way," she said, touching his hand.

"It doesn't feel like it to me," he said gruffly. "All right. Tell me about you, then."

"It's boring," she warned.

He cocked an eyebrow. "Being hijacked by an alien spacecraft was boring?"

"My life is boring. That's the first exciting thing that ever happened." She added, "Except it wasn't exactly a hijacking."

"Tell me about it. What was the name of your courier ship?"

"*Golden Eagle*, out of Viking. We were carrying a diplomatic pouch to Frier's Planet—"

At least in a first reading, the story had the ring of truth.

According to Katherine, she and her robots had been outbound from Viking on the courier ship *Golden Eagle*, along with a pilot and two diplomats. Just before they were about to make their Jump at the fringe of the Viking system, the pilot spotted Aranimas's ship, apparently adrift.

Taking it for an uncharted wreck—in part because of its appearance and in part because they could not raise it on any channel—they abandoned their exit trajectory and went to investigate. Suddenly they were fired upon, and their ship disabled. Katherine and the robots were taken off the courier by the Narwe, and then the courier was set adrift. A short time later the courier exploded, probably, Katherine said, because of a bomb that had been placed aboard.

There were no screaming contradictions in the story, but there were several little points that nagged at Derec. Katherine was vague about just why she was on the courier. At first she seemed to want him to think that she was part of the diplomatic mission. But even though she wanted him to think that she was old enough for such duty, she clearly was not.

When he questioned her on it, she hastily explained that she had been a passenger, using the courier instead of a commercial carrier because she wanted privacy. He wondered aloud at a courier taking on passengers. She responded by hinting that she was important enough to justify any exception that might have been required.

But the biggest sticking point, and the one on which he kept his own counsel, was the behavior of the courier pilot. Couriers carried important people, emergency supplies, engineering prototypes, irreplaceable documents. It didn't make sense that a courier pilot would endanger his cargo by poking around a wreck. It seemed far more likely that the pilot would report the sighting to the Patrol post on Viking, then make his Jump on schedule.

Derec recalled that the first time her capture had come up, Katherine had quickly changed the subject. He wondered now if that was because she didn't have her story ready. Perhaps he was being fed half-truths as some sort of test—Dr. Galen's prescription for crippled minds. If so, he resented it.

But the arrival at last of the Assistant Manager for Station Operations pushed those thoughts to the back of Derec's mind.

"I am called Hajime," the AMSOP said, "Dr. Galen tells me that both of you are recovering from your injuries. That is good news."

"Especially to us," Derec said under his breath.

"I understand that you have questions about your presence here. I hope that I will be able to answer them."

Derec opened his mouth to answer, but before he could speak Katherine jumped in. "Begin with when the station first detected our ship and tell us what you observed," she ordered.

"Yes, madam. The station's sensors detected an unidentified ship immediately after it emerged from its Jump—as you may know, the termination of a Jump is accompanied by a minor spacetime disturbance comparable to the atmospheric disturbance caused by a discharge of lightning—"

"We know all that," Derec said. "Get on with it."

"Forgive me, sir," the robot said with a slight bow. "I only wanted to be certain that you understood how we were able to detect your ship at such a great distance."

"Why? How far out were we?"

"Eighty-three astronomical units. At such a distance, the station's sensors were only able to determine the position and velocity of the vessel. Since there was no direct identification through a transponder or indirect identification through sensor data, this vessel was designated UPH-07."

"UPH?" Katherine asked.

"Forgive me. Unidentified, Potentially Hostile," Hajime supplied.

"Go on, Hajime."

"Thank you, sir. We tracked Oh Seven inbound for two days. We were just beginning to acquire some preliminary data on its mass and profile when an anomalous event took place. UPH-07 divided into two independent bodies, UPH-07A and UPH-07B. The larger vessel, Oh Seven A, made a course correction which carried it out of the station's zone of control—"

"They cut us loose and then turned around and went away," Katherine said.

"Looks like it," Derec said. "Did the big ship Jump?"

"Not while it was within range of our sensors, sir," Hajime answered. "It is not possible to say what happened once contact was lost."

Derec and Katherine exchanged glances that said, So they could still be out there somewhere, waiting.

"And the other vessel, Oh Seven B, it continued inbound?" Katherine asked. "That's where you found us?"

"Yes, madam. A scout with a rescue and retrieval team aboard was dispatched immediately."

"Can you show us a navigational plot of all this?" Derec asked.

"Certainly, sir." The robot went to the hyperviewer and entered a code on the keyboard, and a moment later the far wall dissolved into the black of space.

It was all there as the robot had described it. A blue trace from the top of the plot traced the raider's approach to the station, represented by a golden hexagon at the bottom. One-third of the way there, the blue trace split. A thick green trace angled off the plot to the upper right, while a thin red one continued curling inbound on the original trajectory. Two-thirds of the way down the plot, the red trace intersected a golden trace climbing up out of the station: the rescue ship.

"Can we have a copy of that?" Derec said.

"I will file it in a directory under your name," Hajime said, his touch on the controls turning the far wall into a wall once more.

"Was the boarding recorded?" Katherine asked.

"Yes, madam."

"I'd like to see the recording," Katherine said, beckoning Derec to come sit on the edge of the bed beside her. When he did, she took his hand and gripped it tightly, as though seeking reassurance. The skin contact surprised and unsettled Derec.

"The recording was made by means of a witness robot," Hajime said. "The multicom will not be able to display the full bandwidth—"

"What's a witness robot?" Katherine whispered to Derec.

"I'll explain later," Derec whispered back. Witness robots were odd-looking, with their bullet heads and 360-degree scanning slit instead of eye sensors, but invaluable for such operations. Their sole responsibility was to position themselves so that their scanners and recorders captured unfolding events clearly. Many a bungled operation had been reconstructed from the data supplied by witness robots before they were destroyed.

"—so if you wish to move the window left or right at any point please tell me so."

From the outside, Aranimas's ship looked like a fat arrowhead trailing bits of the twine which had held it to the shaft. The arrowhead was in fact an atmosphere-piercing lifting body, and the twine the tattered remnants of several transfer corridors which had been attached to the hexagonal junction between the engine exhaust bells at the stern.

Together Derec and Katherine watched as the rescue robots fit a self-cutting emergency hatch to the upper hull. When the hatch's contact ring had burned through the hull and fused itself in place, the robots entered—one at a time, the witness first.

"This is where Aranimas had me living," she whispered as the hypervision panned the atticlike upper deck.

"How long were you there?"

"Two months. Believe me, it seemed longer."

When the witness robot led the way down to the main deck, the first thing they saw was a robot standing in the central corridor.

"Alpha," Derec cried.

"Capek," Katherine said at the same instant. "Where's my robot?"

Hajime suspended the recording. "This robot was removed and taken away for diagnostic examination and repair. "

"I want him back, just the way he was," Derec said. "You've got no right to tinker with him without a work order."

"The robot resisted our efforts to rescue you. It was judged to be operating in a substandard and hazardous manner and was deactivated. Standard procedure in such cases is to perform a full examination so that the anomaly may be reported to the manufacturer."

Katherine was nodding in reluctant agreement, and Derec took his cue from her. "All right," he said. "Go on."

When the recording continued, they saw themselves for the first time. They were lying head to foot along one wall in the central walkway of the main deck. Katherine winced and turned away at the sight of her own burn-blistered face and bloody clothing. Derec gritted his teeth and tried not to feel the pain all over again that was reflected in his burned skin.

"I thought so," Derec whispered under his breath. "I thought so."

"What?" Katherine demanded. "What are you talking about?"

"Alpha. He kept us alive."

"You heard Hajime—the robot was abnormal. He wouldn't let them rescue us."

"That was just the PD cube being careful. Look," Derec said, gesturing. "Those aren't positions that you fall into naturally after an accident like that, or even crawl into. We were moved. And more: we were at least five days out when I tripped the booby trap. It took the rescue ship two and a half days to reach us. There's no quarreling with the fact that we were badly injured—"

"No," she said with a little shiver.

"I was wondering how we survived until the paramedics got to us. We should have died right there on the ship. All they should have found were corpses. Alpha is the reason they didn't." Derec looked toward the robot. "Hajime, could you pause the recording and give us privacy, please?"

"Of course, Derec." The image and the robot both froze.

"What? What's going on?"

"I just want to point out that someone else might have been on the ship, too."

"What are you thinking about?"

"I had wondered why Wolruf and the robot were taking so long to get back from their errand. What if Aranimas regained consciousness? They might still have been trying to lock him up when the bomb went off. Alpha would have come running back. He wouldn't worry about Aranimas. He probably wouldn't even worry about what Aranimas might do to Wolruf. Aranimas and Alpha could both have gotten back into Hull A before it was cut loose."

"And Alpha would have protected us from him, just as it tried to protect us from the rescue crew."

"That might even explain *why* Alpha gave the robots trouble."

"He could have hidden," Katherine said thoughtfully. "It was his ship. He would have known where he'd be safe. Until the ship was brought in—"

"Just what I was thinking. If he doesn't have the key, he's looking for it—or us. If he's got it, he still may be looking for us. Either way, the key's not safe, and neither are we. And we can't just sit around and tell ourselves there's no rush. We have to start doing something right now."

Katherine cast her gaze downward into her lap. "All right," she said at last.

"Hajime," Derec said. "You can rejoin us."

The robot stirred again. "Thank you, sir. Shall I continue with the recording?"

"No. Terminate the replay. We've seen enough," Katherine said.

"Very well, madam," the robot said, complying. "Do you have other questions?"

"Yes. Where is Oh Seven B now?"

"I do not know, madam."

The answer brought Derec up off the bed, his face reddening. "What do you mean, you don't know?" he demanded. "You're the second highest ranking staffer on the station."

"That is correct, sir."

"And you don't know where our ship is?"

"I only know that Oh Seven B is no longer in the berth at which it was moored when first towed into the station."

"Was it stolen?" Derec pressed. "Are you trying to tell me it's gone?"

"It was not stolen. It was moved under the authorization of the station manager."

"Why didn't you say so from the start?" Katherine snapped.

"Derec asked if I knew where Oh Seven B was berthed. I do not, and so informed him."

"Then find out where our ship is. I want you to take us to it."

"I am sorry," Hajime said. "I am not permitted to do that."

"Then find us a robot who is permitted," Derec snapped.

"I have been instructed to refer all inquiries of this sort to the station manager."

Derec sighed. "All right. You can go."

"Thank you, sir." The robot paused. "May I make an inquiry, sir?"

"What about?"

"Do you continue to refer to Oh Seven B as 'our ship' out of habit or as a matter of affection?"

"What do you mean?"

"I have been informed that the vessel known as Oh Seven B is no longer your property."

CHAPTER 16
INTO THE DARKNESS

The station manager, a robot named Anazon, would not come to see them, but agreed to a brief vidcall.

"Is the care you are receiving satisfactory?" Anazon asked politely. "I hope that Hajime is seeing to your other needs—"

Derec did not waste any time on pleasantries. "Where is our ship? Where is Oh Seven B?" he demanded.

"I regret, sir, that I am not permitted to tell you," the robot said without a hint of regret in his voice.

"Who gave that order?"

"I regret, sir, that I am not permitted to tell you that, either."

Derec was determined not to be thwarted. "Who is your supervisor? What's his name?"

"My supervisor's name is Aram Jacobson."

"Get him on this channel."

"Mr. Jacobson may not be available at this time—"

"Do it. Use whatever priority you have to to get him to answer. And keep the line open. I want to hear what you say."

The robot reached forward for the hyperviewer controls. "This is Anazon, Manager of Rockliffe Station, requesting a conference with Mr. Jacobson."

A voice said "One moment," and there was a pause.

"Yes, Anazon," a new voice said. The words were muddied by the faint electronic echo which was the telltale sign of a scrambler somewhere in the link. "What is it?"

"Anazon called you on my behalf," Derec cut in. "Your

robots have appropriated my ship. I expect you to order them to return it."

"And our robot," Katherine added. "We want Capek back, too."

The hypervision image of Anazon faded and was replaced an instant later by one of a round-faced man with narrow eyes and shiny black hair. In sharp contrast to the robot's slender physique, Jacobson's stout body was perched precariously on his executive chair like an egg on a teaspoon.

"Excuse me, by whom do I have the pleasure of being ordered about?" he asked with exaggerated politeness.

"My name is Derec. This is—"

"Just Derec? No last name, like a robot?"

"Don't be cute. You know all about me. I'm sure there's a file on me in your library."

"I have many files in my library," Jacobson said. "I'm responsible for facilities which employ twenty-six hundred humans and nearly eight thousand robots. Believe me when I tell you that neither your name nor your face are familiar to me." His gaze flicked toward Katherine. "And you, miss?"

"Katherine Burgess. And don't call me miss."

"My apologies if I insulted you," Jacobson said, bowing his head slightly. "Now if I could ask you to restate your complaint —this is most irregular, to have someone barge in on a private call. I'm afraid it rather distracted me."

Derec was too furious for words, but Katherine took over smoothly. "We were found on a damaged spacecraft and brought here to Rockliffe Station. Now the station manager refuses to allow us access to our ship."

"Refuses you access?" Jacobson asked, wrinkling his forehead. "Whatever for?"

"It won't tell us," Derec said. "It says it's been ordered not to tell us—my guess is by you."

"I assure you not," Jacobson said, reaching for his computer. "If you'll just allow me a moment to check the records—" He turned his back to them briefly. "Oh yes, of course," he said to himself as he studied the screen.

"Of course what?"

Jacobson turned back to face them. "I do recall hearing about you after all, Derec. You're the amnesia case Dr. Galen is studying. That explains a great deal."

"Not to me."

"But it does all the same. You see, the care you've been receiving is quite costly—"

"Dr. Galen said my bill would be charged against a station account."

"I'm afraid Dr. Galen made an error," Jacobson said. "That would be the case if you were indigent and unable to pay, or if the costs of your care exceeded the guarantee made by your homeworld on behalf of its citizens."

"But my case is different—"

"Indeed. Your citizenship is unknown. Your financial assets are unknown. Indeed, there is even some question about your majority under Spacer law," said Jacobson.

"I'm old enough."

"We have decided to presume so," he said. "But in any case, since you have not been able to supply us with identification, we have no choice but to seize your tangible personal assets in payment of your account."

"My tangible assets—"

"Your ship and its contents have been appraised generously, I assure you," Jacobson said, glancing back at his computer. "Even so, I'm afraid there's not much left after subtracting the salvage fee and the expenses of the rescue operation. Still, there's more than enough to cover passage to Nexon on the next shuttle and keep you fed in the meantime."

Derec gaped disbelievingly. "You can't do that. You can't just take everything a man owns."

"It's the judgment of the minister of finance that anyone who has assets enough to own such a ship in the first place can quite afford to pay his bills," Jacobson said, sitting back in his chair. "If we were to let you get away with this, I'd be overwhelmed by freeloaders, all claiming to have forgotten where their funds are held."

"Are you accusing me of making this up? Ask Dr. Galen—"

"Dr. Galen does not set policy for the station. I do."

"At least you finally admit that this is your doing," Derec retorted. "I can't believe you have the nerve to charge me for rescuing me. You'd have gone out to intercept that ship whether we'd been on it or not."

"From our point of view, that ship wouldn't have been there endangering our facility *unless* you were in it," Jacobson said lightly.

"Just a moment," Katherine said. "That ship is half mine. Maybe you can grab his half for payment, but you can't touch mine. You know who I am. I authorized a draft on my account at the Auroran Exchange."

"So you did," Jacobson said. "Tell me, what sort of account was it?"

"A Living Share—a family trust—" Katherine's face was beginning to go gray.

"Which is a revocable trust, is it not?"

"I—I guess."

"I regret to inform you that on May 26, your account was closed and all funds withdrawn. Have you other assets of which we may not be aware?"

"No," Katherine said, her expression acutely pained. "That was my Living Share. How could they take it back? How could they do such a thing?"

"I cannot say. The fact remains, they did. You are legally an adult and responsible for your own debts. Therefore we have been obliged to exercise our rights to your portion of the property as well."

"You won't get away with this," Derec threatened feebly.

"It is not a question of 'getting away with' anything," Jacobson replied. "We are well within our rights. You should be grateful that you're alive, instead of fussing over a ship which I understand is not in flyable condition in any case. Since you couldn't have paid for its repair, you would have had to try to sell it anyway, and I doubt very much you could have gotten anything near the price you were paid by us."

"You—" Derec sputtered.

"Now, if you'll excuse me, I have other business to attend to."

The link dissolved before Derec could reply. "Do you believe that performance?" he exclaimed, turning to Katherine. He was shocked to see how empty of spirit her eyes were.

"Performance?" she asked mechanically.

"This isn't what it looks like. This is just a way of separating us from the ship. To pay us for it they'd have to have proof that we own it—more than our word and the fact that they found us in it. Do you know why they're not asking us for that proof? They don't want to know. Just like they don't want to know whether I'm too young to be responsible for my own debts."

"It doesn't matter," she said. "None of it matters."

Derec stared at her. "What's bothering you?"

"My money. My family took my money—"

"Is that any great surprise? The Patrol probably reported you missing when they went out and picked over what was left of the *Golden Eagle*."

"They didn't even give me a chance to explain—" she said despairingly.

"Explain to who?" he asked gently.

But his question seemed to awaken her to her loss of control. The line of her jaw stiffened and her eyes hardened. "Frost them. Frost them all," she said tersely. "It's ancient history. What do we do now?"

"What are you game for?"

"I'll tell you what I'm *not* going to do. I'm not going to wait around quietly until the next freighter comes and then meekly traipse off to Nexon," she declared. "And I'm not about to let a bunch of robots keep me away from my property, even if they are following the orders of that milkface."

"Sounds like I'm going to need to start calling you Kate."

Surprised, she smiled. "Maybe you'd better."

"Good. Because I think we're going to need her," Derec said. "This isn't going to be easy."

"I know. But there's a limit to how many places you can hide a ship of that size, even in a station this large. If it's still here, we'll find it."

"Probably so," Derec agreed. "Chances are they moved it from the active dock to one of the deactivated ones—in the military wing, would be my guess. Even if the station directory won't tell us where the other dock facilities are, we can figure it out. But that won't help us much."

"Why not?"

"Because the key is what matters, not the ship. Jacobson is right. We don't have any use for the ship."

"We find the ship, we find the key."

Derec shook his head unhappily. "The key won't be there. The robots have it."

"Jacobson didn't say anything about it."

"Why should he take the chance of being the first to call our attention to it?" Derec asked rhetorically. "I just know that the whole time we talked to him, he was sitting there waiting for us to ask about our personal effects or give some sign we know about the key—waiting to pounce if we did. It was a test. We passed, so they're going to let us go. If we hadn't—"

"Why should they take any special notice of the key? It doesn't look like anything special. They don't know what Aranimas went through to get it. I do, and I still don't know why it's so important."

"So you say."

"Do you think I'm lying?"

Yes, he thought. Or at least not telling the whole truth. I'm starting to believe that everybody knows what this thing is but me—that you're pretending that you're just as ignorant as I am, while all the time you know exactly what it is and why it's important.

But he said none of that. "I don't know what to think," Derec said, frustration thick in his voice.

"I think the key's still hidden wherever Aranimas kept it. Jacobson didn't mention the key because he doesn't know anything about it. He's just worried about the ship in general."

"He knows. I'm sure of it," Derec said stubbornly.

"Look, if Jacobson knows about the key and the robots found it, then it went out on *Fariis*. Which means he has it by now. End of story."

"Not necessarily," Derec said, shaking his head. "The packets are contract haulers, not Nexonian nationals. Do you think he'd trust them with something that's probably ten times more valuable than their whole fleet contract? For that matter, do you think he'd put it on an unarmed vessel with the raiders still sitting out there somewhere trying to figure out how to get it back?"

"What, then?"

"Put yourself in their shoes. First you protect your find from being disturbed, and then you get together a team to go retrieve and investigate it. As long as you've done the first one right, you can take your time doing the second. They'll be here when they've assembled the people and the hardware they need. At the very least they'll need to scare up a bulk freighter to carry the spacecraft back and a warship to give the raiders second thoughts."

Katherine sighed. "What a mess. Maybe we ought to just let them have it."

"The hell with that," Derec spat. "As long as Aranimas doesn't have the key, and the raiders don't attack, and Jacobson is still on Nexon—we've got a chance."

"But it's a race."

"Yes. It's a race. And we can't wait around for you to get a clean bill of health from Dr. Galen before we start," Derec said pointedly, bracing for an argument.

The argument never came. "You're right," she said simply, swinging her legs over the side of the bed and feeling for the floor. "Where to?"

Before that question could be considered, there was Dr. Galen to deal with. The robot came bursting into the room before Katherine's bare feet even had a chance to pick up a chill from the floor.

"Please return to the bed, patient Katherine," Dr. Galen requested. "Florence can see to whatever needs you might have."

Derec was girding himself for another protracted argument, but Katherine surprised him. "I'll go where I want when I want," she snapped. "And if you start trying to act like a warden instead of a doctor I'll have your brain reprogrammed for basket-weaving."

"I must protest strongly—"

"Am I in danger of dying?"

"No, patient Katherine. But your recovery—"

"Then save your protest for your medical log: 'Patient Katherine Burgess disregarded recommended rehabilitation program.' Isn't that the phraseology? Derec and I are going for a walk. If you don't want me catching pneumonia you'd better get me some normal clothes. And something for my feet."

Any human addressed in that tone would have been clenching his fists and strongly considering using them. But Dr. Galen only nodded slightly. "I will have clothing brought."

"If it's not here in five minutes I'm going out like this," she warned him. "And don't get any ideas about following us around. If I have any problems, Derec will be there to bring me back."

When the robot left, Derec stared at Katherine in amazement. "How'd you learn how to do that?"

She shrugged. "Medical robots are as bossy as they come, but they can't make it stick unless you're really in some danger. I'm not."

"All the same, it would have taken me twenty minutes to get to the same point, if I'd ever gotten there at all."

"That's because you always let yourself get suckered into arguing with the robots. I just give them orders. Much more efficient."

"I guess it is, sometimes," Derec said. "But you ought to know, in about four hours your dermal analgesic is going to wear off and your skin is going to start feeling like someone's scraping it off with a spatula."

As Derec spoke, Florence entered, wordlessly laid a sleeveless jump suit and a pair of foot pillows on the end of the bed, and then left.

"Thanks for the warning. Let's make a point of being back in three and a half," Katherine said. "Now get out of here while I change."

By the time Katherine emerged from the ward, Derec had decided to go along with her proposal that they look for Aranimas's ship first. He had several reasons for surrendering—that the ship was the last known location of the key, that even if the key had been found and removed it might logically be kept nearby. But the most important reason was that if he didn't show her early that she was wrong, she'd soon be trying to order him around as she did the robots.

The electronic map on the wall of the lobby offered little help. Rockliffe Station was built out of three connected spheres. The central sphere, called C Section, contained some forty levels from top to bottom. Two satellite spheres barely half as large were anchored to it by cylindrical pylons only a few levels in diameter.

Large areas within the station's outline were colored black and labeled "Inactive." No amount of coaxing could persuade the map's controller to reveal what facilities were in those areas or even show the traffic grid.

Less than fifteen percent of C Section was drawn in with the pale blue color, labels, and identifying symbols of the active zone. Most of E Section, which contained the known dock facilities, was blue. But W Section, together with its connecting pylon, was completely black.

"There," Katherine said, pointing to W Section. "They probably had an east terminal and a west terminal."

"Symmetrical design," Derec agreed. "Makes sense."

"It's a good place to start, anyway."

"Let's hope that those sections are just closed down, not closed off."

The hospital was located near the center of C Section, three levels down from the main thoroughfare. Together, Katherine and Derec climbed up to the main level and headed west. There were no physical barriers, though the four-lane express slidewalk was not operating, obliging them to walk.

But past the boundary of subsection 42, the corridor lights were out and the directional "lightworms" were off. Based on what he had seen during his earlier excursion, Derec had thought that might be the case. He had hoped for either a local control option or a presence sensor, but in vain. With eighteen subsections of blackness ahead of them, they were forced to turn back.

They recruited the first robot they encountered to show them where hand lanterns were kept, and soon returned to the subsection 42 threshold. The beams of the powerful portable lights stabbed deep into the cavelike corridor and created a cozy island of light around them. But they were very aware of the darkness beyond, the way their footsteps echoed hollowly, the chill of the unused spaces they were entering.

Ten minutes of walking brought them to the great triple pressure seal doors at the outer boundary of C Section. The doors were resting retracted in their grooves, apparently deactivated. Past the interlock, the throughway narrowed to a single-lane slidewalk in each direction with far fewer jump-offs and side passages than before.

Derec expected to find robots guarding the entry to W Section, and told Katherine so. But when they reached the far end of the slidewalk, they were still alone. The west docks were there, just as they had guessed. But the main public entrance to the complex was not even locked.

"No guards, no locks," Derec said as they stood on the threshold. "This looks very bad. Maybe they had one of the tugs take the ship and stand off a hundred klicks from the base."

"Let's find out," Katherine said, starting ahead.

If the west docks were being held for possible military use as Dr. Galen had implied, it was merely as a line item on some logistics officer's list of resources. There was no sign that the complex had even been or ever would be anything other than a general purpose cargo and passenger transfer node. All the familiar facilities were there: Import Registry, Customs, the travelers' Personals.

Katherine led Derec past the unstaffed security stations and up the loading ramp to the upper concourse. Along the length of the high-ceilinged room were six check-in stations, six glassed-in waiting areas, and six two-story viewports each of which looked out onto an enormous docking slip and space beyond. All six slips were empty and dark. Nothing could be seen through the viewports except a few dim and distant stars.

"Downstairs?" Derec asked.

Her lips pressed into a tight line, Katherine answered by leading the way back down the ramp. The lower concourse seemed like a mirror image of the upper. All six bays on the lower concourse were dark—but one was not empty.

"Bingo," Derec said, sprinting through the check-in station and up the boarding tunnel.

"I don't understand," she said, dogging his heels. "Where are the guards? There ought to be guards."

"Maybe they're inside," Derec said, pulling up short. The boarding tunnel was connected to the emergency hatch they had seen being installed, and across the lock-side seam there was a security seal. It was a token seal, however, meant only to give notice that the hatch had been opened. It could not stop them from going aboard.

Nothing inside had been disturbed, it seemed, since they had been found and removed. For that matter, except for cracks in three of the screens above the great command console, it did not even seem as though there had been an explosion on the main deck. Yet there were a dozen blackened fist-sized pits in the walls and ceiling to mark where the charges had been.

"You don't blow up your house because a burglar breaks in," Katherine observed. "Aranimas's security would have been tailored to his own species. Whatever you want to call what we tripped—"

"Radiation bomb, maybe."

"—must have been designed to kill or disable an Erani without doing serious damage to the ship."

"It did a good enough job on us."

Though they could not find Aranimas's stylus, whatever locked the deck plates in place had apparently been disabled when the ship was powered down. Twenty minutes later, they had torn up the whole floor, but found nothing.

"Shall we put it back?" Katherine asked, gesturing at the mess they had created.

"No point. The robots are going to know we were here anyway."

"They have the key, don't they?"

"Almost certainly. If they don't, Jacobson does."

Katherine sighed. "How are we ever going to find it? The size of this station—even if it were just lying in open view in a corridor somewhere, it'd take us weeks to find it. And you know that they've hidden it better than that."

"There's a lot of places they could put it that you can be sure they didn't," Derec said, looking around the main cabin one last time. "They won't leave it unattended, you can count on that. Not like they left this ship."

"Do you have any idea why they let us in here?"

Derec nodded slowly. "I think so. To send us a message. To tell us just how harmless they think we are. That there's nothing we can do to them." He sighed. "And they may just be right. Let's get out of here, huh?"

Squeak.
 Brush.
 Squeak.
 Brush.
The sounds were soft and distant, but they were there, all right. If either he or Katherine had been talking, as they had been the first third of the way back, there would have been no way he would have heard them. But ever since they had fallen silent in individual introspection, the sounds had played at the threshold of Derec's hearing.

At first he had thought them echoes of their own footsteps, or merely the product of paranoia. But as they were passing into subsection 51, Derec decided that they were real and not imagined. Something was following them.

"Don't say anything and don't turn around," Derec whispered. "You hold both lamps. Keep walking."

"What?"

"Ssssh. Keep walking. Keep the beams angled down so you won't be silhouetted. Try to make it look like you're two people."

"What's this about?" she demanded. But she contained her curiosity to a whisper, and kept walking as he had asked.

Handing the torch to her at arm's length, Derec slipped away into the darkness and squeezed back against the wall. As he waited, he wondered who he was waiting for. One of Dr.

Galen's robots? One of Jacobson's? Or Aranimas? He wished he still had the gas aerosol, or had kept his torch to use as a club.

Have to do it on your own, he told himself, dropping to his knees and huddling against the base of the wall.

The shadow was past Derec before he even saw it. Only when he looked back toward Katherine and caught a glimpse of it silhouetted against the glow of her torch did he move. Gathering himself up, he took three running steps and launched himself at the figure's legs. He struck cloth and bone, not syntheskin and metal, and the stranger came down in a heap on top of Derec, squealing protest.

They wrestled furiously in the darkness, each with different objectives. Derec was trying to get a firm grip on an arm, leg, or neck and pin the other to the floor. His adversary was trying only to break Derec's grip and escape.

Derec was much the more skilled. He had no difficulty getting what he thought were solid holds on the other. The difficulty was in maintaining them for more than a few seconds. Had they been wrestling in competition, he would have been getting the takedowns, his opponent the escape points. Part of the reason was the other's compact strength, and part the slippery fabric its clothes were made of.

But in the dark, luck counted for more than skill or strength, and neutralized both. The two combatants rolled from one side of the passageway to the other, neither able to gain a lasting advantage. Then, with a sudden twist and a lucky grab, Derec found himself on top, straddling the other's waist and with each of his hands locked in an iron grip on one of his opponent's wrists.

Just then Katherine shone one of the lamps full on the shadow's face. His adversary squinted up at him out of eyes nearly hidden by mottled gold and brown fur, and its mouth twisted into a familiar grimace.

"Wolruf!" Derec exclaimed.

"'Ur stronger than 'u look, Derec," Wolruf said, still grinning. "But I 'ope 'u know I let 'u win."

Derec grinned back. "As ugly as you are, I'm awfully glad to see you. I was afraid we'd lost you when we were cut loose."

"Why are you treating it like some long-lost friend?" Katherine demanded. "It's Aranimas's fetch-boy."

"Girl," he corrected. "Besides, you don't understand," he added, helping Wolruf to her feet. "She's my friend."

"Partners," Wolruf said proudly.

"Oh? Then why was it skulking along behind us like that?"

"Following," Wolruf said.

"What were you planning to do?"

"I never 'urt 'u—"

"You were waiting for us to find the key, weren't you? And then you were going to steal it—"

"Katherine—she's sick," Derec said suddenly.

"What?"

"Look at her," he urged. "Look at me," he added, reclaiming his torch and turning its beam on himself. His clothing was covered with long gold and brown hairs. In the light of Katherine's torch, the alien's fur was so thin in patches that Derec could see the pale leathery skin beneath. And there was something about Wolruf's eyes that telegraphed the distress she had been enduring.

"What's wrong with you?" Katherine asked, a faint note of suspicion tainting her concern.

"'Ungry," she said simply.

"Of course," Derec said. "She's starving. There isn't even any food she could steal here."

Katherine squinted at the alien through narrow-slitted eyes. "Is that why you were following us? Not to get the key, but to find out where we were getting our food?"

"I don' care about the jewel," Wolruf said. "Juss 'ungry. I 'ide, follow the robots, look for food. I follow them everywherr and never smell food."

"You don't like the robots, do you? It isn't just Alpha," Derec said.

"Brood-captain tell me a 'undred times, never trust strange animal until 'u've seen its meal table," she said weakly.

It sounded like an attempt at a joke. "And robots never eat," Derec completed. "Well, we'll get you something. I hope we can get you something. Can you eat what we eat?"

"Just hold on," Katherine interrupted. "You were on the ship with us the whole time? And you've been hiding out ever since?"

"I wass coming through interlock—Alpha, too—when heard the bomb go off," Wolruf said. "Noise bring other Erani. Controls dead an' 'u not much better. So I cut us loose. When robots come I 'ide, when ship dock I slip out. Been 'iding ever since."

"Where's Aranimas?"

"Don't know. Left behind." Wolruf was noticeably unsteady on her feet.

"We can sort the rest of this out later," Derec said sharply. "We've got to get her something, quickly."

"Not so quickly," Katherine said, stepping closer. "Where have you been hiding? Here, in the dark sections?"

"Mostly. No robots here. I like the dark better than I like robots."

"How much of the dark sections have you been through, looking for food?"

"Lots," Wolruf said. "But the jewel's not there, if thass what 'u're wondering."

"How do you know?" Katherine demanded. "Because you put it somewhere else?"

"I don' want the jewel. Juss trouble for everyone," Wolruf said. "But I know wherr it iss."

Derec impulsively grabbed the alien by both cheeks and planted a kiss on her forehead. "All right!" he declared. "We're in business!"

Katherine held her enthusiasm in check. "How do you know?" she repeated.

"I follow when they took it from the ship. I think they take it to 'umans, 'umans 'ave food. Wrong. Robots took it wherr therr are lots of robots, no 'umans, no food. I almoss got caught."

"Do you remember exactly where? Can you take us there?" Katherine asked.

"Thought robots 'ur servants," Wolruf said, wrinkling her face in puzzlement. "Why not juss ask them to bring it to 'u?"

"Nevermind about that," Derec said gently. "Answer Katherine's questions. Do you remember the way? Can you take us there?"

"I remember, always, so I can take 'u. Don' want to. Don' want key, don' want to see robots or robots to see me. But 'u be my friend and feed me and I be 'ur friend and show 'u. Okay?"

Derec looked to Katherine. "I'm taking her to find some food," he said. "If you don't like it, you're welcome to go solo from here on."

"Oh, no, you don't," she said quickly. "You can't get rid of me that easily."

"Come on, then," he said as he started brushing futilely at the fur clinging to his clothing. He looked back to Wolruf and smiled. "Let's see if we find you some food before I choke to death on your dander."

They ended up returning to the hospital, both because it was relatively close and because it was one of the few facilities they knew anything about. Katherine entered first, demanding care and attention as she swept through toward the ICU and making sure to gather up both Dr. Galen and Florence along the way. A minute later, Derec and Wolruf slipped inside and headed in the other direction, toward the kitchens.

"Meat, breads, vegetables—what's best for you?" Derec said, scanning the menu of the autogalley.

"Plants," Wolruf said, crouching. "Something to work my teeth on."

"Everything's synthetic, I'm afraid—the farm is one of the things they closed down. Let's see—I think they make the apple wedges with a lot of fiber."

"Do'u know what 'ur going to do with the key when 'u find it?" Wolruf asked from behind.

"No." Derec turned around and presented the alien with a white tray filled with pale yellow pulpy slices of apple. With surprising patience, Wolruf selected a wedge, sniffed it experimentally, then balanced it on her narrow tongue and delicately took it into her mouth. As far as Derec could tell, she did not chew it, but swallowed it whole.

That created a minor paradox—though Wolruf did not appear to be eating quickly, the plate rapidly emptied. She ate as though she were trying to make up for all seven weeks of deprivation at one sitting, and yet was scrupulously neat and almost completely silent. There were none of the wet crunching noises that any human trying to keep pace would have made.

I wouldn't be surprised if she finds our eating habits repulsive, he thought as he watched her.

When the tray was empty, Wolruf offered it up to Derec with a hopeful look. "I guess 'u can trust me now, right?" she said.

"Except I'm not the one you have to win over," he said, taking the tray and turning back to the autogalley for a refill. "Katherine is. Which reminds me—why didn't you tell me she was on board?"

Wolruf shrugged. "No chance to. Always something 'appening, somebody 'terrupting."

"That's true enough," Derec said, surrendering the replenished tray. "There's questions I've been wanting to ask you since that first night and I haven't gotten a chance to."

"Ask," Wolruf said, then rolled out her tongue for another bite.

Derec considered a moment. "This one isn't important to anyone but me. You didn't know I was on the asteroid, did you?"

"Not until gunners spot you. Then thought you were robot."

"Which is why you didn't fire at me—"

"Aranimas's orders—not perfectly followed."

"You meant the robot that was with me? That was a self-destruct."

"Fine distinctions escape Aranimas. Ask gunner who hit him."

Derec smiled. "Did you know the key was on the asteroid?"

"No twice."

"That's what I thought. But then why were you there? Was it just the dumbest luck that you showed up?"

"Purpose, not luck. Aranimas build very fine starglass. Saw ast'roid being made and became very curious."

"Say that again? I didn't catch your meaning."

She cupped her hands and made motions like forming a snowball. "With starglass, Aranimas watched the ast'roid-making. Boss very curious. Not something Erani ever do. 'U do it often?"

"No," Derec said, still blinking in surprise. An artificial world—it was remotely possible. Use a small fleet of haulers to bring in the raw material—maybe just smaller planetoids brought in from the nearest dirty system. Drive the pieces together at just the right speed and fuse them into a larger body—but why?

The answer came to him almost immediately. To hide the key. To bury it away where no one would ever find it, as though it were as dangerous as a cask of plutonium waste. Buried cleverly, not at the heart of the asteroid where the first shaft sunk would uncover it, but tucked invisibly under the surface.

Except that someone saw or found out, and sent the robots to retrieve it.

"Are you sure about this?" Derec demanded.

"Sure. Aranimas saw it all. Very good starglass." She offered up the empty tray hopefully.

Then we're in over our heads, Derec thought as he turned back to the autogalley. Way over—

Wolruf was finishing her third helping when Katherine joined them. She had drawn on station supply for a long-sleeved blouse to wear over the jump suit, and traded the foot pillows for soft-soled shoes.

"I sent Florence on an errand and gave Dr. Galen a task that should keep him out of the lobby for at least half an hour," she said. "And I made Dr. Galen fit me with a loaded medipump just in case it's not convenient to come back. Though my skin really doesn't feel too bad. Are you two almost ready?"

Wolruf made the last two wedges disappear. "I am."

"Then it's time to pay the bill for the meal," Katherine said, reclaiming the empty plate. "Let's go look at the map."

They stood elbow to elbow in the deserted lobby, Wolruf in the middle.

"Here's where we are," Katherine said, pointing. "And here's about the spot you and Derec went to the mat. All you have to do now is tell us where the key is, and we'll go get it. You can go back to the dark and never have to see another robot."

But Wolruf was unable to understand the map in any of its modes or projections, even though both Derec and Katherine made labored efforts to try to explain it. "I know it in my feet and my nose," Wolruf said. "I go with 'u and show 'u."

Katherine frowned and looked to Derec. "How are we going to smuggle her through the halls? It was risky enough bringing her here. And she said she almost got caught the first time."

"I was thinking while we were walking that a place this large probably used to have some kind of personal transport."

"Jitneys," she said.

"That's the word." An image of a three-wheeled utility vehicle snapped into focus in his mind. In automatic mode, they were essentially wheeled robots. In semi-auto, they served as smart taxis for visitors to the station. But in manual mode, they should offer freedom from Central Services control and privacy from Security curiosity. "The robots don't need them, but I'll bet they're all lined up somewhere ready to roll."

"Won't the robots think it's unusual, seeing one out in the streets?"

"I don't think so," Derec said. "When a ship's in port the crew probably uses them. And seeing one of the carts won't strike them as any more strange than our presence alone would. Robots *notice* people. It's the way they're made. But we don't need to be invisible—we just need to be left alone. What do you say?"

Katherine pursed her lips and considered. "I think if we don't find any jitneys, it doesn't matter what I think."

Happily, the jitney accumulator areas were clearly marked on the station map. It took less than five minutes for Derec to walk to the nearest one and return with one of the nimble little electric carts. The version he had chosen had a single driver's seat in back over the solo wheel, and an open passenger cab slung between the other wheels in front.

Wolruf curled up on the floor of the passenger cab under a white hospital robe. Katherine sat in one of the two seats, her legs further helping to conceal the alien, and Derec took the controls.

For Wolruf to find her place in her scent map, they were forced to backtrack into the dark sections. From there it was relatively simple: up three levels, north two subsections, up another level, and then west five blocks into a large plaza.

When Wolruf warned them they were nearing their destination, Derec slowed the vehicle to a moderate walking pace. A moment later the alien stole a peek over the edge of the cab, then jabbed a fat finger in the direction of the circular building at the center of the plaza.

"In there? Are you sure?" Derec hissed.

"Yes, Derec. Thass wherr the jewel iss."

The lightworm sign outside the main entrance said "Station Operations Center—Restricted," and robots were everywhere. The center itself was a single room twenty meters in diameter and encircled with windows looking out on the plaza.

"Great. Just great," Derec grumbled, driving slowly across the plaza at an oblique angle. "How are we going to get in there? We can't sneak up."

"How about the front door?" Katherine said, twisting around to look at him. "Maybe they'll let you in."

Derec regarded her dubiously.

"Go ahead—it's worth a try."

"I still don't understand," Wolruf chimed in. "Aren't robots 'ur servants?"

Before answering, Derec drove the jitney a short distance down a connecting corridor, then pulled to one side and stopped. "I don't know about this," he said to Katherine. "Maybe they're just setting us up, like with Aranimas's ship. If we try to get in there, if we show any interest in the thing at all, maybe that's just going to bring them down on our necks like a tonne of slag."

"You want to just leave it with them? After all we've gone through because of it?"

"When we were prisoners on the ship, I thought it was important to get the thing away from the aliens and back in human hands. Well, that's where it is. Jacobson made it clear they're willing to let us walk away and leave this mess to them. Maybe that's what we ought to do."

"Don't you have any curiosity?" she demanded. "Don't you want to know what this has all been about?"

"Sure, I've got curiosity. I've also got problems of my own to sort out. I don't see where that thing is going to help any."

"What's happened to your nerve?" she said. "Look, these are the same people that stole our spacecraft, spirited away my robot, and then tried to tell us we should be grateful that they're sending us away as paupers instead of criminals. I'm not about to let them get away with it."

"Don't you understand?" Derec shouted angrily. "You think we're going to be able to just walk in there, put it under our arm, and say 'Thanks for looking after it'? This thing came off a heavily armed alien ship—"

"They don't know that," Katherine pointed out. "They never saw Aranimas, or even Wolruf."

"All right," Derec said tiredly. "Maybe you're right. If they did think it was an alien ship, they probably wouldn't let us go.

But these people aren't playing. They wanted the ship, and they took it. They wanted the robot, and they took it. They want the jewel, and they have it. We're not going to be able to take it back. We won't even get in the door."

"Maybe their orders weren't that specific."

"I'd have made them so."

"You didn't give them. Go on—try."

"What's the point? Wolruf's right—the key is just trouble for everybody."

Katherine sighed: "If you want something done—" And before Derec could stop her, she climbed out of the jitney and headed back to the plaza on foot.

In less than ten minutes Katherine was clambering back into her seat. "They let me in, even gave me a little tour," she said breezily. "Very accommodating."

"I figured that out when you weren't back in two minutes. What about the key?"

"It's there all right, sitting out in plain sight. What idiots!"

Derec eased the jitney into motion down the corridor, mulling over Katherine's news. "Not really. Describe what you saw."

"It's a big semicircular room, with glass all around except for the offices at the back. There're five robots at work stations, including Anazon. Then there're two more near the center of the room doing nothing but sitting facing each other with the artifact on a table between them. There was some sort of funny emblem on the shoulder of those robots, a blue *F* in a double gold circle—"

Derec groaned. "Falke X-50s."

"Does that mean something?"

"It means trouble. They have superfast reflexes. If a bomb went off five meters in the opposite direction, they might be distracted long enough for you to get your hands on the key, but you'd never get out of the room with it. If we're going to get it back, we're going to have to have some way to neutralize seven robots at once—and I don't know any."

"Can you explain to me why it's out in plain sight? Could it be a copy, a fake? Maybe you're right about the trap."

"No," Derec said with a shake of his head. "I'd guess the

robots were probably ordered to watch it constantly, in principle if not in so many words."

"If you put it in a vault and nobody opens the vault, it isn't going to vanish into the ozone."

"No," Derec agreed, "but that understanding requires a fairly advanced and rather subtle mental function called object permanence. Robots are strongly biased toward the concrete and away from the inferred. If they lock something away out of sight, they don't really know it's there except when they check on it."

"That's illogical. No human would think that way."

"Some would," Derec dissented. "But you're right, it's not logical."

"So why do the roboticists let that happen?"

"No engineered system is perfect," Derec said with a shrug. "This is just one of those little things that doesn't always behave the way you wish it would. A robot's uncertainty about whether it's satisfactorily fulfilling its orders can drive it into an anxiety state—specifically, they develop an elevated K-integral in the W-14 level. So they begin checking on the thing they're guarding more and more often at shorter and shorter intervals."

"And eventually it ends up sitting on the table next to them," Katherine said.

"Right." Derec fell into a thoughtful silence, then suddenly caught himself. "Damn it all, you've got me trying to figure out how to get to it."

"See, I knew you didn't want to let them have it," Katherine said with a bemused smile. "Any ideas?"

"Not yet." A moment later he added, "Except that no matter how carefully worded and strongly impressed their orders to protect the key are, they're only covered by the Second Law."

Katherine was mute for a time, as Derec drove aimlessly through the streets bounding the Operations bloc.

"Following orders is Second Law," she said finally.

"That's what I just said."

"What if Wolruf and I gave them a First Law reason to disregard them?"

Wolruf peeked out from under the robe at the mention of her name and looked hopefully at Derec.

"That's the way to go, obviously," Derec said. "But how?"

"I've got some ideas. A little—robot theater, shall we say."

"Do you think you can be convincing?" Derec asked skeptically.

"I'd rather try than not," she said. "Let's not stop ourselves. Let's make them stop us."

"Wolruf?" he asked. "Do you want to try?"

"Whatever 'u want, Derec."

The burden was back on him, whether he wanted it or not. "All right, then," Derec said slowly. "Let's go somewhere more private and talk it through."

Peering down the corridor into the plaza, Derec shook his head. "This will never work," he whispered.

"It's worked so far, hasn't it?"

Derec had to admit that it had. The first problem had been to eliminate most of the robot traffic in the plaza. They had considered half a dozen ideas for accomplishing that, from setting up hallblocks with robot monitors to trying to draw them away with invented errands elsewhere in the station.

In the end, they settled for a whisper campaign, a simple variation on the unkind children's game—"Billy is a cootie; pass it on." Derec had stopped a robot at random just outside the Operations bloc and spoken briefly to it:

"Robot. Management has ordered that there be a test of station emergency communications in this subsection. Your instructions are as follows. First, you are not to discuss the test or your part in it over the command link. Second, you are not to enter or remain in subsector 100 at any time between 1200 hours and 1400 hours today. Third, you are to relay these orders to the next robot that you see."

The instructions were innocuous enough that the robot did not challenge them. Like a runaway infection, the whisper had raced through the body of the station staff. Within half an hour, the traffic in the plaza had thinned dramatically. Within the hour, the plaza was deserted, and several robots had even left the Operations Center.

Three robots remained. From where he was crouching beside the jitney, Derec could see them inside the Operations Center— the two X-50s guarding the artifact, and Anazon, darting from one work station to the next trying to oversee critical operations. Their particular responsibilities were too strongly impressed on them for Derec's little trick to pull them away.

"It'll work," Katherine prodded. "Go on. We'll do our part. You just make sure you do yours."

Swallowing hard, Derec nodded and started off down the corridor. He crossed the empty plaza and climbed the single step up into the Operations Center. None of the robots took any notice of him.

"Anazon."

"Yes, Derec."

"I've decided not to wait for the Nexon shuttle. I want to charter a ship to come and get me and take me to Aurora. Tell me the procedure I should follow."

Without ever turning away from the console, the robot began to answer. "There are seven ships of Nexonian registry licensed for Auroran space and available for hire. You may contact any of their owners by hyperwave—"

Suddenly the peace of the plaza was broken by the roaring sound of a jitney in high gear. A moment later the vehicle burst out of one of the connecting corridors, Katherine at the controls. Pursuing close behind was Wolruf, running with an easy loping gait that used all four of her limbs.

Halfway across the plaza, Wolruf got close enough to reach out and catch Katherine by the arm from behind. The jitney veered suddenly, breaking the alien's grip. But the veer turned into a skid that ended with the jitney sliding sideways with a jolt into the rockform base of a tree planter. In a moment, Wolruf caught up and pounced on Katherine. The air was filled with her convincingly terrified cries of "It's killing me!" and the alien's ominous growls.

When the jitney veered, Anazon had started toward the exit and one of the X-50s began to rise. But when the guard robot saw Anazon responding, it sat back down again. Derec knew immediately that meant the guards' instructions were so strongly worded that the expectation that Anazon would handle the First Law situation relieved them of responsibility. Only if Anazon failed would they act.

The moment was slipping away quickly. "Robots—help that woman," Derec said sharply, stepping forward. "She is being harmed. She may be killed."

One of the X-50s stirred slightly. "Anazon will protect her—"

"The creature attacking her is strong and fast. Anazon will not be able to protect her from injury. Go! Help her! Now!"

First one, then the other guard rose and took a halting step or two toward the exit. Then they hesitated, the conflicting positronic potentials having reached a new equilibrium. Anazon would reach Katherine and Wolruf in a few more strides and the stunt would be over, a failure.

Just then, Katherine loosed a blood-chilling cry that even Derec thought real, and the guard robots started forward again. Derec waited no longer. Snatching the artifact up from the table, he turned and ran the other way, vaulting over a console and out through the window.

His heart pounding, Derec fled the plaza and down an empty corridor. He heard the jitney's motors whine, but he did not look back. He could not afford to worry about Katherine and Wolruf. He thought he heard the metronomelike running strides of a robot, but he did not look back. Even if he was being chased, knowing it could not make his legs pump faster.

All he wanted was to reach the dark sections unmolested. All he could think of were the escape route and the rendezvous he had chosen. He ran until his chest ached and his legs were iron, until each breath was pain, until darkness swallowed him and hid him from those who wanted to find him.

CHAPTER 19
THE KEY TO PERIHELION

Derec huddled in pitch blackness in the corner of the room and waited. He could not say how long he had been alone there, except that it seemed an eternity. He held the artifact tightly in both hands and sat, rigid and silent.

Then without warning, he was not alone. Since the corridor outside was as dark as the room inside, Derec could not see when the door opened. But he heard it slide back, and rustling steps as someone entered. His heart began to beat faster and his nerves jangled.

"Derec?"

He sighed, and the tension flowed out of him. It was Katherine's voice. "Here," he said. "In the corner."

She thumbed her torch on and swung it in his direction, and the polished surface of the object he held in his hands sent an answering beam of light back at her and Wolruf. "You did it!" she exulted. "Let me see."

Derec crossed his arms protectively over the artifact. "No. Don't come near me."

"What's going on? What's happening to you?" Katherine demanded. "We did it. We've got it."

"So we do. It's confessions time, that's all," Derec said, sliding up the wall to a standing position. "I've had some time to sit here and think about things. It's amazing how being scared will focus your thoughts."

"What are you talking about?" Katherine demanded.

176

He waggled the key above his head. "It's real simple. Which one of you is going to stop playing dumb and tell me just what it is we've got?"

Katherine stared at him. "If you're trying to say that I've been holding out on you—"

"Haven't you been?" Derec interrupted. "You and Wolruf both. I'm tired of being the one in the dark, the one who's always one step behind. I want to know everything you know. I'd rather give it back to the robots than have it and not know what it is."

"Derec, I don't know anything more than I already told you," Katherine said pleadingly, taking a step forward.

Derec stiffened and gripped the artifact even more tightly. "Don't try it. Talk to me."

Katherine retreated a step. "Derec, I don't want to fight you. But this is crazy. We're all part of a team. I'm not keeping any secrets from you. I never saw or heard of that thing before Aranimas asked me about it. I couldn't tell him anything and he didn't tell me anything."

She turned and looked into the half-shadow where Wolruf stood. "But Wolruf *was* Aranimas's top aide. And when the robots took the key from the spacecraft, she thought it was worth the risk to follow and find out where it was taken. How about it, Wolruf?"

"I was 'ungry. I thought there would be food."

"Really? How hungry? Not six weeks' worth. Three days, that's all. Is that hungry enough to send you out where the robots were and take the chance of being caught by them? Especially considering how you feel about robots."

"If anyone's keeping secrets, p'rhaps iss 'u, Derec," Wolruf said challengingly. "The key was found on the asteroid 'u claim 'u were shipwrecked on. Why did 'u go to that spot when 'u were escaping? Because 'u knew that it was therr? Maybe because 'u'd put it therr and wanted to get it back?"

Without warning, the lights in the room suddenly flared to life. The only one who did not jump was Derec; he had been expecting it. "The robots are looking for us," he said. "They've reactivated this section, maybe the whole station. They can use the environmental systems to find out where lights are being used, where the oxygen demand is up."

"We can't stay here," Katherine said simply. "We've got to move. We've got to get the key hidden again before they find us."

Derec shook his head. "Wrong. Unless one of you starts talking, I'm going to wait right here until the robots show up and then hand it to them," he said with quiet calm. "It's up to you."

"If you let them have it back, we'll never be able to get it again," Katherine said angrily.

"I think you can count on that," Derec said, undisturbed.

She turned on Wolruf. "If you do know something, you'd better tell him straight and tell him fast, or the key's lost," she ordered. "If you wait any longer we'll never get away."

A wild look in her eyes, Wolruf backed away a step. "'U'll take it and leave me and I'll never get 'ome," she said desperately.

"That won't happen," Katherine said. "We won't abandon you."

"I already promised you that," Derec said. "I meant it."

"Tell him," Katherine prodded. "Tell us."

Wolruf's darting eyes fixed first on Katherine's face, then on Derec's. "Iss one of the Keys to Perihelion," she said finally.

"Perihelion? What's that?" Katherine said.

"Iss said to be the place nearest to every other place in the universe," Wolruf said. "'U 'old the key to the room which is the center of all. With the key, through Perihelion, 'u should be able to travel anywherr."

Derec shook his head in disbelief. "Some kind of matter transporter?"

"No," Wolruf said. "It is a key that opens the door to Perihelion."

Her anger forgotten for the moment, Katherine looked to Derec. "Could it be something that uses the same principle as the Jump?"

"In a package this size?" he asked skeptically. To Wolruf he added, "You said one of the keys. How many are there?"

"By the stories Aranimas 'eard, seven."

"What stories? Where did he hear them?"

"Therr werr three ships before this one came aboard," Wolruf said, gesturing toward Katherine. "Aranimas learned much from the 'umans aboard before he 'urt them so much they died. Learn 'ur language. 'ear many stories."

Katherine looked at Derec. "I've never heard any stories about a Key to Perihelion. They must have been Settler ships."

"That fits—otherwise Aranimas would have run into robots sooner." Derec turned to Wolruf. "Where did the keys come from?"

Wolruf twitched her cheeks, a gesture equivalent to a shrug. "Aranimas could not even learn wherr the tales came from."

Derec looked back to the key and turned it over in his hands. "How does it work? Where are the controls?"

"There iss only one control that Aranimas could find," Wolruf said. "Push each corner in turn. A button will appear."

"Press the corners clockwise or counterclockwise? Starting where? And which side?"

"It does not matter," Wolruf said. "Turn it any way 'u choose. The button always appears in the last corner 'u touch and always on the side facing 'u. If 'u do nothing, the button disappears again."

"And if you push the button you go to Perihelion?" asked Katherine.

"No," Wolruf said sadly. "That is what should 'appen, I think. But it does not. The key does not function."

"You tried it? With Aranimas?"

"Many times."

Derec looked down at the glittering metal bar resting in his hands. Its finish was mirror-smooth and seamless. There was no sign of a concealed switch. When he squeezed the upper right corner between thumb and forefinger, there was no give, no sign he had done anything at all.

But when Derec pressed the fourth corner, it pressed back against his thumb. A three-centimeter square section on the corner sprang smoothly upward, looking just like a button waiting to be pushed. At the same time, it seemed to be an immovable part of the rest of the artifact, as though the silver covering was some sort of metallic membrane.

Katherine looked back to Wolruf. "If it doesn't work, why were you so eager to get it back?"

"Maybe Wolruf can fix," was her forlorn reply. "Only way to go 'ome now."

Just then, they heard a voice calling them from the corridor outside. "Derec—Katherine—come out," it said. "Derec—Katherine—you do not have to hide."

Wolruf dropped to her crouch and loosed a barrage of guttural moaning sounds. "Shut up!" Katherine hissed at the alien, then turned to Derec. "Do something," she urged.

"What?" Derec snapped back. "This room has only one exit."

At that moment the door slid open, drawing Derec's attention away from Katherine. He glimpsed a golden robot filling the doorway and advancing across the threshold. Then suddenly Katherine was blocking his view. She had moved closer and was reaching for the key, a determined expression on her face.

Derec's immediate thought was that she was going to grab the key and try to run. He did not have enough time to snatch the gleaming artifact out of her reach. There was time only to tighten his grip.

Too late he realized Katherine had never meant to take the key. Her hands closed firmly over his, locking them in place. Her thumb drove the small square button back down into the body of the key.

"No!" cried Wolruf.

"Wait—" Derec started to say.

But there was nothing anyone could do to stop it—not Derec, not the robot, not even Katherine. There was a soundless burst of color that stabbed deep into Derec's eyes, driving out the sight of all else. And when the light faded to gray and his sight was restored, Wolruf, the robot, and the room had all vanished.

They found themselves standing as they had been standing, both gripping the key, at the center of a tiny place within a great space. There was nothing to prevent them from seeing vast distances, except that there was nothing to see.

All around them was a soft gray light that was to the eye what a hum is to the ear. The air had the fuggy, dusty odor of a house that has been closed up for the summer. There was no sound except their own tight, frightened breathing.

They clung to each other and to the key and tried to understand and accept their sudden displacement to this unreal reality. It was a place which could be nowhere in space. They were somewhere outside, thrown there by the staggering power of the little silver bar. It was a place without time, without life.

"Perihelion," Katherine whispered.

"Wolruf said that it was the nearest place to everywhere," Derec said. "It feels more like the farthest place from anywhere."

Katherine twisted her head around, looking. "Where is she?"

"Back on Rockliffe Station, I guess. Left behind."

"Why didn't the key bring her with us?"

"Maybe for the same reason it wouldn't work for her," Derec said. "Maybe because she was too far away from us. Maybe you have to be touching it, or touching someone who's touching it. I don't know. But we have to go back and get her."

"But the robots—"

Derec shook his head. "It was Alpha. You didn't even look. It was Alpha."

"I didn't know," Katherine whispered. "Press it again. Let's go back."

"How do we know we will?"

"I was thinking about escape when I pushed it. Think about going back."

Wordlessly Derec complied. The button appeared as before. There was another flash of color, and another few seconds of adjustment. Then their returning vision told them something that should not be, could not be. They were not at Perihelion, but neither were they back in Rockliffe Station.

They were standing in open sunlight atop a great pyramidal tower, looking down at a still greater city spread out before them. The tower they were on was taller by half than any other building in sight. It was like standing on top of the world, like looking down from an eagle's eyrie.

"What is this?" Katherine hissed. "Where did you send us?"

Derec stared unbelievingly at the towers, cubes, and spires stretching from the base of the pyramid to the horizon. "I don't know," he said hoarsely. "I had Rockliffe Station in my mind."

She released her grip on the key and grabbed tight to his arm. "Are we on Earth?" She asked it as though the prospect frightened her.

Derec looked west at the low-hanging disc of the sun. "No," he said. "The star is too white and too small." But he knew why she had asked. No Spacer world had a city this vast. Only on Earth had city-building ever been practiced on this scale, and they were not cities but Cities, enclosed and largely underground. "You don't recognize it?"

"I've never seen such a thing before," she whispered. "Is it Wolruf's homeworld? Or Aranimas's?"

"I don't know," Derec said. "We can find the answer easily enough, though."

"How?"

"By going down there." He gestured toward the city spread out below them.

"No," she said with a shudder. "Send us back."

Derec realized that he was still gripping the key in his unfeeling hands. "I don't know if I can," he said.

"Try," she urged. "Or let me try."

"We'll try," he agreed.

Holding an image of the gray emptiness of Perihelion in his mind, Derec called up the control button and pressed it. This time, nothing happened. "What it did has to take a lot of power. Maybe it has to recharge—or be recharged," he said. "Either way, it looks like we're here for a while at least."

"I don't want to go down there," Katherine said. "It'll be night soon. Let's stay here until morning and then try the key again."

The sun had indeed slipped a fraction of a degree toward the horizon, lengthening the already long shadow of the tower on the city below. "Aren't you afraid of going over the side in your sleep?" he asked. There was no railing or footwall enclosing the table-flat top of the pyramid.

"I don't expect to be able to sleep," she said soberly.

As the sun descended toward the horizon, a breeze kicked up, teasing at their hair and clothing. It carried with it no scent Derec knew. In fact, for a world so obviously teeming with life, it carried remarkably little scent at all.

Below them, the city was becoming alive with light—light cascading down the sides of buildings, light puddling in the streets. In those streets, hundreds of other lights were in restless motion, reminding Derec of the bustle within a colony of bees or ants.

Too emotionally numbed even to be afraid, they avoided talk. Katherine withdrew into herself, sitting in the lotus position near the center of the tile-covered plaza. Derec wandered near the edges, looking out and trying to abstract the pattern on which the city had been built.

When the stars came out, he studied them, hoping against hope to recognize their patterns. There was a red star as bright as a planet that might have been Betelgeuse, and a fierce white one that might have been Sirius.

But each could just as easily be any of a thousand other stars named or merely numbered. There was no way to tell without a spectrometer to take the optical fingerprint of each suspect and a general astrographical catalog in which to search for matches.

"Do you remember what the stars look like from Aurora?" he called across to Katherine, sitting huddled against herself on the other side of the plaza.

"I never knew," she admitted. "I wasn't interested."

Giving up, he went and sat facing her. She was idly rubbing her right bicep through the sleeve of her Lindbergh blouse.

"Having trouble with the pump?"

"That's not what hurts," she said, tugging the sleeve up and showing him a purple crescent bruise.

"Nice."

"My most convincing scream," she said with a rueful smile.

"Wolruf?"

"She got carried away and bit me. She's not as harmless as she wanted us to think."

"Anything living knows how to defend itself," he said, then added wistfully, "I wonder what's happened to her."

"I don't understand why you liked her."

"She's a victim—a prisoner—just like us."

"I have trouble thinking of her that way."

Derec sighed. "Doesn't matter now, I guess. I've abandoned her again."

Conversation lapsed after that. "I don't understand why it

was Alpha that came after us," Katherine said finally. "It can't have been roaming free like Wolruf since we came to the station, can it? Looking for us?"

"Just another one of Jacobson's tricks," Derec said. "He knew we wanted the robot back. What better bait to draw us out?"

They were silent together for a while, sitting close but not touching. "Your first name is David," she said unexpectedly.

Hearing the name brought no sudden revelations, and caution born out of experience kept him from feeling any gratitude. "Why tell me now?"

"So I can stop the mental gymnastics every time I start to talk to you. Because I thought you'd want to know."

"And because we don't know what's going to happen to us?"

"I won't think like that," she said. "I don't believe in it."

"I should have known better," Derec said with a faint smile. "Are you going to drop more than one crumb? How is it you know me? Where did we meet?"

She turned her head to look at him. "You were the engineer's mate on a Settler merchantman—the *Daniel O'Neill,* I think it was called," she said. "Does it sound familiar?"

"No," he said unhappily. "What else can you tell me?"

She hesitated. "I'm afraid I don't know you as well as I let you think. We crossed paths in the spaceport."

"If I'm a Settler drudge and you're a Spacer topcrust—"

"Your captain was having trouble with Customs coming in and we were delayed going out by mechanical problems. We ended up in the same waiting area. We talked for a while." She hesitated, then added, "You were funny. You made me laugh."

"Did I talk about my family—my home—"

"You don't remember any of it, do you? Meeting me—the *O'Neill*—"

"No."

"I'm sorry." She hesitated. "Even so, I thought you'd be happier, knowing."

"I'd be happier remembering," he said, and was silent for a moment. "Anyway, it doesn't seem to matter as much at the moment. I don't know a thing about this David. At least I know a little about Derec. I think I'll just stay Derec for the time being."

"I didn't tell you everything," she said. "I didn't tell you about—"

"Don't," he said. "If my name didn't bring it back, nothing will. Save the rest. You'll be able to tell me whether I'm remembering or inventing."

"I know your memory will come back. It has to."

He nodded absently, acknowledging her words without accepting them. "If you want to try to sleep, I'll watch to make sure you don't get restless and try to air-walk."

Shaking her head, she said, "I can't sleep without a pillow."

Derec stretched out on his back and tapped his left shoulder with his right hand. "I have an unoccupied pillow available, no charge."

He expected her to refuse the offer. But she crawled wordlessly to where he lay and snuggled against his left side, her head resting on his arm. Closing her eyes, she seemed to fall asleep almost at once.

They fit together easily, and, innocent though the embrace was, there was something pleasing about her closeness. Probably it's just that she's not talking, Derec told himself. He lay there looking up at the stars and listening to her slow, peaceful breathing until his own eyelids were too heavy to keep open.

David Derec, he thought just before sleep took him. It *would* be nice to have two names again—

CHAPTER 20
MORNING ON THE MOUNT

They woke thoroughly chilled from their night on the exposed promontory, and the early rays of the rising sun did little to warm them. Despite the cold, Katherine quickly separated herself from him as though embarrassed by the contact.

"Let's try the key," she said nervously as she stood up.

Derec pulled himself up to a sitting position. "No hello? No good morning?" he said with a half-grin. But he reached for the key, lying an arm's length away on the tile.

"Come on," she said impatiently. "I had a bad dream that I'd like to rule out as quickly as possible."

"What happened?"

"I was stuck here with you."

Smiling, he stood and held it out toward her. "Do the honors?"

She quickly went through the activation sequence, then glanced up and met Derec's eyes. "Ready?" she asked.

"What do we think of? Perihelion or the Station?"

"Perihelion first. I think we have to."

He inclined his head in agreement. "Ready if you are."

Her thumb went hard against the button, as though the vehemence with which she pushed it would speed their return. Light exploded against their retinas, the sunlight vanished, and they found themselves in the gray world of Perihelion once more.

"Now the Station?" Derec asked.

"How about Aurora?" she asked, her eyes glowing with excitement. "Wolruf said we could go anywhere with it. Why should we take ourselves back to trouble?"

"No," Derec said. "First we go back to get Wolruf. I owe her."

"I don't want to go back there," Katherine said anxiously. "We won't be able to use the key again to get away, not for hours. They'll have us locked up and it locked up by then, and we won't have done anything for Wolruf. You could get help on Aurora—get a ship and go back for her."

"How?"

"I have friends on Aurora—"

"The same ones that closed your account?"

She winced at the reminder, but was adamant. "More friends than we have on Rockliffe Station."

"You'll have to do the steering. I don't have a clear enough image of Aurora in my head."

"Happy to do it. Hold tight," she said, and triggered the key once more.

Perihelion vanished on cue, but it was not the pastoral landscape of Aurora which replaced it. It took only an instant for Derec to realize that they had returned to the top of the tower that looked out on the great mystery city.

A heartbeat later, the same understanding impressed itself on Katherine. "Frost!" she declared, throwing her hands in the air and rushing to the edge with a vigor that alarmed Derec. "What went wrong?"

Derec looked past her to the nearer structures of the city. "Hard to say, since we don't really know what happens when it goes right," he said. "Obviously there's more to controlling the key than just thinking about where you want to go."

"But why here, then, a place that neither one of us knows?"

"I don't know," Derec said. "But it could be worse."

"I'd like to know how," she said, turning to face him and planting her fists on her hips.

"Well, just consider," he said, stepping closer. "Wherever we are, we're a long way from Rockliffe Station, and the way we left we're not easily going to be followed. That means in one fell swoop we got away from Jacobson, Anazon's robots, and the raiders. And as a little bonus we got away with the key."

"Which we don't know how to make work right. We've lost Alpha, we don't know where we are, we have no ship, no money, no food, nothing but the clothes we're wearing and that useless key." It could not have been more of a tantrum of self-pity if she had ended it by stamping her foot.

"I didn't say it was all good. I just said it could be worse." Squatting on his heels, he stared at the key as he passed it from right hand to left and back again restlessly. "I can hardly believe what this thing does. For a machine this size to be able to transport matter ten feet, much less ten light-years, is the most fantastic feat of engineering—damn near magic. I can't tell you how much I'd love to take it apart and see how it works. And finally I understand why everybody wants it. What I don't understand is why someone tried to hide it."

"What do you mean?"

He looked up. "Something Wolruf told me. The asteroid that I woke up on—it was artificial. Somebody meant it to be the final hiding place for this."

Katherine was quick to pick up the implication. "As though it were dangerous, not just powerful."

"Exactly."

"Well—just think what a terrorist or assassin could do with it. Or an army where every soldier had one. Especially an alien army."

"It'd be impossible to protect yourself against them," Derec said, staring at the key again. "A lot of responsibility goes along with ownership of this thing. Maybe more responsibility than I want."

"The monkey getting heavy already?"

Derec nodded. "On top of everything else, I still don't know what I'm doing mixed up in the middle of this." He looked up at her. "I suppose you think the pod was from the *Daniel O'Neill*, that I ejected in some emergency."

"It's the straightest line between two points."

"I guess it is. But you know, there's something that doesn't fit in. Why did Monitor 5 think it was so important to give the key to me? Me, who'd been nothing but a nuisance to the robots up till then? It said something like 'I found the key, Derec. You have to take it.' How do you explain that?"

She gestured helplessly. "I don't."

Derec stood and walked to where she stood, at the edge of the plaza. "And this place," he said, spreading his hands wide to take in the city surrounding them. "Just look at it. It's glorious. Doesn't just seeing it make you feel exhilarated? Can't you sense the unifying vision, the way it all fits together as one seamless whole? Look at the turrets with mansard roofs—beautiful! Look at the way the five Pythagorean perfect solids are used as structural shapes to focus—"

As he looked to the north, he stopped short. "That's funny," he said, puzzled. "I would have sworn that last night there was a grouping of three icosahedrons right there along that boulevard."

"Icosahedrons?"

"The most complex perfect solid—twenty triangular faces." He shook his head. "I must have been mistaken about the grouping. Maybe I was dreaming about this place last night. Anyway, I'm almost looking forward to going down there. If we'd managed to get back to Rockliffe Station last night or on to Aurora this morning, I'd have felt cheated by not having my chance to explore."

"Have you bothered to notice that this city isn't just a collection of buildings?" she asked petulantly.

"What do you mean?"

She pointed down over the edge at the small figures moving in the streets. "You go down there and you're going to have to deal with the creatures that built this city. Is it as much fun thinking about having a hundred thousand monsters like Aranimas after you? We're trespassers, you know. We weren't invited."

Derec folded his arms over his chest and scanned the city outward to the horizon. "I'd say more like a million or more inhabitants in a city this size. But they won't be like Aranimas —or like Wolruf, for that matter."

"What makes you so sure?"

"First, because Wolruf told me about his world and the Erani world, and this doesn't fit the description—"

"She could have lied."

"True. But you say you didn't pick this destination, and I know I didn't. That means it was the key that decided to bring us here."

"So?"

"So, the key wasn't made by Aranimas's people, and it wasn't made by Wolruf's. If it was, they'd have known how to make the key work. They could probably even have made one with a lot less trouble than they seem to have gone through to find this one," Derec said. "So why should it take us to either of their worlds?"

"Maybe they did learn how to set the destination," she pointed out.

"Maybe. Or maybe the key was built to return to a certain place when it's activated without guidance—as a way of reclaiming them when they fall into the wrong hands."

"Then the creatures down there—"

"Might be not only the builders of this city, but the builders of the key," Derec completed. "Which means that maybe we were invited."

She squinted in his direction. "You're going to go down there whether I do or not, aren't you."

"Yes. I'll leave the key with you, if you want."

"I thought we were a team."

"Are we still?" he said, raising an eyebrow questioningly.

"Don't you want to be?"

"I don't know if we want the same things," he said slowly. "You want to get back to Aurora. I want to do something to help Wolruf—and then look into this business of the *Daniel O'Neill.*"

"Both of which require getting off this planet," she pointed out. "Our interests overlap at least that far."

"They do, indeed," Derec admitted. "All right, then. We're still a team."

"At least until we beg, borrow, or steal a spaceship."

"Or learn how to control the Key to Perihelion, whichever comes first," he amended.

"Or Aranimas shows up with fire in his eye and uses us for thrust mass," Katherine said with a grin. She peeked over the side again. "Or we kill ourselves trying to get down from here. Maybe we can make them come to us?"

Katherine's concern was justified. The only way down from the promontory seemed to be to climb down one of the sloping faces of the pyramid. Those faces were steep, much more nearly vertical than the faces of the Incan and Mayan temples of ancient Earth which the tower otherwise resembled. But unlike those temples, there were no wide ceremonial staircases cut into any of the four faces.

Instead, there was a regular pattern of holes down the center of each plasticrete face, a pattern that seemed to extend all the way to the ground. Each hole was wider than his handspan and twenty centimeters deep, and they were spaced in such a way that they would make convenient handholds and footholds.

It was possible they had been placed there purely for decorative reasons. "The fact is, I can't see why anyone would want to climb up here—there's nothing up here except a good view," he told Katherine. "And if the view was important to them, they could have run a lift up through the center of the tower."

Even so, the holes were in some ways better than a staircase. Hugging the face of the tower, with both hands and feet to provide good purchase and their backs to the view out and down that could inspire vertigo, they might just make it.

"You're going to be hurting by the time we get to the bottom," he told Katherine.

"I've got an eighty percent charge in my medipump and I feel fine. Besides, didn't anyone ever tell you that women have more endurance than men?" she teased. "Let's stop talking and get going."

The worst part was going over the edge and feeling for that first foothold. Derec led the way, being careful not to dislodge the key from its spot tucked into his waistband. A moment later Katherine was beside him, clinging more tightly than she needed to the lip of the holes she was using as handholds.

"I almost hate to bring this up, but I wonder what sort of creatures might have decided these holes would make great nests," Katherine said breathlessly.

"Flying snakes," Derec said straight-faced. "A meter long with three rows of sharp teeth. Nothing to worry about."

"You're so considerate," she said crossly, starting down.

"No charge," he said with a smile, and followed after her.

If he had ever thought that Katherine would be the kind to pick her way timidly down the wall, letting him lead the way and guide her steps, the first few minutes would have banished that notion. Katherine—Kate—was agile and aggressive and, most of all, fast. In ten minutes they were a fourth of the way down the tower's face. Since he had to be wary of moving too quickly and dislodging the key, Derec had trouble keeping pace.

"Hey, partner," he called down to her. "Time-out for a conference."

"I thought you were already taking a time-out, as slow as you move," she shot back. But she stopped and waited for him all the same. "What's up?" she asked as he joined her.

"A thought about the key. Do we really want to take it down there, not knowing what we're walking into?"

She frowned. "That would be taking a risk, wouldn't it? If we knew how to control it, I'd say keep it with us. We could always use it to escape from a tight spot—"

"If we knew how to control it, we wouldn't have to do this," Derec said.

"You want to leave it here, in one of these holes?"

"That's what I was thinking. The key is heavy enough and the holes deep enough that nothing's going to dislodge it."

"I don't much like the idea of being separated from it," Katherine said, her eyes clouded by concern. "It's one of our two chances to get out of here, maybe the better one, for all we know."

"I like the idea of being separated from it by force even less," Derec said. "What do you say?"

She nodded reluctantly. "You're right. Let's hide it."

At Katherine's insistence, they left the key right there where they were, in the leftmost hole of the pattern.

"It's going to be a harder climb up than it is down," Derec warned as they started down again.

"For them, too," she said.

Freed from his burden, Derec could more readily keep pace, and the rest of the descent turned into an undeclared race. But the race ended prematurely when, sneaking a peek over her shoulder to see how much farther they had to go, Katherine saw something that made her want to start climbing upward again.

"Reception committee," she hissed, reaching out and seizing Derec by the sleeve.

Letting go with his right hand, Derec twisted at the waist and looked down. At ground level, a hundred meters below their feet, a dozen figures stood in a half-circle. All twelve faces were tipped upward, looking back at him.

A happy grin spread slowly across Derec's face. "But look who's on the committee," he exulted. "They're robots!"

Katherine stole another glance down. "Considering recent history, I don't know why that's such good news," she said.

"It means that this has to be a Spacer world—"

"Rockliffe was a Spacer station," she said.

"—which means that our biggest problem from here on out is going to be bureaucratic red tape."

"Optimist."

"You'll see," he said, starting down.

The only response came from one of the robots waiting below. "Please move slowly and exercise all possible care," it called up to them. "Climbing the Compass Tower is a dangerous activity."

CHAPTER 21
ROBOT CITY

Eager to hasten the meeting, Derec skipped the last few steps, swinging out and jumping down to the ground. As Katherine clambered down behind him, he turned to face the robots.

Several were already leaving. Derec presumed that they were medical specialists who had been there in case of a fall, plus perhaps a few riggers who could have climbed up the wall to help them. Their skills no longer needed, they were efficiently moving on to other tasks.

The robots that remained were similar in appearance to each other, but not identical—variations on a theme. One had a seemingly purposeless swatch of blue enamel above the right ear, a second brilliant green optical scanner, still another sensor mesh wrapped around its skull like a headband.

"What's your name?" Derec asked, singling one of them out.

The robot took a step forward. "I am M-3323."

"Very well. M-3323, take me—us—to the city manager."

"The city as presently constituted does not have a manager," the robot replied. "What is your name, please?"

"Derec," he said. "David Derec. But—"

"And I'm Katherine Burgess," she said, stepping forward. "Look, we don't need to talk to the person on top, no matter what you call them—city manager, king, president, god. We need a place to see to our hygienic needs—something with a shower and a Personal. While we're busy with that, you can arrange a meeting for us with someone who can help us with our other problems. Is there any problem with that?"

"No, Katherine," M-3323 said. "Arrangements are now being made. If you will follow me, I will lead you to the appropriate facilities."

Mercifully, the house they were taken to was less than a minute's walk away. It was nestled between two great six-sided towers like a child hiding amongst its mother's skirts. The interior was startlingly new and pristine, as though the house had not only never been occupied, but never entered.

But the house contained everything they needed, including two Personals that opened off a room containing a futonlike sleeping platform. The three robots which had accompanied them inside waited downstairs, which afforded them an extra measure of privacy.

"There," Katherine said, emerging from her Personal after twenty minutes. "More presentable?"

Derec rose from where he had been seated on the edge of the platform. "You're very easy on the eyes."

"A quaint expression," she said, obviously pleased. "Do you have any idea where we are?"

"None whatsoever," Derec confessed.

"But we're on our way out of this," she said with some anxiety. "I'm going to get to go home. You're going to get to go find home."

He held up crossed fingers.

"You promised me there'd be nothing more than red tape," she said warningly.

"That was a prediction, not a promise."

"Still stand behind your forecast?"

"Sure," Derec said. "Let's go start hacking through the tangle."

M-3323 led them out of the house and guided them back the way they had come, up the street toward the great central tower. It was a strange little procession—a pair of robots in the lead, matching stride for stride—M-3323 walking between Derec and Katherine like a vigilant chaperone—another pair of robots trailing a few steps behind.

Were the extra robots an honor guard, bodyguards, or prison

guards? The pair following silently behind bothered Derec the most. Before they had gone half a block, he glanced back over his shoulder to check on what they were doing. What he saw behind the robots—or, more to the point, what he did not see —made him do a double-take. The house they had just left was gone. The gap between the two towers which had flanked it had closed.

He shook his head and chided himself for foolishness. It must be the angle, he told himself. The house is set farther back than you realized. It's there, between the towers. You just can't see it. Then he remembered the grouping of icosahedrons he had seen, and then not seen, from the high plaza.

"Excuse me," he said to Katherine and M-3323. "I'll be right back."

He ran back down the street until he had gone far enough that he should have been able to see the house, and then slowed to a walk. He could scarcely believe his eyes. The house *was* gone. The two towers now flanked an open courtyard.

He looked around wildly, wanting to believe that he had taken a wrong turn, that he was the victim of some sort of illusion. The house had been just what Katherine had asked for, and so conveniently located. Could they possibly have built it just for us, and then torn it down again?

It was an insane thought, and he did not want to deal with it just then. Demand-driven architecture—a modular structure that swapped whole buildings around like toy blocks or fabricated them from elemental forms—what kind of society was this? How could people live in a city like this?

With an effort, he tore himself away from the sight of the empty courtyard and found two of the escort robots standing two steps away behind him.

"Are you finished here, sir?" one asked politely.

He grunted. "Yeah, I'm finished."

There was no keeping the troubled expression off his face as he rejoined the others.

"Is there a problem, David Derec?" asked M-3323.

"You bet there's a problem. What happened to the house we were just in?"

"My apologies. Did you have other needs that you did not previously identify? Or do you have additional personal needs?"

"I *need* a straight answer. Where's the house?"

"That facility has been released to the general inventory."

"So I'm not just imagining that it's gone—you brought it there for us and then cleaned up when we were done."

"Yes, David Derec."

"Do you do that all the time around here?"

"All physical resources are managed for maximum efficiency."

"I'll take that as yes. Crazy," Derec shook his head.

"But it doesn't matter to us," Katherine said.

"No," Derec agreed. "So forget it and let's get on with this."

They walked on until they came to a great plaza at the convergence of several main streets. In the center of the plaza was a great white tetrahedron perhaps fifteen stories tall. Their guides directed them toward an entrance on the right.

"M-3323—"

"Yes, David Derec?"

"Is this part of the city exclusively used by robots? I didn't see any people along the way here."

"Yes, Derec."

"I thought so. Where *are* all the people?"

"I do not know, sir," M-3323 said. "This way, please." It led them through a lobby area which was itself a tetrahedron and down a corridor. At the third door, the robot turned and paused. "In here, please."

"Who are we meeting?" Katherine asked, pausing in the open doorway.

"Rydberg and Euler," M-3323 said. "They are waiting for you in the inner office."

Rydberg—Euler—The names gnawed familiarly at Derec's memory as he followed Katherine first through one doorway, then through another. *Where have I heard them before*—

Preoccupied, he entered the inner office with his eyes lowered. When he looked up, he received a jolt. The spartan compartment contained three straight-backed chairs, a quarter-circle work station with a sophisticated hypervision computer terminal, and two blue-skinned robots with silver slits for optical sensors.

This can't be—A chill went through Derec as he stared at

robots that were clones of the supervisors on the asteroid. *It's all connected. I don't understand—*"Kate—" he started.

Just then the robot on the left stepped forward. "I am Rydberg."

"I am Euler," the other robot said.

"I'm afraid there's some mistake," Katherine said. "We want to talk to people."

"There is no error. We are the representatives assigned to your case," Euler said.

"Kate, this is wrong," Derec said hoarsely.

Pursing her lips, Katherine decided, "If they want to do it this way, I don't care." She addressed Euler. "We need to see about transportation to Aurora and Nexon—that is where you're going to go, isn't it, Derec?—and temporary accommodations."

"I am afraid that that is not possible," Euler said, shaking his head gravely.

"What?" exclaimed Katherine. "Why not?"

"Friend Euler's statement was imprecise," Rydberg said. "It is possible to leave. But there is a problem. A human being has been killed—"

"Why does that involve us?" Derec asked.

"It would be an unthinkable violation of the Laws of Robotics for a robot to harm a human being," Rydberg said. "I am unable even to form the thought without experiencing distress."

"Of course it wasn't a robot," Derec said impatiently. "Another human being did it, obviously."

Euler said, "Disregarding yourselves, there are no other humans here."

"Our guide said something about that," Derec said. "But just because they have no business here doesn't mean that they didn't come over from some other sector anyway. Someone who'd murder wouldn't worry too long about proper travel passes or whatever it is you use here."

"I will clarify," Rydberg interjected. "Friend Euler meant to say that there are no other human beings in this city."

"Then from one of the other cities—," Katherine began.

"There are no other cities on this planet."

"What are you saying? Where are we?" she demanded.

"I regret that I may not identify this planet or its star," Rydberg said. "But we who live here call this place Robot City."

"There's nothing but robots here?" Derec said slowly, an uncomfortable idea pricking at him.

"Discounting yourselves, that is correct," Euler said.

Katherine gaped. "No one in this whole city—it must be fifty hectares—"

"Two hundred five," Euler corrected.

Derec interrupted. "Where are the inhabitants? The builders? Where did they go?"

Rydberg cocked his head slightly. "We are the inhabitants, and the builders, Friend Derec," he said matter-of-factly.

It was the answer he had been expecting, but he still resisted its implications. "Where are your owners?" Derec persisted. "Where are the people you report to?"

"Your question is based on an erroneous assumption," Euler replied. "Robot City is a free and autonomous community."

"That can't be," he protested. "Maybe there are no humans here now. Maybe you're not presently in contact with any. But they must have brought you here, or sent you here. You must still be following their directives."

"No, Friend Derec. We are self-directed," Euler said. "But we are not unaware of human beings. We have a vast library of book-films by and about human beings. And we have accepted our responsibility to see that humans do not come to harm."

"I hope you understand, Friend Derec, why we are obliged to delay your departure," Rydberg said. "This is our first experience with death. We need your help in understanding how it happened, and in understanding how the experience of death should be integrated into our study of the Laws of Humanics."

"The Laws of Humanics? What are they?" Katherine asked, puzzled.

"The human counterparts of the Laws of Robotics—those guiding principles which govern human behavior."

Euler continued, "At present the Laws of Humanics are a theoretical construct. We are attempting to determine if Laws of Humanics exist, and if they do, what they are. This incident has placed the research project in crisis. You must help us. I assure you that you will be afforded every possible comfort."

As Euler was speaking, Katherine had slowly edged closer and closer to Derec, and now was standing at his elbow. "This is crazy," she said under her breath. "A city of robots, with no one to guide them? Doing research on human beings, like we were some curiosity?"

And in that moment, Derec stopped fighting the truth and embraced it: *The community on the asteroid and the great city surrounding him were products of the same mind, the same plan. He hadn't escaped at all.*

But at least he at last understood why—why he was given the key, and why it had brought them there. For the last to touch it had been Monitor 5, an advanced robot desperate to fulfill its First Law obligation to save him. Knowing what it was and what it was capable of, the robot could do nothing other than give it to him—programmed for what it knew would be a safe destination, a sister colony of robots light-years away.

"Sssh," he said to Katherine, then looked to the robots. "Could you excuse us for a moment? We need to talk."

"Certainly, Friend Derec," Euler replied, "We will—"

"You stay. We'll leave," Derec said, taking Katherine's hand and leading her out the door.

"Where are we going?" she asked breathlessly as he guided her a dozen meters down the corridor. "They're going to follow us."

He stopped short and released her hand. "We're not going anywhere. At least I'm not. I really did want to talk privately."

"What do you mean, you're not going anywhere?"

"I'm going to stay," he said. "I won't tell them that, though. I'll offer to stay and cooperate on the condition they arrange transportation for you. They don't need both of us."

"No!" she said emphatically. "You don't have to do that. They've got no right to hold us. They have to let us both go. They're robots, aren't they? They have to help us."

"They're robots, yes. But not like any you're used to. I don't think they'd agree with your definition of their obligations," Derec said, shaking his head. "But that's not the point. I'm not going to stay just to appease them, or to get them to let you go. I'm staying because I want to."

"Want to! Why?"

Derec flashed a tight-lipped smile. "I started thinking about how I'd feel if they did what we asked and put us on a ship to

Aurora, or wherever. How I'd feel if I never found out any more about the key—"

"We could take it with us."

"—never found out where this planet is or why the robots are here—never went back for Wolruf or found out what happened to her. I thought about it and realized I couldn't just walk away. It's true that I don't know who I am. Even so, I know that's not the kind of person I want to be."

There was a studied silence, which Derec finally broke. "Part friends?"

Her eyes flicked upward and her gaze met his. "No," she said, shaking her head. "Because if you're staying, I'm staying, too."

It was his turn to protest. "You don't have to do that. They're my causes, not yours. This is a safe world. I'll be fine alone."

"You don't like my company?"

He shrugged. "We get on all right."

"Then are you trying to tell me that this is something a girl can't handle or shouldn't worry her head about?"

"Of course not."

"Then it's okay if I stay just because I want to?"

Derec surrendered. "Sure."

"Then let's go tell Euler and Rydberg."

"After you," he said, bowing with a flourish of his hand.

Wearing a contented smile, Katherine led the way back to the office. As the door opened, she turned and whispered back over her shoulder. "Just tell me this—when do our lives turn normal again?"

Derec laughed aloud, startling the robots. "Maybe never, Katherine," he said. "Why are you complaining? You said your life was dull, didn't you?"

"Dull isn't so bad," she said wistfully. "Dull has its good points."

Chuckling to himself, Derec picked out a chair and settled in it as though planning to stay for a while. "We'll do what we can to help," he said to Rydberg. "Tell us the story. Who're the suspects?"

But the robot's dispassionate answer erased the smiles from both their faces so thoroughly it was as though they had never been there. Like a bitter aftertaste to a sweet drink, it stole all the pleasure that had come before.

"Yes, David Derec," Rydberg said. "There are two suspects. Yourself—and Katherine Burgess. We are most curious to learn which of you committed the act, and why."

DATA BANK

by Paul Rivoche

DEREC: An amnesiac who awakens inside a Massey survival pod, marooned on an asteroid composed of ice, his past and identity are total mysteries to him. Despite his amnesia, his intelligence remains unaffected, and he knows a great deal about robotics. He has adopted the name found on his clothing, apparently the name of the manufacturer.

ARANIMAS: Like all Erani, he is ambitious, aggressive, inventive and acquisitive. The Erani are the dominant species in their solar system and treat all other races as their servants and inferiors, including humans, whom they have only recently encountered.

Aranimas is the youngest member of one of the larger, more powerful Erani clans, which are organized into trading groups. Aranimas is a perfect exemplar of one of his race's most important traits: he is a technical genius. He invented the hyperdrive that powers his patched-together mega-vessel. Due to the politics of Erani, he didn't share his invention with other Erani clans, or even within his own clan. He kept it to himself in hopes of enriching his trading house and enhancing his personal prestige. Aranimas is also a gifted astronomer. His invention of a special long-range telescope helped him discover the asteroid where he encountered Derec.

Physically, Erani are tall and slender, with pale, hairless skin. Their eyes are large, set in the sides of their heads, and are capable of independent functioning, like a chameleon's. Their voices are high-pitched, and when speaking Galactic Standard they tril their "r"s.

CARGO "PORTER" ROBOT:
There are various classes of
non-supervisor robots within
the asteroid community. The
one shown here is the basic
porter, a large, wheeled robot
with a forward cargo platform
and articulated loading arms.
Their intelligence is limited
and non-positronic.

AUGMENTED WORKSUIT:
This is a self-contained field-repairable hardsuit for humans working in hostile environments. The suit sports high-intensity worklamps and a radio equipped with an omni-directional antenna. The suit systems are completely computerized and include diagnostic computers for on-the-spot trouble-shooting and field repairs.

The name derives from the fact that the suit augments the worker's movements. In addition to greatly amplifying human strength, the suits are extremely flexible. They carry extra "hands" for the tips of the extensors, which are stored in re-sealable pockets on the thighs of the suit. The basic "hands" are multi-purpose grapples, but the suit also comes equipped with illumi-nated micromanipulators, for fine work in darkness, and laser spot-welders, among others.

THE KEYS TO PERIHELION: The Keys are transport devices capable of transporting the user to Perihelion, the place nearest all other places in the universe. Keys are metallic silver in color, mirror-smooth and seamless. They are operated by pressing each of the four corners, one after another, which makes the operating button appear in the last corner touched. When used properly, the Key will first transport the user to Perihelion, then to the selected destination.

Rather than being preprogrammed for different species, the Keys are "initialized" when first used, and thereafter will only work for that type of organism, although it is possible to "reset" a key to an "uninitialized" state. The Keys can be used by any species, even robots, so robots don't need a "robot specific" Key.

BREATHER: These masks are made of gray plastic and are designed to fit over the middle third of the face, like a pair of wraparound sunglasses. The breathers' straps are hollow elastic tubes that meet behind the neck. A flexible gas delivery tube leads from the back of the neck to the cartridge pack, which is small enough to strap to the upper arm. The bottom edge of this particular style of mask does not fit flush with

the wearer's upper lip, creating an imperfect seal that allows outside atmosphere to mix with the pure oxygen flow produced by the cartridges. This arrangement not only reduces the size of the cartridge pack, but leaves the wearer's sense of smell unimpeded.

MASSEY G-85 SURVIVAL POD: This is a limited-duration, self-contained emergency survival pod equipped with a positronic companion.

The G-85 provides a complete environment for stranded survivors, including food, water, oxygen, a viewing screen, and entertainment facilities. The positronic companion is programmed to act as a therapist and ensure the best chance of survival for a space-wrecked castaway, even to the point of sedation.

Massey survival pods are not equipped with windows. Instead they have a limpet pack, a disc-shaped sensor array capable of sliding across the outer surface of smooth-hulled spacecraft. The G-85 does not have a full environmental recycle system, and its resources are limited to approximately two weeks. They are also equipped with locator beacons, which broadcast the pods' locations constantly. Massey survival pods are the primary safety system on most of the large commercial carriers, the equivalent of the life-boat.

MONITOR 5: Supervisor robots are marvels of simplicity and elegance of design. Their structure is composed of flexible, inert, non-organic duodecahedral fragments capable of directed rearrangement (morphallaxis). These fragments contain kilometers of circuitry and megabytes of programming. With the right command codes, the forms of these robots are infinitely malleable.

Supervisor robots are an infinity of specialized forms with one generalized package. Their skin is a metallic pale blue. The supervisors Derec encounters lack the customary red tracking marker that telegraphs the direction of the robot's visual sensors. Like all robots, they are incapable of violating the Three Laws of Robotics. Their positronic brains are also incapable of forgetting.

ALPHA: This robot is constructed by Derec from salvage aboard Aranimas's ship. The basic data library is contained in five removeable memory cubes in a compartment located in the chest area.

Its extensive positronic memory is reserved completely for the business of learning from experience. Its artificial intelligence is expandable and flexible. The positronic brain is a three-pound lump of platinum-iridium that is the repository for the fundamental positronic potentials governing its activity, for the temporary potentials representing thought and decision, and for the pathways representing learning.

Like Derec, Alpha is an amnesiac, though in this case its memories were wiped when it was destroyed. As an essentially new construct, it has been re-programmed. Alpha's new arm comes from a Supervisor robot and is constructed of the same infinitely malleable material that all supervisors are composed of.

ABOUT THE AUTHOR

MICHAEL P. KUBE-McDOWELL has been called "the finest new writer of cosmic science fiction in twenty years" (Orson Scott Card), and his writing praised as "reminiscent of Arthur C. Clarke at his best" (*Newsday*). Since 1979, Kube-McDowell's short stories have been featured in such magazines as *Analog*, *Asimov's*, *Amazing*, *Rod Serling's Twilight Zone*, and *Fantasy and Science Fiction*, as well as in various anthologies. His 1983 fantasy "Slippage" was chosen for Karl Edward Wagner's *The Year's Best Horror Stories*, and was subsequently adapted as an episode of George Romero's television series *Tales From the Darkside*. *Emprise*, Kube-McDowell's first novel, launched the thousand-year "Trigon Disunity" future history, and was a finalist for the Philip K. Dick Award. His most acclaimed work to date is *The Quiet Pools*, a selection of the Book-of-the-Month Club and nominee for the Hugo Award for Best Novel.